BECOMING MY SISTER

V.C. Andrews® Books

The Dollanganger Family
Flowers in the Attic
Petals on the Wind
If There Be Thorns
Seeds of Yesterday
Garden of Shadows
Christopher's Diary: Secrets of Foxworth
Christopher's Diary: Echoes of Dollanganger
Secret Brother
Beneath the Attic
Out of the Attic
Shadows of Foxworth

The Audrina Series
My Sweet Audrina
Whitefern

The Casteel Family
Heaven
Dark Angel
Fallen Hearts
Gates of Paradise
Web of Dreams

The Cutler Family
Dawn
Secrets of the Morning
Twilight's Child
Midnight Whispers
Darkest Hour

The Landry Family
Ruby
Pearl in the Mist
All That Glitters
Hidden Jewel
Tarnished Gold

The Logan Family
Melody
Heart Song
Unfinished Symphony
Music in the Night
Olivia

The Orphans Series
Butterfly
Crystal
Brooke
Raven
Runaways

The Wildflowers Series
Misty
Star
Jade
Cat
Into the Garden

The Hudson Family
Rain
Lightning Strikes
Eye of the Storm
The End of the Rainbow

The Shooting Stars
Cinnamon
Ice
Rose
Honey
Falling Stars

The De Beers Family
"Dark Seed"
Willow
Wicked Forest
Twisted Roots
Into the Woods
Hidden Leaves

The Broken Wings Series
Broken Wings
Midnight Flight

The Gemini Series
Celeste
Black Cat
Child of Darkness

The Shadows Series
April Shadows
Girl in the Shadows

The Early Spring Series
Broken Flower
Scattered Leaves

The Secrets Series
Secrets in the Attic
Secrets in the Shadows

The Delia Series
Delia's Crossing
Delia's Heart
Delia's Gift

The Heavenstone Series
The Heavenstone Secrets
Secret Whispers

The March Family
Family Storms
Cloudburst

The Kindred Series
Daughter of Darkness
Daughter of Light

The Forbidden Series
The Forbidden Sister
"The Forbidden Heart"
Roxy's Story

The Mirror Sisters
The Mirror Sisters
Broken Glass
Shattered Memories

The House of Secrets Series
House of Secrets
Echoes in the Walls

The Umbrella Series
The Umbrella Lady
Out of the Rain

The Girls of Spindrift
Bittersweet Dreams
"Corliss"
"Donna"
"Mayfair"
"Spindrift"

Stand-alone Novels
Gods of Green Mountain
Into the Darkness
Capturing Angels
The Unwelcomed Child
Sage's Eyes
The Silhouette Girl
Whispering Hearts

BECOMING MY SISTER

V.C. ANDREWS®

Gallery Books
New York London Toronto Sydney New Delhi

G

Gallery Books
An Imprint of Simon & Schuster, Inc.
1230 Avenue of the Americas
New York, NY 10020

Following the death of Virginia Andrews, the Andrews family worked with a carefully selected writer to organize and complete Virginia Andrews's stories and to create additional novels, of which this is one, inspired by her storytelling genius.

This book is a work of fiction. Any references to historical events, real people, or real places are used fictitiously. Other names, characters, places, and events are products of the author's imagination, and any resemblance to actual events or places or persons, living or dead, is entirely coincidental.

First Gallery Books trade paperback edition March 2022

Interior design by Erika R. Genova

Manufactured in the United States of America

10 9 8 7 6 5 4 3

Library of Congress Cataloging-in-Publication Data

Names: Andrews, V. C. (Virginia C.), author.
Title: Becoming my sister / V.C. Andrews.
Description: First Gallery Books trade paperback edition. | New York : Gallery Books, 2022.
Identifiers: LCCN 2020054030 (print) | LCCN 2020054031 (ebook) | ISBN 9781982156305 (paperback) | ISBN 9781982156312 (hardcover) | ISBN 9781982156336 (ebook)
Subjects: GSAFD: Ghost stories.
Classification: LCC PS3551.N454 B43 2022 (print) | LCC PS3551.N454 (ebook) | DDC 813/.54—dc23
LC record available at https://lccn.loc.gov/2020054030
LC ebook record available at https://lccn.loc.gov/2020054031

ISBN 978-1-9821-5631-2
ISBN 978-1-9821-5630-5 (pbk)
ISBN 978-1-9821-5633-6 (ebook)

BECOMING MY SISTER

prologue

"I've seen you here from time to time," the elderly man said after I entered the lobby of Golden Ages.

He surprised me. I hadn't seen him there in one of the big cushion chairs until I was well into the waiting room and past the shaft of light streaming through the open walnut shutters.

His glasses seemed wrong for someone his age. They had pinkish frames and extra-large lenses, which made me think of a young Elton John. He wasn't gaunt; however, the thinness in his frame suggested he might be in his late eighties. Gray hair ran a little long around his ears and down the back of his neck. Small brown age spots peppered his forehead. He must have been a redhead or maybe a blond with a fair complexion because he still had freckles, too.

He wore a dark blue turtleneck sweater with a pair of fading baggy blue jeans and couldn't have been more than five foot seven or eight. Yet he appeared to have long legs. With his black running shoes and thick white socks, he had the look of someone who had once been quite athletic, perhaps a runner.

"Yes, you have," I said, and sat on the beige leather settee across from him and slipped my paisley triple zip messenger bag off my shoulder, clutching it in my lap like someone who feared it would be snatched. Today I was wearing my Bohemian V-neck long-sleeved single-breasted dress. I wasn't always so fashion-conscious. My sister, Gloria, was more like our mother than I was, a *fashionista*, who would fine you for matching the wrong shirt with the skirt.

Although long-sleeved, my dress was a light cotton. It was early fall, but by the tips of its fingers summer was hanging over the gorge of darker, cooler days and nights. Leaves had yet to turn, even at the higher mountain elevations.

"I thought so," the elderly man said, looking relieved that I had verified his suspicion.

However, I was a little defensive about it, annoyed that anyone had been watching me and keeping track of my visits.

"From time to time, when I can, I come," I said, sounding more like my mother, who could turn a consonant into a razor blade in your ear when she was even slightly irritated. "I live some distance away. Laguna Beach. On a hillside just across from the beach. It's not an easy ride, traffic the terrible way it is all day in both directions."

"Ahhhh," he said, as if I was examining his throat. "It's still very nice that you try to visit as often as you can. Sometimes I'm here almost all day and no other visitors for anyone else appear. House of the Forgotten."

"Yes, it's easier to forget and not confront something you cannot change."

He nodded and smiled. "When my partner has a lucid moment, he accuses me of putting him in storage." He shrugged. "What else is it, really? I know there is no hope he'll recover. Once everyone accepts it, including me, he'll really go into storage."

He uncrossed his legs and sat straighter in the way a man might who thought that to continue to do otherwise when speaking to a woman would be impolite. I relaxed a bit because it brought a hidden smile to my face. Long ago I had learned that a smile leaves you vulnerable. You look too innocent, too gullible and eager to please. Spend fewer smiles, suffer less disappointment. That was what I had come to believe.

But there was something old-fashioned and romantic about his appreciation of the way a woman sitting across from him might feel looking at a man who appeared so indifferent, slouched with his legs apart. My father had been aware of how important the little things could be, especially with women. He was always rising to pull out my mother's chair and opening and closing doors for her. "Your wife is your queen," he often had said, especially if another man looked surprised or didn't do as he did.

My father was gallant and my mother graceful and elegant, especially in public. I would reluctantly give her that. She moved slowly, her posture perfect, and when Daddy did something courteous for her she always made sure to say, "Thank you, Alan dear." She smiled at my father as if they had just started dating and he was doing it for the first time.

My sister, Gloria, and I would look proudly at each other. Who didn't think we were the perfect family? Other husbands and wives surely dreamed of someday becoming like our parents, who seemed to wear invisible crowns. They could part a sea of people, everyone vying for their personal greeting. My mother never shook hands; she bestowed a touch or blew an air-kiss like an actual queen might. She clung to my father's arm when they walked in public or entered a room. They moved with such synchronicity that someone would think they were attached at the hip. He never walked ahead of her.

I thought about couples dating today or young marrieds. I didn't know whether to blame the women for wanting to appear independent or the men for being self-absorbed, but rarely did I see a couple practice such chivalry. Whatever the reason, the gaps between generations often seemed like canyons. My generation especially appeared to be oblivious to the little things that made their partners comfortable. Some couples looked as if they were moving in separate dimensions. As we were growing up, especially when we were in our teens, I often pointed that out to my sister, who would laugh and tell me I was being hypercritical. "But they ignore each other," I insisted. "They're not like Mother and Daddy."

"I'm sure they care for each other deeply," Gloria would say. "They simply show it in other ways, private ways, Gish. Don't worry about it."

I wasn't worrying about it, not like she was implying. I was worrying about ever meeting a man who would be as devoted to me as Daddy was to Mother.

Besides, Gloria was so forgiving. I had despised her faith in the goodness of people and then eventually envied her for it when I came to understand that cynicism and cold realism baked a crust over your eyes. Everything beautiful, everything hopeful, gets filtered until it's too thin to matter. Cynicism verifies the inevitability of unhappiness. No one knew that better than I did.

The old man in the lobby was waiting for me to say something insightful, something beyond small talk. I could see the hope in his eyes. He would finally have a real conversation with someone here.

"What does your partner have? What's the diagnosis?" I asked.

This wasn't exactly an adult residence. *Clinic* was the operative word. *Expensive* followed on its heels. And as the old man had suggested, from here a hearse might take you off or an ambulance might transport you to the sister facility with a similar but not as stylish waiting room and what was known as hospice care. Anticipating Mother going there soon, I had visited it and couldn't leave fast enough. There, clocks ticked down, oxygen tanks emptied, and death swept through like some eternal vacuum cleaner sucking up souls.

"Dementia, creeping dementia," the old man said. "It became dangerous to leave him alone. That included my taking a nap or oversleeping. Twice he wandered off and the police brought him back. I resisted as long as I could. I've never liked facing reality. I'm the dreamer; he's the realist. If he could, he would have checked himself in here and then called to tell me. That was my guy, my guy," he said, his voice drifting. "We had a wonderful life together."

"I'm sorry," I said. It wasn't simply something I would say because it was expected. I cherished my words. And I really had come to think of old age as more of a disease, something worthy of pity and compassion. Maybe that was because I could see it eventually waiting out there for me, too, hungrily rubbing its palms and holding out its arms, despite how young I was. Mother had tried to wrestle it down with her plastic surgeries, her hair treatments, and her expensive makeup. In the end, age wove its persistent wrinkles through her like a spider would weave a web.

"It's funny," Gloria once said, "but when you see an elderly man struggling to walk or something, you can't help but feel sorry for him, even if he was just released from prison for doing something terrible."

"Lady Jesus," I called her, and she laughed. We were in high school by then. People paid more attention to your words when you were beyond just being cute.

"I like your hair," the old man suddenly said, surprising me. With the light in his eyes and the softness in his smile, he looked like he had suddenly fallen back in years.

"Thank you."

I had my espresso-brown hair in a layered bob. Older men were usually a little hesitant about commenting on my hair or my clothes. Some looked uncertain about how their words would be taken, even afraid they were crossing a line. Despite being in my twenties, I knew I still looked like a teenager. But most men I had met certainly would risk it. Women rarely flirt when they're older; men never seem to stop, even to their last breath. Daddy was like that, especially when he was introduced to an attractive woman. There was a brightness in his eyes, the green specks dancing around the blue. Mother's friends said his smile could melt an iceberg, not to mention their hearts. She nodded, forcing her own smile. She was never good with jealousy. It brought out the knives.

"What are those flowers woven into your hair?"

"Baby white roses," I said.

He closed his left eye like someone aiming a rifle. "Poet, artist?"

"I'm an artist, painter."

He nodded. "I used to design custom-made furniture. My partner was an accountant. He was the one who looked after us, the stable one. He had a very good 401(k) in place, thus we could afford this. I'm probably not that far behind him. I'm already quite forgetful." He leaned forward to whisper. "I have a note on the inside of the front door that reads, *Did you zip up your fly?*"

He laughed, but I simply stared at him. I was never very good at pessimism. His face quickly folded into the serious puddle of age again.

"So who are you here to visit?"

"My mother," I said.

"And your father?"

"Died a little over ten years ago. Heart failure. In his sleep."

"Oh? Sorry." He thought a moment and then said, "I wonder if women still outlive men."

"I don't know. I never paid much attention to statistics. There are always too many exceptions."

"Exactly. Hope is based on that," he added. "So . . . your mother . . ."

"Is being given a bath."

"Ahhhh," he said again. "Dementia?"

"No, it's a little different. Complicated," I said. What a perfect word, I thought, so serviceable, the perfect *I don't care to discuss it* answer.

He nodded and looked around the waiting room, shifting his eyes from me because I had established a firm boundary around what was clearly personal.

"I came in here a little while ago because I started to feel alone. My partner drifted way off, so I figured I'd wait another hour or so and go back to see if he'd returned to earth."

He clasped his hands in his lap and looked down at them. His age began rushing back again as if the tide of time had instantly changed.

"You call him your partner? Never legally wedded or . . ."

"Civil stuff. Neither of us cared about titles. Although I wouldn't pass up a lordship."

He smiled. Neither of us spoke. One of the nurses stopped by, looked at us, and walked on.

"We almost adopted, you know."

He was so eager to talk about himself that it felt like a sin to ignore him.

"Really? Adopt?"

"I wonder how we would have done as parents, whether he or she would have come to see either of us in a place like this, whether they would have cared at this point, and whether they would have realized the importance of it."

"There's one test of that," I said. "One question to answer."

"Oh? What?"

"Is your daughter or son visiting for you or for herself or himself?"

"Very interesting thought. And how do you answer that, if it's not too personal?"

"No, it's not. I'm here for myself," I said. "My mother stopped needing me long ago, long before she was brought here."

He widened his eyes and froze for a moment. Before he unfroze completely, another nurse came to the door and nodded at me.

"Nice meeting you," I said, rising. "I hope your partner returns to earth, at least for today."

He stared, looking like someone unable to speak. I could see it in his eyes.

He was still trying to digest what I had said about my mother.

chapter one

For me more than for my sister, Gloria, our house was always full of echoes, and not because our house was vast and cavernous with high ceilings and long hallways. It was bigger than most homes, but it wasn't a castle. These were the echoes of voices from the past speaking softly. I remember playing alone in my room with a hand-me-down doll that originally had been given to Gloria, and hearing whispering outside my door, sometimes so loud I finally had to get up to peek down the hallway. If I looked, the whispering always stopped. I'd wait and wait and then rush back to the doll and hug her, patting its almost human hair.

"Don't be afraid," I'd assure her with my eyes on the doorway. "These aren't bad ghosts."

Our house had once been the home of a famous silent-movie star who frequently threw glamorous parties right up to and through most of the 1960s. According to Mother, anyone who was anyone during the golden age of Hollywood and right after had come here, slept here, and partied into the "wee hours" in our living and dining rooms. Chefs and servants ran back and forth from the long, restaurant-sized kitchen with trays of hors d'oeuvres. Champagne bottles were popped so quickly that they "sounded like a tune." Often the guests reveled outside on our beautiful grounds, sitting and dancing on the patios. Musicians played under large umbrellas. There were dramatic lights. There always had to be lights. These were movie stars.

As if she had been there at the time, Mother described in great detail how the house had been filled with laughter, music, and the clinking of champagne glasses, all of it being more significant because of the overlay of fame.

"These weren't just any parties," she bragged. "They were parties that were written up in the newspapers, reported on the radio and on television. These were parties with pictures of our house and grounds in magazines! Sometimes a producer would premiere a movie here."

Many times I heard my mother claim that the spirits of cinema as well as stage theater greats still walked the halls, which explained the ghosts she claimed inhabited our house. Although she had redone most of the floors, replacing all the wood with rich marble tiles that didn't creak, she would swear to her friends that she still heard their footsteps late at night. She claimed that she often woke, opened her eyes, and listened to the voices, the laughter, the singing, and the applause. "As if it was happening in the here and now."

Of course, my father had slept through it and simply smiled and nodded when she described it all to us in the morning. Our nanny, who was with us both since birth, Mrs. Broadchurch, smiled, too, but took my hand and Gloria's for a quick, reassuring squeeze. Mother insisted nobody should be frightened by it, but sometimes I thought Mrs. Broadchurch was frightened as much and as often as I was.

Gloria never seemed afraid. In fact, now that I think about her more, I don't recall her ever having a nightmare. But she was at my side whenever I did. Our bedrooms were next to each other's, and our parents' was to the right at the end of the hall. I started to believe Gloria had her ear to the wall anticipating my sobs. She was always there before Mother, who took one look at us lying together and went back to bed, content that Gloria had done what had to be done with me. She had little patience for me. My fears annoyed her. "How could these ghosts frighten anyone? They were stars!"

"Gish has a big imagination, Mother, bigger than mine," Gloria would tell her.

Mother would throw her right hand up in a smooth motion and dramatically dismiss me. She had seen it done that way in some silent movie. She unraveled through our house every day like a reel of film.

She was unstoppable when it came to convincing everyone that the movement of famous spirits through our house was real. I'd look at the way Mrs. Broadchurch's eyes would widen as Mother detailed her colorful descriptions, pinpointing laughter, the tinkle of glasses, and the whispers of secret love at this corner of the house or that. She made it sound so logical and true and with such vivid detail that my four-year-old heart, so willing to accept wondrous new things, would begin to race with my own memories of voices heard just the previous night.

On one occasion, one of her more skeptical friends asked Mother how she was so sure these spirits lived on for decades.

"And here?" she added, looking like she had collapsed Mother's house of cards with her logical question.

"The more famous you were, the longer you could haunt the settings you had enjoyed," Mother replied, as if the answer was as clear as day. "Ordinary people evaporate instantly, but celebrities whose names linger on the lips of the living and whose voices and faces are still resurrected on television and the internet are immortal. And they are that especially in this house, our house!"

She would say all these things to all her friends and visitors as well, while brightening her beautiful amber eyes with their yellowish golden and coppery tint, hypnotizing her listeners with even more detail about this celebrity or that, some of those facts astoundingly personal. It was as if she was immortal and really had known them all. She'd sit in her favorite vintage English Victorian carved high-back armchair, looking like a monarch with her dark brown hair styled in what she called the Garbo bob, named for the actress Greta Garbo, "who most certainly had been here."

She'd sit with her regal posture and deliver her descriptions and references with an air of authority that kept her listeners mesmerized. As if she had promised these celebrated spirits to live up to their expectations, she never greeted any guest without her makeup carefully applied, including on her long eyelashes. She had taken lessons from a movie makeup artist. Her ears and neck sparkled with her diamonds. For years, she had been collecting vintage clothing, and at times she bought something some actress was said to have owned. She'd dress in one of those when she was going to have one of her get-togethers, her famous Celebrity Talks. It was as if she was ready to go onto a movie set herself.

"Her words rang with the timbre of church bells," Gloria recalled when as teenagers we reminisced about our childhood and Mother's famous afternoon recitations. "Why wouldn't her gullible friends believe her?"

We had seen it ourselves. When Gloria and I were little older than infants, we'd sit quietly with Mrs. Broadchurch and listen to our mother ramble on and on to new and older friends about the history of the house. I really would rather have not been there, would rather have been outside playing, but she told Mrs. Broadchurch she wanted us present for these gatherings so we would know how lucky we were to be living where we were living. The two of us would sit quietly with our hands in our laps, trying to look like we were proud of her and were enjoying it. I could see the birds outside, circling and inviting me to run over our carpet-like lawns with my arms out like wings, screaming to be free, to glide off and escape.

Often Mother glanced at me with something of a scowl because I couldn't hold a smile or look grateful that I was there. I was afraid to tell her how her "hallways at night" stories slipped into my sleep and had me envision hands and arms floating along our walls, her famous faces flashing a smile at me, and sometimes, in my dreams, coming into my room to hover above me. If I woke, I wouldn't open my eyes until the sunshine washed the ghosts away in the morning. I knew how much Mother wanted me to be thankful for and be happy about the wonder of our spiritual houseguests, but it wasn't easy for me, as easy as it seemed to be for Gloria, and she could see that in my expression and discomfort.

"Too many young people have no appreciation for their history. A fifty-dollar video game is a far more important way to spend their time than walking through a historical site like ours," our mother said, sounding so mournful.

She directed those words of criticism more at me than at my sister, Gloria. When Mother spoke of her celebrities, Gloria would look like Daddy and wear that soft, amused smile of hers, as if Mother was telling some sort of fairy tale. I was still young enough to believe in fairy tales, Mother's and the ones Mrs. Broadchurch read to us. I can't say I ever stopped believing in Mother's stories, even years later when fantasies and magic were supposed to have faded.

I had one particular memory that would never fade. One night when I heard whispers and laughter again, I got out of bed slowly and went to my door. Opening it just a little, I peered out and was sure I saw Mother walking through the hallway in her sheer white nightgown, the hem of it floating around her, looking like she was talking to someone. She was laughing, too. I rushed back to bed. In the morning, when I told Gloria, she said I was probably just dreaming. However, I thought Mother would be proud of me and love me more, so I told her what I had seen and heard and asked her if I had been dreaming.

"Of course not, and of course you could have seen and heard all that," she said. "It wasn't a dream. However, it wasn't me you saw. It was more likely Mary Pickford. Little children have more contact with the spiritual world."

I looked at Gloria, who simply smiled that smile of hers, looking as if she had known this for a long time, but it still frightened me a little, maybe more than a little.

"We're so lucky," Mother told us when we sat with her

fascinated audience again. "We not only live with the rich and famous now, but we have the memories of them locked within our walls. Practically every day, I learn about another famous person who visited or partied here."

How did she learn? Did a ghost tell her? I wondered. I was afraid to ask her, and Daddy provided no clues. He was never at these gatherings because they were only with Mother's friends, Mrs. Broadchurch, and us. Often he was working at his office, either here at the house or downtown. He even worked on weekends. Later, at dinner, she would describe a recent meeting of her celebrities club to Daddy. Gloria and I would have to relive it, almost word for word. She was often not very nice to some of her guests. She would act so surprised, even insulted, that they knew so little about famous people. I could swear I saw Mrs. Hume's eyes tear up and her lips quiver when Mother practically called her an idiot for not knowing who Norma Shearer was.

"She was the first person to be nominated five times for an Academy Award for acting!" she practically spit at her. "And she won for *The Divorcee*. Have you never seen *The Divorcee*?"

Mrs. Hume shook her head and looked at everyone fearfully. I thought no one there had seen the movie, but no one else dared to admit it. Mother seemed so powerful to me then, even with her soft, dainty hands and thin frame that Daddy compared to Audrey Hepburn's. "My wife's like the princess in *Roman Holiday*," he'd say, and only those who came to Mother's movie nights or watched TCM knew what he meant.

"You'd be shocked," she told Daddy after one of her tea parties. "It's one thing to forget who Norma Shearer was, but none of them knew who Rudolph Valentino, Charlie Farrell, and Janet Gaynor were."

"Really? Well . . ."

Before he could offer an explanation, she said, "They're too into themselves and their meaningless gossip. I don't know why I bother with them."

Daddy nodded. Maybe her friends were into themselves, but when I looked at their faces, I still saw that most were impressed and even envious that Mother was so schooled in celebrities and could somehow connect with them. Why would anyone be surprised that it made Mother special in my eyes, too?

Even though the very thought of something supernatural would frighten most of her guests, these people were continually intrigued and looked forward to Mother's gatherings, her little parties with wine and cheese. Pictures flashed on walls, and old singers like Rudy Vallee were played on an antique Victrola to provide atmosphere for her talks. An invitation was highly cherished. In their eyes, Mother was part of the world of the rich and famous, and fame was something everyone sought. Who didn't want to live forever, at least on the lips of future admirers?

"Mother's sessions make her guests feel as if they're learning things most people don't know, could never know. They want to believe her," Gloria told me when we were a little older, but even at six, she had explanations for practically everything that puzzled me.

I was never really sure whether or not Mrs. Broadchurch believed Mother when she told her stories. She knew most of the celebrity names. She was in her early sixties, widowed. Daddy had tempted her away from a well-to-do family in England by offering her twice the salary. She called our home "posh." I never knew what that meant until she was gone, but it sounded good. She was almost as proud of our home and living here as Mother was, but when I asked her if she heard voices and laughter at night, too, she said no, but not to take anything from that because she was hard of hearing.

"However, if your mum says she did, she did," she added. "Mums don't lie about such things, especially to their own children."

I didn't know what to believe. Aside from telling me I was dreaming when I heard voices and laughter and what I had seen Mother doing, Gloria never came right out and said that what Mother was telling her friends wasn't true. The most she said about it back then was, "It doesn't hurt us to believe it, too, Gish, and it makes Mother happier if we do. The least we can do is be proud of where we live. It's what Mother wants."

I did come to believe that our house was a piece of history, like some national monument and, as Mother said, "far more important than houses with signs that boasted 'George Washington Slept Here.'" Everyone laughed, even Mrs. Broadchurch, when Mother said that, but Mother was very, very serious about our house. She didn't laugh after she had said it. She never meant it as a joke. Her lips would tighten and her eyes would widen. Everyone would instantly stop laughing, as if she had thrown a switch.

"By buying it, we saved it from disappearing and rescued it from practically melting in the desert sun. Those of us who have the money also have the obligation to preserve what was and is important," she told her wealthy friends—lectured them, more like it.

Daddy was a very successful investment manager. Early on, Mother told us, "Your father is one of those men whose work is their life. Never blame him for something he cannot control because it's in our family's interest."

She meant he was as obsessed with his work as she was with

our house and her research. She didn't seem to mind how often he was gone. Other wives would surely have complained at how frequently their husbands missed dinner or had to be on business trips. Because of Daddy, we were as wealthy as any of the people Mother invited. Besides, she had her celebrity projects to keep her occupied whenever he wasn't home anyway. In her mind, the buying of this house and saving it from termites, rats, and the weather was akin to winning a great battle for the country, even the world. It was as if she was challenging all her rich friends to do something nearly as significant.

"You should be proud of your mum," Mrs. Broadchurch always told us. "I come from a place where there are many historical houses that are in great need of a woman like your mum. Look at how well she's kept your home and, as she says, for good reason. It has history. If we don't preserve our history, all of it, we lose a sense of who we are."

That did make sense and made what Mother was doing very impressive. How could Gloria, I, or Daddy really ever disagree? She certainly kept our home looking elegant and important. She changed drapes, replaced windows and molding, and had some areas repainted. Every change was carefully coordinated to keep our house and grounds looking like they belonged in the golden age of Hollywood.

There was a wall that Mother hadn't repainted or even touched, a wall that gave her claims some authenticity. It was just inside the main entryway. On it were dozens and dozens of autographs, some so faded that you had to guess at the names. No one challenged my mother's interpretation of the scribbles or that they were genuine. This one was definitely W. C. Fields, and that one was assuredly Cary Grant.

"You know that wasn't his real name," she would explain when pointing out his signature to someone, and then proudly declare that his real name was Archie Leach.

"Yes, he was English, too," Mrs. Broadchurch whispered to Gloria and me.

Mother spent much of her time researching celebrities and covered two of the walls in the den with old photographs and movie posters that featured the stars of stage and screen who "surely had dinner here." There were even framed pictures in our formal living room where other homes would have family pictures. It was as if, to Mother, the celebrities were related to us.

She would often call Gloria and me to watch her place a new framed celebrity photograph on a shelf or table. Of course, she'd tell us all about whoever it was and warn us that she might ask us to repeat some of that later. We knew more about George Raft or Ida Lupino than we did about our grandparents, who had evaporated like raindrops years ago. Mother seemed ashamed of her parents. She didn't want to dwell on where she was born and how she had lived. Daddy's mother died young, and his father was barely alive in an adult residence in Los Angeles. Only he visited him and, from what I understood, not so often.

So instead of our personal family history, there were volumes and volumes of autobiographies of celebrities, official and unofficial biographies, books with pictures from hundreds of films, as well as histories of studios and executives and discussions of the greatest movies ever. They took up a dozen shelves in our den. If someone asked Mother a question, she could pluck the right book with the answer off the shelf in an instant.

Just as full were the shelves in the cabinet that held all the DVDs of old movies she had collected. Some had autographs on them, too. Often, she would have movie nights and then lecture about the films and the actors until the eyes of her guests began to droop. Committees of this organization or that would invite her to speak about our house and its history. The local television station came often to interview her whenever someone or some famous movie was being celebrated. She had become something of a celebrity because of the celebrities.

And it wasn't only the historical famous who Mother thought should be cherished. For Mother, attending galas and charity events where some recent television or movie personality would be present was more important than any holiday, birthday, or anniversary, even her own. She added the photographs taken beside someone newly famous to the ones of older actors in the den. Many didn't have my father in them, just her. He wasn't upset. Daddy never challenged Mother's enthusiasm for her famous people. On the contrary, anyone could clearly see he was basically doing everything he could to please her. *Whatever makes her happy* was a motto he could have had chiseled over the front door or tattooed on his forehead. Even Mrs. Broadchurch told us, "Your mum gettin' your father angry is harder than turnin' a battleship on a dime. The man's a saint," she added, almost under her breath. I had no idea what that meant. Sometimes I wouldn't ask Gloria questions just because I was jealous that she always knew the answers.

She knew the answer to this one but didn't tell me until I was in the fifth grade and we both saw Mother bawl Daddy out as if he was nothing more than one of our employees. He had forgotten to buy something she needed for one of her talks.

"When they were married," Gloria said, "Mother's family was the family with all the money. She funded Daddy's investment business."

"If they were in love, why would that matter?" I asked.

She didn't answer. Not really. She just shrugged and went on to talk about something else.

We knew that Mother had ordered Daddy to arrange for the purchase of this house before we were born. From the way she described the purchase to Gloria and me, Gloria suspected she wouldn't permit herself to become pregnant until he had. She was six and I was almost five at the time Gloria explained it further.

"She wouldn't start a family, us, until he had bought it," she said, her small hands curled, with her arms up and moving as if she was shaping the truth right before my eyes the way she would mold interesting figures out of clay. "And Daddy really wanted a family. They're both only children, no brothers or sisters. It mattered more to Daddy."

For me, this whole business of making babies was still quite unclear. "Were you in her stomach waiting to be born?"

"Yes," Gloria said.

"Were you crying?"

"Probably," she told me.

"Wouldn't that keep Daddy awake at night?"

"It's why he bought our house so fast," she said. "The owners at the time wanted a lot more money for it, and Daddy had to use all his skills to get them to lower their price. I heard him describe it all to his partner, Mr. Hemsley, in his office."

"Why didn't I hear him?"

"You were in the lobby telling the story of *Charlotte's Web* to Mrs. Norris, their secretary."

Gloria had what Mother called "a photographic memory." She had only to look at something once or experience something one time to recall it easily even years later. Still, I wondered if Gloria was telling the truth about being in Mother's stomach so long. Even then, I suspected she told me things to keep me happy or from wondering anymore about something.

She said that Mother and Daddy had been married only a little more than a year and were renting a house not half the size when Daddy bought our home. She immediately named it Cameo and had that name printed on a copper plaque and placed above the outside entry. The name had something to do with the movies.

This house with its property was one of the biggest in what was known as the Movie Colony in Palm Springs, California, a classic Spanish revival with a central courtyard, and a separate casita that became Gloria's and my playhouse, our private getaway where we would reveal our secret thoughts and dance like television stars. A veranda connected it to the four-bedroom main house.

Pathways led through the terra-cotta-tiled courtyard, surrounded by nearly five acres of rolling green lawn, palm trees, more tile walkways, and a dramatic swimming pool shaped like a violin and redone in blue and white Pebble Tec with a pink stucco pool house beside it. To the right of that was our tennis court, where Mother claimed Douglas Fairbanks Jr. had played against Errol Flynn. "Even Charlie Chaplin once played on it."

There was flowing white and red bougainvillea everywhere, with gardens carefully designed to feature any and all desert flowers. The fountains scattered over the property were never turned off. Sometimes, with the windows of my room open, I would hear the gurgle and fall asleep to it, just like many movie stars had, according to Mother.

When anyone entered through the gateway of the ten-foot-high solid white concrete-block walls that surrounded us, they thought they had left one world and stepped into another, a world Mother said was designed to be a "way station" between earth and heaven. Why not believe that movie and entertainment stars still haunted its beautiful grounds?

Our parents couldn't move into it for nearly a year after they had bought it, because Mother wanted to carefully update the electric fixtures with ones she had found in antique shops, including chandeliers. She improved the dramatic lighting all over the property. Only because they were getting to be problems, she replaced bathroom and kitchen fixtures, but insisted on keeping one original bathroom sacrosanct as a sort of historical site. No one used it. It didn't even have running water or a door, but it was there because "Marilyn Monroe sat on that toilet and peed." Above it Mother had placed a copy of the famous picture of Marilyn Monroe having her skirt blown.

Once when I was nearly six, almost a year after Mrs. Broadchurch had become too ill to remain with us, I pressed the tips of my fingers as hard as I could on the Wall of Signatures, expecting to force out words and cries absorbed years and years ago. When my mother saw me, she screamed.

"You're smudging William Powell!"

I pulled my hand back as if I had touched a hot stove. She rushed out, got a cloth, and ever so carefully wiped the area I had touched, screaming about the desecration of our valuable property. I saw no difference in the signature when she was finished, because I didn't think it was so clear to read anyway. I stood there watching her, the tears, mostly tears of fear, streaming down my cheeks. Gloria came running to save me from Mother's rage. She had done that many times, because Mother would get almost as angry if I dropped a crumb on the floor or smudged a mirror. Sometimes, she'd be angry at me for days. This time, Mother did calm down when Gloria promised to make sure I never did anything like that again.

"You'd better," she warned her. "Your job is to keep an eye on her, maybe for the rest of your life."

Her job? The rest of my life? She made me feel like some kind of wild animal who was slow to learn and become housebroken like some pet. All I wanted was to please her as much as Gloria obviously did. Both she and Daddy never stopped complimenting her for this or that, especially her reading and writing and her drawings, whereas their words to me, mainly Mother's, were usually warnings and threats.

Mother rarely, if ever, growled at Gloria, but I could make Mother so furious that she looked like she might explode sometimes. Holding her hand over her heart and gasping, she would accuse me of rushing her aging. Wrinkles were a direct result of the stress and aggravation I had caused. Once, she cut off a few of her premature gray hairs and put them on my pillow.

"Maybe if you sleep with that, you'll realize what you're doing to me," she whispered sharply into my ear, her lips so close that I could feel the breeze of the words, stinging like the kiss of a bee.

I was afraid to let my face touch those hairs and cried until Gloria came into my bedroom, took them away, and flushed them down the toilet.

"It's all right, Gish," she told me. "She's just afraid of getting old because some of her friends who aren't much older look so much older and makeup won't help them. It's not your fault."

Maybe, I thought, *but you're never blamed for a gray hair or a wrinkle.* I swallowed back my sadness but wondered, do those tears you hold back soak inside you forever and ever so that eventually you drown from the inside out? It occurred to me that I never saw Mother make Gloria cry. Certainly, neither Mother nor Daddy did or said anything to her that even made her eyes well up.

Early in my life, I realized that when my mother looked at me, she saw someone other than whom I saw in a mirror. I think that was because she, and my father, for that matter, were blinded by the light they saw in Gloria's face. When they turned from her to me, I could clearly see the changes in their eyes, the tightness in their lips. A stranger had appeared. There were times when I seriously questioned whether Gloria and I were sisters, even though there were clear resemblances.

Often, I'd wonder why they wanted me anyway. They had everything a parent could want when my mother had given birth to Gloria. After I learned the difference between the words *compare* and *contrast*, I immediately realized my parents never compared us. From day one, they contrasted us. *Compare* means to see the similarity, but *contrast* means to see the difference, and that's what they saw. Always. My father was not as obvious about it, perhaps, but I still sensed it in his voice, in how he held my hand and hers, and especially in his smile, always deeper and wider and brighter than the smile he gave me. He loved bragging about her to his friends. When he finished, he'd look at me as if he was struggling to find anything similar to say.

Essentially, the day Gloria was gone, all smiles died in our house. One day, I realized how I might resurrect them, but to do so meant we had to live in a different reality, yet still one in which we heard the voices we needed to hear.

How much love had gone from Cameo after that? Mother lost interest in keeping our "historical" property pristine and precious. The spirits kept away. "They abhor sadness and depression." Eventually, my parents seemed to drift from each other as much as they drifted from me. I often wondered if love could be measured the way you measured teaspoons of flour, sugar, or salt. Could you add up how many times your parents told you they loved you and measure that against what every parent told his or her child? Do you contrast expressions of love for you against how many more times they told your sister or your brother? Or do you have to just hope it's there? I certainly couldn't imagine asking either of my parents if he or she loved me, especially after Gloria had left us. What good would it do? Of course, they'd say "Yes" or, worse, "Don't be silly." No matter what, I wouldn't believe them. How could I? Growing up, I sometimes felt like one of Mother's famous ghosts.

I was born a little over a year after Gloria, whom Mother had wanted to name after Gloria Swanson, considered the silent screen's most successful and highest-paid star in the 1920s, the silent-movie era. I didn't think there was another person with my name, Gish. She named me after another famous early movie actress, Lillian Gish. My father didn't oppose it. No one foresaw that other kids especially would tease me and call me Pish, but never when Gloria was around.

Daddy had wanted a son, and my mother never failed to remind me. "The look on his face when he realized he was having another daughter almost gave me a miscarriage," she said many times as I grew up, sometimes right after she had chastised me for giving her another wrinkle or another premature gray hair. They were always premature. How could I not accept that my father had resented me and wished I had somehow slipped past his swimming sperm so it could go on to find a boy?

"Oh, Mother, don't tell her that," Gloria would say whenever

Mother tried to shock me with the threat of almost being aborted. It sent chills right to my heart. Go to sleep with that on your mind and see how fast your dreams turn grotesque.

"You're frightening her," Gloria would say, shake her head, and put her arm around me, looking as if she was going to cry harder than I would.

Mother would become a little sorry. She never apologized, but only Gloria could make her swallow back words. After all, she was the "golden child"; nothing she said or did was wrong. From the way our parents described her birth, it was as if the doctor thought her first cry was an ingenious composition of notes. In contrast, Mother claimed my cry was so loud that she was convinced I would have returned to the womb if possible.

I wondered. Would she have taken me back? Maybe. If she could start over and guarantee a boy, she surely would. "Why didn't they?" I wondered aloud one day.

"It wasn't part of their agreement," Gloria said. The whole idea of agreeing about children confused me. I thought they just happened. Gloria whispered the rest of her explanation. "I heard them talking about it once. Mother wanted so much to be a movie star herself. She tried before she met Daddy, but no one would have her. After they were married, she kept trying for a while. Daddy paid for everything, but they agreed they would have two children, only two. So," she said, smiling the way she always did when she solved a problem for me, "here we are. No one is going to replace us."

That helped me to feel better. Besides Gloria, Mrs. Broadchurch was still there to comfort me during those early years, but always with the admonition, "Think first before you act, especially in front of your mother." Truthfully, I didn't understand her warning back then and why she told it only to me. Also, why only my mother? Why not my father, too? Or anyone, for that matter? What did she know that I didn't? Maybe even Gloria didn't know back then, either.

Because of her distressing health concerns, Mrs. Broadchurch left us just a week before Gloria entered kindergarten. Almost immediately, Mother hired a nanny for me, Lila Jenkins, whose husband had died a year before and whose three older daughters were all married and living in other states and places, one living thousands of miles away in the U.S. Virgin Islands. Someone told Mother how lonely Lila was and how she would make a perfect nanny to take the place of Mrs. Broadchurch. Mother leaped at the opportunity. Taking me off her hands was like someone snatching a hot frying pan out of her fingers. "What would I do without Mrs. Broadchurch and Gloria all day anyway?" Mother wanted to know.

"She'll be like a fly buzzing around just to annoy us," I heard her tell my father, not that he would have opposed her no matter what she decided. She practically confessed her disinterest in caring for me by claiming she was "too busy with community business" to be chasing after an infant all day. "You know how full my day is, Alan."

"Do what must be done, Evelyn," Daddy said. Anyone hearing him might think he was condemning someone to be hanged.

It didn't upset me as much as it should have. Lila was quite different from Mrs. Broadchurch and my mother. Physically, she was at least four inches taller than Mrs. Broadchurch and probably twenty pounds lighter. But her voice was softer. Mrs. Broadchurch was most always firm and correct. I never saw her with her dark gray hair down. It was always in a tight bun. When Gloria and I talked about her years later, she told me she used to believe Mrs. Broadchurch "ironed herself like a dress before she came out of her room in the morning."

Gloria had a gift for capturing everyone and everything in an image or a simile. Mother stood "like a dress mannequin" when she greeted her dinner guests at the door. Sometimes Daddy rose and walked through the house "jerking like a puppet whose strings Mother tugged." When Lila was just sitting quietly, she had the face of someone deeply wounded, "wounded to the bottom of her soul."

Lila never wore makeup, not even lipstick, but she was not an unattractive woman. Daddy always had one of his nice smiles for her. She had salt-and-pepper hair, neatly pinned on the sides and halfway down her neck. Although she obviously didn't have her hair pampered in a beauty salon every two weeks like my mother pampered hers, she never looked disheveled or haggard and didn't dress in colorless clothes like Mrs. Broadchurch had dressed.

When my mother was present, Lila wore a dark, serious expression, as if she accepted that she had been given a difficult assignment and agreed with my mother that I needed special care and stern discipline, but the moment my mother was gone, Lila burst into a warm, loving smile to show me how grateful and happy she was to take care of me. She read to me, took walks with me, and taught me almost as much as Gloria was learning in kindergarten, so that when I finally was sent there, I did very well.

Gloria and I attended a private school. I was eager to rush home to show Lila my first test paper. It had an A on it. Mother had abruptly terminated Lila one day shortly after I had begun kindergarten. She never told me she was going to do that. Disappointment washed over me as if I had lost another mother, more like my real one. Mother barely looked at my test; she was preparing for another lecture about the house and celebrities and couldn't be disturbed. Gloria took it and immediately pinned it to her corkboard, which was nearly covered with her own. Daddy enjoyed bringing his friends to look at it when they came to our house for dinner. He beamed so brightly when he talked about her achievements that I thought he'd burst into a torch.

When I entered the private school with Gloria, Daddy's limousine driver, Miles Compton, took us there and home. He was a tall man, almost as tall as Daddy, with a thick coal-black mustache and gray eyes "filled with road signs." I once heard Mother describe him as the perfect driver, someone who "heard no evil, saw no evil, and didn't spread personal stories." He did sit erect and kept his eyes on the road. We barely heard him grunt "Good morning" when we got in, and usually, he said nothing when we came out of school. He held the door open for us and closed it without a word. Early on, he had sharply told us we must wear the seat belts. We rode home without his saying another word. There could have been no one else in the car as far as he was concerned.

Sometimes, if Daddy had to go somewhere and wanted Miles to drive him, he'd ride to school with us, sitting between us, and ask Gloria questions about her classes and occasionally ask me questions about mine, but not with the same interest and enthusiasm. It was more like something he was supposed to do.

Daddy wore a strong manly cologne and dressed immaculately in either his black and gray suits or a black sports jacket, tie, and slacks. The crease in his pants was so sharp that you might think you could cut your fingers on it. Riding with us was often our only time alone with him all day.

Daddy was tall and stout, with powerful-looking shoulders. He had been a wrestler in college at Yale. At six foot three, he towered over most men, but I think what made him a commanding figure was the intense way he would focus his eyes on whoever spoke to him or whomever he spoke to. It looked like he could drill past or through their words right to the core of the truth, no matter how they tried to disguise it. He was meticulous with his questions, which Gloria said was the reason he was so good an investor for his clients. He knew how to separate truth from fiction.

Consequently, I tried to never lie to Daddy. It would be as difficult as trying to kill a mosquito with a tennis racket. However, I did look forward to those mornings when he rode with us to school. I knew I didn't impress him as much as Gloria did, but at least I felt like I was really there. So many other times, his eyes seemed to glide over me to get to her.

And of course, after Gloria was gone, he rarely looked at me at all. And Mother practically refused to see or hear me.

After Daddy died, it didn't take me all that long to realize that I had to be gone, too.

chapter two

My disappearance was different from Gloria's primarily in that I had wanted mine to happen years before Gloria was gone. There was only one way to fill the emptiness I felt in my home and family: step out of it. Truthfully, after Gloria had vanished, I moved about as if I was merely a shell of what had been me anyway. Maybe I had always been little more than a shell. Was I ever really noticeable by myself? Was anything that different after she was gone?

Sometimes I would dream about a tombstone with nothing on it and nothing buried beneath it. That was my grave. I thought of that probably because Miles drove us past a cemetery on the way to school. I was just beginning the first grade, and I really never thought much about the cemetery, but suddenly Gloria made a joke that made Miles laugh the one and only time I could recall him laughing on the way to or from school. "People are just dying to get in there," she said. She was only seven. I think she had heard Daddy say it one time when he rode with us. I don't think it was a new joke for Miles; it was simply that Gloria, a seven-year-old, was telling it.

And then there was a story we overheard Mother tell Daddy. One of her friends had told her that her parents were so concerned she wouldn't have the right things written on their tombstones that they bought them and had them engraved with everything but the dates of their passing. They actually visited the site and brought friends there as if they were proud of their achievement.

Daddy said he thought it might be a good idea for an investment of some kind. "Most people aren't creative enough to think of their own inscriptions. We could hire poets and provide an internet site where—"

"Everything is dollars and cents to you," she snapped at him. She often ridiculed or belittled him, but he would simply laugh. It was as if long ago he had decided she had become one of her famous spirits and all her words would float away like smoke. Maybe that was what Mrs. Broadchurch had meant when she warned me about Mother: she was a spirit. Thinking back now, I realize Mrs. Broadchurch spoke like she had respected her, but truthfully, she feared her. In the end, she was probably happy she had to leave us.

Daddy's business idea wasn't so terrible. I was surprised Mother had jumped down his throat. I knew for certain that not having the perfect inscription on her tombstone would bother her. After that conversation, I saw her spend hours looking at famous movie quotes. Her inscription had to come from a movie for sure. I think she always believed she would wander the halls of Cameo after she had passed away. Why wouldn't her famous spirits want her with them? She had earned the status. Look at who she thought she was in our community. Daddy was instrumental in getting her a star on the Palm Springs Walk of Fame. It read *Evelyn John, Movie Historian.*

After that, even though we had another BMW sedan, Mother had Miles take her to wherever she was going, just the way her celebrities would be transported. Occasionally on weekends, Daddy drove himself, her, or all of us somewhere unless he and Mother were going to an event, especially one that was held down valley or east in Palm Desert or Indian Wells. I was sure that Mother felt having a chauffeur take her here and there was expected.

Because we were one of the most prestigious families in the entire Coachella Valley, "desert royalty," as Mother often called us, she had to have all the trappings. She loved stepping out of the limousine after Miles had opened the door for her, her jewelry dripping over her breasts and dangling from her ears. Strangers would take pictures with their smartphones. Mother and Daddy did look like celebrities. Why take the chance of missing an opportunity, just in case? So many celebrities came here. Palm Springs was always a playground for the rich and famous during Hollywood's golden age and still was.

When most people who don't live here think of the desert, they think of places like the Sahara or movies like *Lawrence of Arabia* with camels and drifting sands. They see people getting lost and then being burned and baked by the glaring sun. These desert victims hallucinate water holes and crawl into nothing.

To be sure, there's drifting sand here, and people do get lost hiking in the mountains, but at the center of it all is the booming and glittering world of Palm Springs, with a Main Street that makes you think you closed your eyes and found yourself in New Orleans because music is being blasted out of restaurants and cafes, hundreds of tourists are walking and laughing, and there is a constant stream of cars, motorcycles, and trucks. During the season, October through April and sometimes even into May, banners wave over Palm Canyon Drive announcing this festival or that. Palm trees line the streets. Hotels seem to rise every morning, their windows opening like eyes, and wake up. People pour into and out of them as if there was a subway or train station inside.

It's true that spring and summer sometimes seem indistinguishable here, and winter, although we think of it as getting cold, is a spring day in most of the country. There doesn't seem to be a fall, because it's nothing like the East Coast with wave after wave of orange and yellow filtering the pollen-filled dying summer air. It turns that world into a crisp and fresh place, if only for a few months before it all disappears and the dreary gray of winter spreads like a Rip Van Winkle blanket putting most living things to sleep or driving them away. The Eastern, Northern, and Midwestern residents thicken with overcoats and hats.

Nick O'Sullivan, who oversaw the people working on our grounds, was born in Wisconsin. He was as tall and wide in the shoulders as Daddy. His thick reddish-brown hair seemed to turn brassy in the sunlight, and his face always seemed sunburnt. His parents had emigrated from Cork, Ireland, a year before he was born. I once heard him tell a worker that during the Wisconsin winter, the dead are easier to recognize outside. There is no puff of breath here "like there is for the livin' souls in Wisconsin or the Emerald Isle a good slice of the year."

During the season here, people mainly from states like Washington and Oregon and places in Canada think, *Time to go to the desert.* They envision the sun and sand and imagine the warmth, the pools, and the outside restaurant patios. Gloria and I thought of Palm Springs as just our hometown, but we always loved the excitement, especially on weekends when droves of young people poured in to celebrate whatever they could. It was especially true when we were teenagers, too, and there was the infamous Spring Break.

"It's always so easy to find a reason for a party," Gloria said once. "Mother could have one every day celebrating this actor or that actor's birthday," she whispered, and described closets filled with balloons anxious to escape. We both laughed. It wasn't that much of an exaggeration. Mother had actually had a party for John Garfield's birthday once, not that either of us and some of her guests knew who he was until Mother had a movie night to show one of his films.

Whenever either of us said anything critical or made fun of something Mother had said or done, we had to whisper. One of the ghosts might overhear us and tell her. Maybe living in the desert made it easier to believe in ghosts, especially ones being punished, because there were pockets of hot hell everywhere, especially in the summer.

Occasionally, our parents would take us farther east to shop or see the new development down valley that Daddy's clients were constructing, and we'd see rolling hills of sand that did look like the Sahara. I remember asking why there weren't any camels. My father laughed, but my mother turned and looked back at me as if I had just arrived from another planet.

"People don't have to travel over the sand, Gish," Gloria explained before Mother could speak. I think she rushed a response because she was afraid my mother would say something nasty or mean to me. "No one really lives out there, so they don't have to ride a camel. There are roads close for cars, too."

Gloria was clearly more intelligent than others her age. I didn't have to have anyone tell me. I think I sensed it from the moment we had begun talking to each other. Her first-grade teacher had told our parents, "Your daughter is already reading like a third-grader, and she's clearly artistic."

"Thank God for your sister," my mother said when Gloria explained why there weren't camels. It was as if Gloria had lifted some burden off her shoulders. After Lila was let go, Mother did depend on Gloria to get me organized every day, dressed and ready for school, despite there being only a little more than a year between us. Gloria was the one who kept me entertained and therefore out of everyone's hair, as if I was made of tar or something.

"Take her to the study; take her to your room; take her outside," my mother would say when she and my father were watching one of their favorite shows or he was reading his financial magazine and she was talking to friends or thumbing through fashion or movie magazines. Maybe I had dropped something that had startled them or I had asked a question neither my mother nor my father had the patience to answer, especially if it was from me.

I grew up holding Gloria's hand more than I held my mother's or father's. She never tired of answering my questions and explaining things, and when we were both in grade school and in secondary school, she looked after me, making sure I was dressed correctly and never looked sloppy, which I probably would have looked if it wasn't for her. My mother stepped back and let Gloria manage that part of my life, too.

We spent so much time away from our parents that Mr. O'Sullivan once referred to us as "them orphan girls with parents" when he was talking to the pool maintenance man. Of course, neither Mother nor Daddy ever heard him say it. I don't think they'd have liked it, but I understood why he had said it. He didn't witness us doing much as a family. We really didn't spend much time together at the pool when it was warm enough to swim, and if we did, it was part of Mother entertaining some of her friends. In the beginning, Mrs. Broadchurch would be with us, and then Lila was with me. Our biggest family event was when we left Cameo for periodic trips during the summer months. Summer really began for us by May.

Daddy had bought a house in the hills above Laguna Beach, where the temperature could be forty degrees cooler in the summer. It was nowhere near as big as Cameo, but it had a beautiful, wide Spanish-tile patio and great views of the ocean. Daddy would take us to the beach, but only occasionally, and whenever he did, he carried Gloria on his shoulders, and I had to take hold of his bathing suit or shorts and walk beside them. Gloria would ask Daddy questions, and he would point out things about the ocean and describe some fishing trips he had been on with clients. Sometimes it felt as if both Gloria and he had forgotten I was there. With my other hand, I carried a pail and shovel for the sand.

These beach trips were occasional because Daddy was just as busy in the summer and Mother detested the beach. If the sand didn't get into her shoes, it surely got into her hair. We had a sizable playroom and lots to keep us occupied, but sometimes, after only two days there, Mother would decide she had to return to Cameo for some thing or another. Neither Gloria nor I could understand what that was. There were people caring for the property. Mr. O'Sullivan was still overseeing everything. He was not someone to take advantage of our absence. He couldn't have been more attentive if he had owned Cameo himself. At times, because of the way he berated his workers, I thought he sounded more like a slave owner before the Civil War. Finally, it was Gloria who decided why Mother wanted to return: "She just misses her spirits."

I think we could have stayed by ourselves in the Laguna house even when we were younger. When Gloria was fourteen, Mother decided we could. She'd say she would be back in two days. Often that stretched to four, and a few times, she was gone almost a whole week. Daddy was usually on a business trip. If he was there and Mother wasn't, we'd cook for him, and Gloria would get him to go to the beach or take us out to eat. He usually didn't talk about his business, but when Gloria began asking questions about investments, he enjoyed elaborating on the subject, and despite my disinterest, I learned quite a lot, which would eventually come in quite handy. But Daddy wasn't there as often as we would have liked.

Actually, Gloria and I grew independent of our parents very early in our lives, mainly thanks to her. When we were old enough, we shopped for our own necessities when Mother took us to El Paseo, a high-end street in Palm Desert. She'd go off to one of the fashion boutiques, and we'd shop for clothes and shoes in the less expensive stores. Sometimes she let us off in the mall and came back for us two hours later. Gloria was trusted with the money and either decided or helped me decide on exactly what to buy for myself. She knew exactly what I needed because she looked at my clothes in drawers and closets. Mother never washed anything or ironed anything, so she had no idea what I had to replace.

"Your socks are washed out," Gloria would say. Or "You need new running shoes."

Mother never disagreed with anything we bought because Gloria was deciding. Like anything else that had to be done for me, Mother was happy Gloria was so involved and in charge. When

Gloria was only nine, my parents, mainly my mother, decided we could be left alone even when one of our maids was not there.

"It's not necessary for anyone to babysit you now. Gloria is responsible enough to manage any crisis or issue. And," she said, glaring at me, "she'll make sure you don't mess up anything or break anything. You listen to your sister."

Even Gloria was a little stunned at how much responsibility was laid at her feet. We could have had one of our three maids stay over all the time, but Mother didn't want a live-in maid. She could keep all or one of them as late as she wanted.

She did favor one of our maids, Danita Rosario. Her husband was a chef at a Mexican restaurant in Indio. They had two daughters attending the College of the Desert. What my mother liked about Danita was that she was a perfectionist who on the first day here treated the care and cleaning of our home as a personal achievement. She did behave as if our house was a national treasure. She often went beyond what my mother had requested, never complained about the hours, and was available to assist during any dinner or party event. She even worked a dinner the night of her own birthday. Why would my mother want a live-in maid as long as she had Danita?

Danita had begun to work for us when Gloria was seven and I was six. By the time Gloria was eight, because of Danita, she was speaking fluent Spanish, which was just another in a long line of reasons my parents were so proud of her. I learned some Spanish, but I was never as good at explaining or pronouncing it as Gloria was. She was actually fluent. Whenever my father and mother had any Mexican businessmen or couples over, they called on Gloria to perform or translate, which she did just like anything else she could do, without any fanfare or arrogance. Danita would stand by and watch with pride. I sensed it was different from the pride my mother had in her. It wasn't like bragging pride; it was more like what a mother's pride should really be, trailing love instead of just being another line in some social column.

It was Danita who asked us questions about our schooling when we returned home. It was Danita who complimented and approved of how we were dressed, mainly because of Gloria. And Danita was always there with some family remedy when either of us had a cough or a cold. She did most of our cooking when it came to dinner. We had a professional chef only for important dinners.

However, when we were only twelve and thirteen, Danita had to spend more time at her own home, caring for her husband, who had suffered a nearly fatal heart attack. Other maids handled the cleaning of our house, but Gloria and I gradually began to take over the preparations for our dinners and our breakfasts, especially breakfasts on weekends, because our mother liked to sleep late and Daddy avoided the kitchen as if he believed he could catch some disease from stoves and ovens. Mother was never that excited about Danita's or any of the maids' cooking anyway. According to her, it was "tolerable," probably because she and Daddy ate out so often and the dinner was prepared mainly for Gloria and me.

Eventually, Gloria knew how to plan out the week's menu. She knew what we had in the pantry and the refrigerator and kept a list of what had to be replaced. She did that even better than Danita had. Although she always asked my opinion, I never disagreed with what Gloria chose for us to eat.

It got so if Mother and Daddy were staying home for dinner, he would turn to Gloria and ask, "What are we having tonight?"

If Gloria wasn't nearby, he'd say, "Go ask Gloria what we're having tonight. Your mother is on the phone."

I knew what we were having and that Mother wouldn't know anyway, but I had the feeling that if I told him, he wouldn't be convinced until Gloria had confirmed it. That was how completely Gloria loomed over everything, especially me.

And why she continued to, long after she was gone, until I found her voice among the echoes and brought her home again. Maybe she didn't realize it or want to realize it as much as I did, but I knew she could never leave. Long ago, Mother had turned her into one of her celebrities, embedded her in the history and soul of this house.

If Gloria had asked me, I would have told her: "You can't escape. Even if you die, Mother will seize your spirit and force it to walk our halls."

I'd say, "Just look at what she's done now while you're alive."

Someone might think she was worshipped. Along with the celebrities, there were pictures of Gloria and me in the living room and in my father's office, but there were many more of Gloria, probably because a photo was taken of her winning this award or that. Even in the pictures of both of us, Gloria seemed to be more prominent. Probably it was all my imagination, but it wasn't unusual for Mother to say, "Look at how she looked here," and show someone the picture of both of us, referring, however, only to Gloria. I began to wonder if only I was able to see me in the picture. There were many more baby pictures of Gloria than there were of me as well. Sometimes Gloria would rearrange them so that I wasn't so lost in the background.

My parents made sure to frame and hang certificates she had won or had earned. One picture they cherished in particular was of her at her grade-school graduation. She was the head of her class from grade one on, so at graduation, the principal handed her an academic award, a pewter plaque with her name inscribed and the image of an eagle above it, with *Sure to soar* inscribed below. Our parents framed it in a dark-cherry wood and removed their wedding picture from over the fireplace mantel to put it there. I would have been quite flattered and overjoyed, but Gloria never looked happy about it and hated whenever anyone pointed it out. She wasn't ashamed; she was just trying to look humble, I told myself.

My grade-school graduation picture wasn't even framed. They slipped it into a family album that lay on the under-shelf of the living-room glass-top oval table. Gloria suggested we look at it from time to time, but my parents never did. My sister was winning awards and recognition so often and fast, it drowned out anything or truly everything I did or could do anyway.

Would there ever be an end to her special gifts, made so much more special because of her age when they had appeared? I often wondered back then.

That was the first question that came to my mind the day Gloria completed her first watercolor painting when she was only nine, a painting her teacher and the principal decided they would hang in the school lobby. It wasn't a simple landscape or a picture of fruit in a bowl, either. It was a picture of a little girl dressed in a pink ballet costume dancing on a cloud. Everyone remarked about the way Gloria had woven in pink, white, and blue and somehow created a glow around the girl. She looked more like a young angel. Gloria on her own had come up with the title, too: *Dance of the Butterfly Girl.*

Her teacher said the little girl had my face, and Gloria told her and the principal that she was drawing her sister. No one was more amazed at that than I was. I could see from the way my mother tucked in the corners of her mouth when she was told that she didn't believe it.

"Your sister is just being nice to you by saying that," she told me in the lobby when she, my father, Gloria, and her teacher were gathered to watch it being hung. My class and Gloria's had been brought out of the classrooms to witness the event. Daddy had left work to attend, and Mother canceled what she said was an important chamber of commerce meeting about creating a movie museum in the city. The school photographer was there taking pictures of Gloria beside her painting and then a picture of Mother and Daddy with her. She asked to have a picture with just me.

When Daddy turned one of our rooms in the house into an art studio for her, Gloria encouraged me to draw and paint, too, but my hand trembled so much, probably because I was afraid of how poorly my work would be in comparison, that it did indeed look immature and silly. The best I achieved put me in what I thought was my accustomed place, ordinary.

I really began to think that the only thing special about me was having Gloria as my sister. Maybe that was really why I panicked so much when she was gone. She was taking me with her. I didn't have to imagine that. My parents eventually believed it, too.

Years later, sitting in Laguna Beach with my boyfriend Brad Thomas, who managed a seaside restaurant called Surf City, we sipped some cappuccinos and watched families of tourists walk by, the kids talking too loudly or walking in front of other pedestrians and creating a general air of annoyance.

"Who would you say is a child's worst enemy as he or she grows up?" Brad asked. Brad was nearly ten years older, had been married for less than a year, and fortunately had no children to suffer in any divorce.

"His or her parents," I said.

He nodded. "Exactly. Mine were."

So were mine, I thought, but I wondered now if they ever had any real idea why they were.

chapter three

I will never forget the day I screamed so hard that I felt my vocal cords strain to the point of snapping. Gloria would joke about it for years and quote Franklin Delano Roosevelt's famous line after the attack on Pearl Harbor on December 7, 1941. She'd tease me and call what happened to me that day "a date which will live in infamy."

"Well, it will always be for me," I'd say.

She'd laugh and hug me and tell me she was only joking because she loved me.

"You tease only someone you love," she said. "Otherwise, why bother?"

Gloria would always see the good in people, maybe because

people could see only the good in her. She was certainly like that when it came to Mother and Daddy.

Another reason I would remember that day of infamy forever was that it was the first important thing I had done before Gloria had done it, although it was certainly not something I was eager to do. Ironically, it was only because of Gloria's explanations and descriptions that I knew anything about what was happening to me physically as I grew older. Mother never so much as mentioned anything about my sexual development to me. In her mind, even though I was more than eleven, I was still a baby. Sometimes she made me feel as if I would never get older. "We'll talk about that later," she would say. When was later? As far as Mother was concerned, I would never catch up to Gloria. I would always be standing in her shadow waiting to emerge into myself. Shadows and ghosts of Mother's rich and famous people were always on my mind as well as my mother's.

Once, when we were riding to school with Daddy and we came upon that cemetery we always passed, I asked him where all those people's shadows went when they died. He looked at Gloria like always, expecting her to have the answer.

"They go into the darkness we see every night, Gish," she said, "making it thicker and thicker."

Daddy smiled. "Now, that makes a lot of sense," he said. He looked at me and nodded as if I should have known.

It got so I was afraid to ask either of my parents any questions.

I suppose there were lots of reasons for me to scream on my own day that would live in infamy. I screamed again, even more shrilly, my hands clenched and pressed against my thighs. I could feel the strain in my neck and the redness in my face.

Both Mother and Gloria rushed to my en suite bathroom,

where I stood over the toilet, shocked at the trickle of red down the inside of my left thigh. It felt like it was slicing my leg. The cramps made it hard to breathe. Tears of panic that had been locked just under my eyelids burst out to cross each other as they zigzagged down my cheeks.

"For crying out loud!" Mother said. "You nearly gave us all heart failure. I should be the one screaming, not you. I had to hang up on the chairman of the Palm Springs film festival. It's not the end of the world, Gish Agnes John. Clean yourself."

I hated it when Mother called me by my full name. Ironically, it made it sound like I was not a member of the family.

Gloria moved first to get me a washcloth, and then I sat on the toilet. I knew what this was and that it was coming, but I knew it as something that was supposed to happen much later and surely after it had happened to Gloria, even though my breasts had been developing faster than hers. I tried to tell Mother that something was happening. I had cramps on and off, but she told me to stop being silly and just keep clean. That was another of her answers to any question that might involve a question about my body: "Just keep clean."

I certainly couldn't ask Daddy anything about a girl maturing. As usual, I'd turn and run to Gloria. She was always there for me. When it came to our sexual development, she had done more research for us both just recently because of how quickly I was developing. Just last week, she had read from an article she had found on the internet. It explained that breast development could occur before a girl's menstruation. However, neither of us expected it would happen to me before it had happened to her, especially since her breasts were developing, too.

"Wait right there," Mother said.

I covered my face with my palms, and Gloria put her hand on my shoulder.

"It's all right," she whispered. "You know there's nothing wrong with you."

Mother disappeared, and then moments later, she brought in the tampons she used. She practically tossed the box at me, as if getting too close to me would cause her to have her period, too.

"Gloria will read the directions and show you how to use it," she said. "I'm sure she's read about it and can explain everything to you anyway."

She looked so sure of that. I always suspected that Mother eavesdropped on our conversations and knew the subject of our most secret talks.

"Yes, we've discussed it, Mother," Gloria said. She looked at me. "Gish understands why she's had the cramps and what's happening. She knows she'll be all right. Right, Gish?"

I wiped the tears away and nodded.

"Good." Mother stared at me a moment and shook her head. "Now I have something new to worry about," she said.

"Why?" I asked, looking from her to Gloria, who smiled reassurance at me.

"You don't have anything new to worry about, Mother," Gloria told her.

Mother grunted skeptically and left us.

"What does she mean?" I asked as Gloria took out a tampon for me.

"Just what I had read to you, Gish. She means when a girl starts her period, she can become pregnant."

"But now? What does she mean? I'm only in the sixth grade."

"Let's do this first. We'll talk about it," she said calmly.

Afterward, that was just what we did. It wasn't the first and last personal sexual talk she and I would have, but it always loomed in my memory as one of the most important. It was probably then that I most appreciated having a sister like Gloria, someone who was so much more mature and intelligent than other girls her age. Lots of mothers were like ours, reluctant to have sexual discussions with their daughters; everyone joked about the girls' bathroom being "The Feminine Sexual Research Center."

I think I appreciated Gloria mostly because of her easygoing, balanced way of handling her emotions and now mine as well. Nothing ever panicked her. If something did bother her, she had a way of retreating into herself so that no one else would be disturbed; but she always managed to be there when I needed her, when I was disturbed.

I loved her and I hated her for being so superior in almost every way, even though she never looked down at me. How often I wished she had. The jealousy in me was always looking for an excuse to be mean to her.

"Let's go to the playhouse," she said when I was done with the tampon that day. I brushed aside my tears and followed her out of the house. Everything we did and said in the casita always did feel special and more private, especially when we danced and unashamedly tried to be as provocative as we could. Even though she had more confidence, I thought I could keep up with her, each of us looking for some special move, some special step to teach the other, and mostly, another way to be sexy.

The casita had a small living room, a kitchenette with a marble-top round table and black leather chairs, and a large bedroom with a king-size bed that had a half-moon, oversize headboard. It looked like it was constructed out of pearls. Mother called it a "Hollywood bed." Above it, Mother had hung a blown-up photo of Frank Sinatra at a pool party at Cameo before we had bought it. There were other celebrity photos scattered about the casita as well, but that didn't make it any less our place.

Often, holding hands, we would hurry across the veranda and then, just after we had opened the door, we would look at each other and screech to scare away any ghosts of old movie stars who had once stayed there. Still holding hands and laughing, we'd dive onto the bed, turn onto our backs, keep holding hands, and look up at the cathedral ceiling with recessed lights, both of us catching our breath.

Besides our dancing, she always came up with interesting games and questions like "What do you think of when I say, 'Why'? The word or the letter?"

I tried to be careful with my answer. Which one was stupid? Whatever I said, she admitted to the same. It was as if she was proving we did think alike, felt alike about everything, and sometimes even dreamed the same dreams or had the same fantasies. Maybe she was reinforcing that we really were sisters, no matter how differently our parents reacted to me and to her. I admitted to her that sometimes I felt more like someone who was adopted. She didn't disagree, but once she said something that she wouldn't explain. She practically denied saying it. Instead of arguing with me about my feelings, she said, "Sometimes I wish I really was adopted."

It lingered in the air even though she quickly laughed. It was always in the air.

Gloria had come up with a totally new game shortly before I had gotten my period, maybe to stop me from thinking about her comment about being adopted.

"First word," she said, and then explained that either I or she first would state the word that came to mind, and then the other would have to make a sentence that involved a boy in our school. Once one of us did that, the other would continue to build a short story or incident. So if I began with *wind*, she would say, "The *wind* blew Gerald Patrick's hair all over his forehead."

"Which made him look stupid."

"Until he smiled at me."

"You like him?" I asked, because she sounded so happy about it.

She shook her head. "I'm just making sentences that work. Choose a boy in your class now."

"Ugh," I said, and she laughed. "What's so funny?"

"You won't say 'ugh' all the time, Gish. And I bet there's someone you don't want to say 'ugh' about right now. And don't think you can pretend not to," she warned.

There was a boy I liked, but I knew he liked another girl. I never told Gloria, and I did act like I wasn't interested in boys, but sometimes I thought she could do what Daddy could do and see right through any false face. It was true. I had a difficult time lying to her. I was sure I told her more about myself than any other girl my age told her sister or even her mother, especially my mother. It always seemed safe to confide in Gloria anyway. She never made fun of anything nasty or mean I had said. She would simply smile and tell me why I shouldn't have said it. Here in the casita, we had kept nothing secret from each other. At least, I thought we hadn't.

Gradually, the sentences that followed the first word became more and more suggestive, like "Chris Pauling rubbed my backside with the palm of his left hand as we all walked out of the classroom today."

"He made it seem like an accident?"

"He held it there too long for it to be an accident."

"So you looked at him angrily?"

"Until I smiled."

"No. Did you?"

She laughed. "And I said, 'That's pathetic, Chris Pauling.' He turned so red that I thought he might bleed."

I turned on my side and looked at her, my face inches from hers.

"Did that really happen?"

She pressed her lips together like she did whenever she was holding in some secret and nodded.

"What did it really feel like?"

She thought a moment and shrugged. "It wasn't nice, but I did feel a little excitement," she confessed.

"Did you? Really?"

She nodded. Her secret wasn't finished. "I've flirted with him. It was like an experiment."

"Experiment?"

"To see what I could do to affect a boy. I suppose it's a bit dishonest. I haven't met any boy I really like yet. Who knows what will happen then?" she said, her eyes wider.

Her confession took my breath away. Suddenly, seemingly overnight, all this wasn't really a silly game anymore. We were peeling back whatever had been covering our budding sexual feelings. I could feel the new enthusiasm for our talks. We were no longer playmates; we were sisters.

That day, after the start of my first period, one of the most important in my personal history, we lay on the bed and talked in more detail about sex. Actually, she talked about it and I listened, asked questions, and then tried to envision myself willingly doing with a boy what she had described in such vivid detail.

"Painful?" I asked after her description.

"Losing virginity can be a little painful," she said, and went through the physical description.

"It sounds horrible," I said.

"Yes," Gloria said, "at first I thought so, too. I've read enough about it and enough descriptions of lovemaking to realize it isn't always. And then there are things I've heard some of the girls in the senior high tell each other, different ways to do it, how many times they've done it . . ."

"How many?"

"Some girls brag more than ten times and with different boys. I listen to them compare notes. A couple of girls did it with the same boy."

"You never told me that."

"I was going to."

"Where did you read descriptions that made you think it would be nice?" I asked, now a little more suspicious.

"In novels. We have some that Mother and surely Daddy would be surprised I've read. They were Mother's, although she claims they were here when they bought the house."

"You never told me about them. You never told me any of this, Gloria."

"I'm telling you now," she said before I could pout. "And I'll give you the books to read."

I was nowhere near as much of a reader as she was, but reading suddenly seemed more exciting. I knew what she had meant by "now," too. She hadn't thought I was ready for this discussion until this moment. It should have made me angrier. She was only a little more than a year older, but she was miles ahead of me when it came to most everything, and she knew it, too. She went on to talk about things she had read and heard about romance and love.

I sat up and looked around the bedroom after she had finished her detailed description of the romance in one of the novels. The man in the story was compared to a famous movie star, James Dean.

"Do you think that sort of thing happened in here, Gloria?"

"Of course, Gish. Probably many times."

"Many?"

"We call this our playhouse, but it was probably more of a honeymoon suite or what they sometimes call 'a lovers' lair.'"

In here? On this very bed? I was sure the expression on my face was enough to bring on a burst of laughter, but Gloria held hers back.

"If these walls really could talk," she said, and lay back again. So did I, and for a few long moments, we were both silent, swimming in our imaginations.

"So when do you think it will happen to me?" I asked.

"It's not something that happens to you, Gish," she said. She ran her right forefinger around a curl on my forehead. "Don't think of it that way."

"I don't know how to think of it. So much of what you said only gets me more confused."

"You won't always be. Someday you'll be in love with someone who will be in love with you, and doing it will be the most natural thing, like the most natural next step. If you're really in love, it will make your love stronger."

"How do you really know all this?"

"I told you. Reading," she said. I looked at her warily, and she laughed. "I haven't done it yet, Gish. I promise."

"What happens if I do and I make a baby?"

"There are ways to do it and not to get pregnant, Gish. I'll tell you everything. Don't worry."

"Mother thinks I will, right? She doesn't think I'm smart enough. That's why she said that about her worrying."

"She's just being a mother," she said. "Mothers are supposed to worry about it when they have daughters. She'll say the same to me when my time comes."

"I doubt it."

She looked at me. "No, she will. She expects a lot from me before I really fall in love and get married. I wish I was half as ambitious about myself as she and Daddy are for me, especially Daddy."

"He probably expects you to become a well-known artist. Mr. Longo, the art teacher, thinks you might."

She smiled. "Everyone transfers their own failed dreams to you sometimes, Gish."

"More than likely, though, Mother would prefer you to become a movie star?"

"Maybe, but I don't want to."

"What do you want to be?"

"Me," she said, smiling. Then she stopped and looked so thoughtful I thought we'd lose our moment together. I wanted to talk more about sexual intercourse and how it could be enjoyable and dangerous at the same time. Mother's eyes had been so condemning. She seemed so positive I would do something to ruin this family.

"What about Daddy? What's he going to think about me now? I'm sure she'll tell him. Will he worry I'll have a baby, too?"

"Sure."

"What?"

"Fathers worry more about their daughters than mothers do. It's already giving him nightmares to realize we're no longer like boys, but could *like* boys."

She laughed and squeezed my arm gently.

"Gish's a woman," she said, looking proud of me.

"What about you? When do you think it will happen?"

"Soon."

"Well, why are you so happy about it? It's not pleasant. I still have cramps."

"The world is going to change for us both, Gish. Everything will be different, especially a touch and a kiss."

I stared at her, still suspicious. She would often say things to make me feel better.

"Really," she said.

"I want to read one of those books tonight," I said.

She laughed harder and hugged me.

How wondrous she was, my sister Gloria. Despite the cramps and the shock, lying next to her in the playhouse, I felt secure and safe and very happy. She slipped her hand into mine, and we lay there side by side for nearly an hour, dozing, talking about silly things, laughing at the expression on Mother's face, and dreaming, I suspected, of when we would both fall in love.

That day in the casita, my day of infamy, would always loom brightly in my memory. It would always be easy to close my eyes and drift back into it and think of a time when we were deeply sisters and were like two astronauts about to be rocketed to a new and wonderful world, together.

I wished those moments never had ended. We spent a similar time talking, holding hands, and dreaming about her romantic future when she had her first period. By then, I was a lot wiser, having read two of the books she had given me, one almost straight through the night. I did feel like we had been launched. The first stage of our rocket, our childhood, fell back into memory forever and ever.

The changes that came over both of us now seemed to come overnight each time. In a new burst of energy, we went shopping for bras and bought sexier panties. We started to pay more attention to our makeup and began to change our entire wardrobes, from the wardrobes of children to the clothing of young adults. Gloria tried to buy us different things.

"We each want to be who we are," she said.

We shopped more than ever and read fashion magazines, imagining ourselves dressed in this or that, talked about boys in school, and when Daddy and Mother were out for the night, we sampled different alcoholic drinks, so that we'd know what to avoid or what to be careful drinking when we went to parties and "boys could take advantage of us," as Gloria said.

"Would they always?" I wondered aloud. "You make it sound that way, Gloria."

"Probably," Gloria said. "It's in their nature. We have to be more mature and control them."

"How?"

She thought about it and said, "By controlling ourselves, Gish, always, as difficult as that might be."

How wise that sounded. Even though I wasn't ashamed of how I was developing and what I looked like, I couldn't help but be in jealous awe of Gloria. Maybe I was becoming attractive, but Gloria was evolving into a world-class beauty. I knew that the eyes of men as well as teenage boys were fixating on her, not me, wherever we walked and in whatever room we entered. We both felt it, however. We were coming into our own. With maturity came independence, and with independence came more responsibility. More than once, Gloria would say, "I wish we could be children forever. Children are not responsible for what they do. Even the legal system recognizes that."

"Is it just age?"

"Yes, but when you start to drive . . ."

"What?"

"It all changes, Gish. In so many ways."

When Gloria got her driver's license and Daddy bought her a BMW hardtop convertible, Miles no longer drove us everywhere. Gloria drove me to my dental and eye appointments. Gloria picked me up if I remained longer after school. She always took me shopping for something I needed.

As I drew closer to driving age, I wondered if Daddy would think of buying me my own car, too. Before I could even approach the hope, Mother, noting my passing the driver's education program, said, "You two will just share Gloria's car when it's free." The implication was clear. I'd have to ask Gloria first, not that Gloria would ever deliberately refuse me. She was simply assumed to be the more responsible of the two of us.

That wasn't fair. Gloria was always an A-plus student, but I was a good B student. When I grew older, I never brought any unnecessary grief to my parents, either. Even through my teenage years, I never smoked or did any drugs. I always kept to our curfews and never once got into any trouble at school. But it was as if I was so ordinary that I couldn't be noticed. The best my mother could offer when someone complimented me for anything was to nod and say, "She's a nice girl." It got so that that word, *nice*, was another four-letter word, a profanity I'd never utter.

Maybe Gloria intimidated me, although never deliberately. Perhaps I could have done better. I know my parents seemed to believe that whatever success I had in school was thanks to Gloria's help, Gloria's tutoring me. My mother actually came out and said, "You're lucky you have a sister who can help you keep passing grades."

My grades weren't just passing, but she made it sound like they were just because I wasn't always on the honor roll or winning any awards. All my parents' expectations of me were so small, so limited. After a while, I stopped trying to get their appreciation.

I know I could have studied more, read more, but even though deep down inside I wanted to, I never wanted to appear like I was competing with my sister. Mother was always there to discourage me anyway. On more than one occasion, she told me not to expect to do this or that as well as Gloria could. That even extended to how we worked at being pretty.

Gloria had espresso-brown hair and greenish-blue eyes. She was always stunning, even as a little girl. No wonder Mother fantasized about her becoming a movie star. She'd introduce her as "our Shirley Temple."

From the first time our mother took us to a beauty salon, Gloria liked her hair short, a layered bob style. It was her choice, and our mother said it was brilliant and illustrated her artistic "equilibrium" and her "cinematic eye," especially at so young an age, whatever that meant. When it came to me, Mother said I didn't have the face for the short hairdo.

"It will exaggerate your features," she told me. That was like saying, *You have a blemish or some distortion. Don't do anything to magnify it.*

I wanted to disagree or whine that Gloria's features would be exaggerated, too, but in my heart of hearts, I knew that Gloria's could and should be magnified. She had the perfect button nose, the soft, full feminine lips, the graceful chin, and naturally long eyelashes. She was sculpted in the image of a mythological beauty, destined to go smoothly from cute to beautiful and alluring.

I was far from ugly, but I knew that I wasn't ever going to stand out like Gloria did and would. I was afraid to even try. I was safer sinking back into the ordinary, even though our differences weren't really the differences between the beautiful and the plain. I knew I could be pretty enough to attract the interest of boys. We had the same color hair, mine maybe a shade lighter, and almost the same blue eyes, hers just slightly more greenish blue. I just didn't want to work at it and appear to be vying for more compliments than she was getting. And anyway, when someone praised her for her beauty when I was beside her, she would always include me and say, "We're lucky. We inherited good genes."

We did resemble each other in so many ways, but Gloria had the glow. The candles behind my eyes were still unlit. Imitating her would not ignite them. I wouldn't insist on wearing my hair like she wore hers. My lighter brown hair was shoulder-length until soon after the day Daddy died. I tried to go with the flow, as they say, and agree with Mother. Gloria was worried I was upset about not having short hair, too.

"I'm not upset. Maybe Mother is right. I look better with longer hair."

"Yes, she is, and you do," Gloria said. "Your hair is thicker and richer. Why shouldn't you wear it longer?"

The thing I most hated about Gloria's compliments was that they were so sincere. Despite all the natural reasons for it, the anticipated sibling rivalry didn't seem to exist for Gloria. I think Mother making me Gloria's responsibility kept those feelings subdued.

I was the exact opposite. I looked for reasons to argue or to be angry at her as we became older. But even if I had found something, she would eagerly accept the blame and promise to make amends. Gloria was clearly the reason I hated angels. When my friends in high school complimented me on having such a beautiful and nice sister, I said, "She isn't perfect."

"Really?" Karla Bishop, one of my best friends at the time, said. "Why not?"

"Because she is perfect," I said, and they all looked at me as if I had lost my mind. "How would you like your mother constantly telling you to be more like your sister? And when you moved up a grade the following year, to have your teachers look at you and expect you to do as well as your sister?" I added, and that got them to rethink it all.

It did no good to express how I felt to Gloria, either. She would only look puzzled and troubled, so that in the end, I'd be the one who felt guilty.

"It bothers me, too, Gish," she said often.

"Sure," I said, clearly showing doubt, which did strike her like a dart.

But that didn't bring me any satisfaction. It was never easy or comforting for me to hurt Gloria or even just make her feel bad. There was something about seeing a face as beautiful and peaceful as hers take on the burden of pain and unhappiness that squeezed regret like a sponge and had it drip through my body and around my heart. Whenever I did that, I could feel my tears building and ran off to bury my face in a pillow.

She always followed to see if I was all right. She would say something like "I know you're unhappy, Gish. I'm sorry."

Why was she apologizing? And for what? Being more beautiful

and so intelligent? I'd swallow a scream of frustration and suck in my sniffles.

"Let's do something fun," she'd say. "Let's walk to town."

"Now?"

"Why not? We can get some frozen yogurt. Bubble and Pop has your favorite, pistachio. Okay?"

Despite how stubborn I wanted to be so I could sulk and sulk, I nodded.

Before I knew it, I'd forget my unhappy words and even my thoughts. Laughter was soothing and therapeutic for both of us. Gloria knew just how to do it, how to make me put aside my unhappiness, even for just a little while.

Eventually, I learned how to bury my jealousy almost completely and bask in the wide circle of respect and admiration she radiated. I convinced myself that it was enough to be Gloria John's sister. Something good and wonderful of hers surely would be shared with me. I did begin to appreciate and learn how to take advantage of that, even with my teachers, with boys, and eventually, with my parents.

It got so that my most cherished compliment from my father was, "That's good, Gish. That's how Gloria would have done it." By the time I was sixteen, I was actually happy to hear him say it.

I had learned that it's only when you accept your fate that you have even the smallest opportunity to change it. I suppose I was my own worst enemy in so many ways when we were younger. If you didn't believe things like this about yourself, you wouldn't do much of anything to change them. No one forced me to look plain, to have less ambition and self-respect. No one forced me to eat stupidly and become a good ten to twelve pounds too heavy by the time I entered high school. Gloria would literally search my room and confiscate candy bars and cookies hidden in the closet or under clothes in drawers. She would never tell me she had done it, and I never accused her, but we both knew she had. The maids wouldn't have dared touch any of it.

"I don't care about looking perfect like you," I'd say, to let her know I knew what she was doing.

She'd smile and say, "Of course you do, Gish, not that I'm perfect. Besides, I care about you."

"Why?" I challenged.

"Why? Because I love you, silly. You're my one and only sister. I never forget that."

Why was it always easier for her to say that than it was for me? I would soon learn why and, along with it, what she intended for both of us, even more so for me.

At the beginning of November of my junior year, Gloria came into my room after school and sat on my bed. I could see she had something very serious and important to tell me. Whenever she did, she would trace circles on the blanket and keep her eyes low until I said, "What?"

Then she would look up and say whatever it was, usually fast and in one breath. Most of the time, it wasn't anything earth-shattering, and it usually had to do with something I could do to please Mother and make both of our lives easier. Whenever Nick O'Sullivan saw me pouting and Gloria trying to cheer me up, he'd stop to say, "Whatever your problems, it's nothin' compared to what's happening to real people out there." He nodded at the world beyond our wall and then walked off.

"Real people? What are we? Fake people? What's bothering him today?" I asked Gloria.

"Same as yesterday—life," she muttered.

Today Gloria looked like she had something very different to tell me, something that made my own heart skip beats.

"Lee Aaron asked me to go out with him this Thursday."

"Lee Aaron?"

She nodded, that tiny soft smile on her lips.

"Out where?"

She looked up. "To watch a basketball game in Indio and then go for pizza afterward. He's scouting for our game with the Indio team in a week. Most of the team is going, as well as Coach McDermott."

I grimaced. "A basketball game?"

She laughed. "I know. Doesn't sound like much of a date, going somewhere with the school basketball team and their coach."

Lee Aaron was a senior and star of our basketball team as well as the student government president. He was six foot three, ginger-haired, with kelly green eyes and a smile that belonged in toothpaste commercials.

Probably just like every other girl in my class, I couldn't count how many times I had fantasized about being romantic with Lee Aaron. I knew that many boys had crushes on Gloria, so it didn't surprise me that the most popular boy in the school would eventually turn to her.

"Did you say yes?"

She nodded.

"Did you ask Mother and Daddy?"

"Just did. Mother said yes almost before I was finished."

"She's friends with his mother," I said, nodding. "One of her adoring fans at her celebrity coffee gatherings."

"Mother and Daddy are both friends with his parents. Daddy handles some of Mr. Aaron's investments."

Because of his work, Daddy knew so many rich people. Paul and Mary Aaron owned five car dealerships in the Coachella Valley. They had a big house on the road that led up to what had been Bob Hope's house. Mother and Daddy had been to dinners there, but neither of us had.

I sat up. Everyone at school knew Lee Aaron had just broken up with Kaylee Donald, a senior who had actually been in a beauty contest. Of course, I thought Gloria was far more beautiful, but Mother would never permit her to enter such a contest. She thought they were the only places real "dodos" could stand out. Besides, as Mother would quickly say, "Gloria John doesn't need anyone's stamp of approval on her beauty."

I could see some laughter in Gloria's eyes. How she could be so casual and relaxed about the most exciting romantic thing in her life intrigued me.

"Why are you smiling like that about it, Gloria? Were you expecting him to ask you once he broke up with Kaylee? You were, weren't you?" I followed before she could deny it.

She shrugged, again with the infuriating casualness about something I would treat as earth-shattering.

"I thought about it but didn't dwell on it, and I didn't give him any special attention. I see how most of the girls practically melt if he looks at or talks to them. I know he's a bit too conceited, but who isn't in the age of selfies?"

"Maybe you ignore him, but I've seen him look at you, even when he was walking with Kaylee," I said, secretly wishing I was saying that about myself.

"Yes, I know."

How casually she could admit it, and without the slightest hint of arrogance. Her being the most beautiful and intelligent girl in our school had somehow become an ordinary fact. It irked me and yet filled me with admiration at the same time. Nothing surprised her. She could end up on the cover of *People* magazine with the caption *The most beautiful teenage girl in America*, and she would look at it and say, "That's sweet of them to do."

"So you think he always wanted to be with you?" I asked, with a clear hint of annoyance.

"Maybe." She looked up and smiled more. "I have some other suspicions."

"What other suspicions?" I asked. "Do you think he was just trying to make Kaylee jealous?"

"Anything would have made her jealous, but no."

"Then what? What other suspicions?"

"Maybe our parents and his talked about his asking me out, especially after the end of his marquee romance."

"What's a marquee romance?"

"You know . . . he and Kaylee were always on everyone's lips. They were seen kissing in a corner, cuddling during an assembly, whatever. Truthfully, he turned me off most of the time with this public display of affection."

Turned her off? Was she kidding?

"Right," I said sarcastically. "Seeing that could make you throw up lunch."

She laughed. "Anyway," she said, "I was a little suspicious when he asked me out so soon. Then I remembered our parents had gone out with his parents after he broke up with Kaylee. Mother can be very persuasive, as you know, especially when it comes to planting something she wants in someone else's head."

Despite my immediate flush of jealousy, it was easy to imagine Gloria and Lee together. Mother didn't have to do a lot of planting. If someone was producing a movie about the perfect teenage couple, he or she would surely have cast them in the lead roles. However, Gloria might not be wrong in her suspicions, I thought. I could easily see how Mother would have thought of this first.

"No one had to convince him to ask you out, Gloria. He'd have had to be brain-dead not to have thought of it before Mother and his mother."

"It's okay either way," she said. "Despite his big head, I decided I like him enough to give him a chance."

Give him a chance? Give me *the chance*, I thought.

"What convinced you? His looks, his winning personality, his popularity? I'm sure it was a difficult decision," I said, with such sarcasm that I could taste the blood on my lips.

She laughed. "I might have misjudged him. He was a little more insecure than I imagined, almost tiptoeing around me."

"Insecure. How can he be arrogant and insecure?"

"Most arrogant people are, Gish. It's how they overcome it."

"Dr. Gloria. I keep forgetting you have that degree in psychology. So now you like him a lot?"

"Enough. For now," she added.

"What does *enough* mean? Enough to hold hands, to kiss, what?"

"We'll see."

"You'll see?" I couldn't imagine having any doubts.

"Yes, I really don't think people 'fall' in love at first sight, Gish, no matter how often it happens in Mother's movies or most of the books I told you to read."

"So how does it happen, Dr. Gloria?"

She laughed and then grew serious. "You start liking someone, maybe you're initially attracted, and then that grows stronger, if it's supposed to. Lee really liked Kaylee, or at least everyone thought he did. I know she thought he did."

"Thought?"

"Something happened, and they broke up. Their love didn't go on."

"What did happen? No one's told me anything."

I wasn't really surprised at that. I wasn't part of any gossip chain. Maybe it was my fault; I showed so little interest in it. Why did I need a best friend anyway? I had Gloria. Most of the girls in my class seemed to realize that. Few, if any, tried to get me to be closer, share secrets. Whereas everyone wanted to win Gloria's favor.

"A little gossip bird named Alice Thomas told me Kaylee secretly had started seeing a boy named Kurt Adams, a student at College of the Desert. Lee found out through a friend who is a waiter at Ruby's. So everyone's heartthrob had his own heart broken."

"Why would she leave him? Was this boy better-looking than Lee Aaron?"

"I don't know, Gish. Looks don't always have everything to do with it."

"Well, why would she do it, then?"

How could there be someone better than Lee Aaron? I didn't know any girl who didn't drool over him. I fantasized about being with him more than I wanted to admit, especially now that he was going to be involved with Gloria. It brought him closer to me. Maybe he wouldn't ignore me as much as he did.

"So?"

"Maybe she thought it was more impressive to go out with a college boy. Maybe she has an attention disorder."

"What's that?"

"She gets bored too easily."

"Bored? With Lee Aaron?"

"I don't know him well enough to answer that, Gish. Ask me after I date him a while, if it lasts a while."

"Maybe he is happy she cheated on him."

"Maybe. She could be one of those people who will be unhappy all their lives because they can't be happy for long. They always think there's something better, something they're missing. Too many of the girls we know are like that."

"You mean girls *you* know. I don't really know them," I said. "Everything is so complicated."

"Especially relationships." She reached for my hand. "Don't worry so much about it, Gish. When things like this are supposed to happen, they do." She leaned in to whisper. "You'll be the first to know if it's supposed to happen for me with Lee Aaron. I promise."

"It? Do you mean the same *it* we often discussed?"

She tilted her head. "Maybe. Eventually."

I felt the flush of excitement wash over me. Maybe? And with Lee Aaron? To my way of thinking, no matter what her reservations about him were at the moment, that had to be super special.

"How will you know it's supposed to happen with him? How long will it take? Will you tell me right away?"

She shrugged. "I just will, and of course I'll tell you," she said. "The same will be true for you, too, when the time comes."

Would it? She was so relaxed and confident about things that put some girls into therapy. I wondered if I would ever be as sure of myself when it came to my feelings. Could Gloria teach me how to be that way? Was it even something possible to learn, or was it simply in you or not?

"You promise and hope to die you will tell me if *it* does happen?"

"Of course. You'd be the first to know." She tightened her grip on my hand as if she was afraid that I'd float away. "Don't we share all our secrets? I promise. It will be like it's happening to you, too. But let's not get ahead of ourselves. As I said, I have to see what he's really like, and I think that may take some time, because he's always surrounded by his admirers. Boys, especially, can be very different when they're alone with you."

"What do you mean? How different?"

"They don't have to prove themselves so much. They can be . . . vulnerable, naked."

"Naked?"

"Emotionally, Gish, as well as physically. Maybe one leads to the other," she added with a Gloria laugh, short but full of subtle meaning.

"And you'll take me along on this emotional and romantic journey with you?"

"Every step of the way, if there is a way. Nothing is for sure."

Why was she being so cautious and even somewhat skeptical of something I saw as one of my best fantasies?

"Besides, if you're too anxious for something to happen, you are the one who's most vulnerable. Remember that, Gish, especially when it comes to boys."

"I don't understand where you get all this wisdom, Gloria, and don't tell me from books."

"It's a mystery. So what? Remember what Daddy always says. 'Don't look a gift horse in the mouth.'"

"Ugh. Who wants to look in a horse's mouth anyway?"

She laughed. "I love you, Gish," she said. It was unexpected, but so sincere that it brought tears to my eyes. "Unlike you, I'm glad we aren't twins. We'd have less to give each other."

That surprised me. "What do I give you?"

"More than you'll ever believe you do," she said. She looked like she was going to hug me.

"Yeah, but meanwhile, live up to your promise about Lee Aaron. I want a minute-by-minute report."

"Okay," she said, smiling. "I will."

It was truly the sort of promise that sisters as close as we were would make to each other.

But later she would be sorry for it.

Even Gloria could be trapped in a maze of promises better kept unfulfilled.

I knew this. I knew something she didn't know, but there was no way I could help her.

Or maybe . . . help myself.

chapter four

As I had anticipated, no one was surprised at Lee Aaron's pursuit of Gloria, and if she was truthful, she, especially, should not have been. Despite how modest and humble she was whenever she was complimented for anything, she was never oblivious of her popularity. She always had that twinkle of awareness, that soft smile of deep inner satisfaction. Maybe only I could see it. As strange as it might sound, I loved observing my sister when she was unaware that I was. It was like looking through one of those one-way mirrors.

Everyone admired Gloria for not being stuck-up or arrogant about her looks and achievements, especially her artistic talent, but I never doubted she believed she was superior to most everyone around her. She knew it, but she cloaked it well in her modesty after any and all praise, honors, and awards. For a long time, even I was astonished at her look of amazement when she was chosen for this or that or was told she was the best student her teacher had ever had. Somehow she was able to balance herself between a lack of self-confidence and an abundance of it. Would her humility ever be shed?

Somewhat frustrated by her perfection, I demanded that she explain herself to me once when we were both in high school. I was in my sophomore year, and she had just won another prize, this time for first place in a countywide essay contest. The principal made a big deal of it in his morning announcements. It was the first time our school had won. Even the school nurse stopped us on the way to lunch to congratulate her. Listening to Mrs. Mills's compliments, someone would think Gloria had invented a cure for cancer. Gloria thanked her, and we started away.

"How nice and unexpected of Mrs. Mills," she said.

"How unexpected? What did you think she was coming over to say to you when she approached us, Gloria? How healthy you looked?" I asked, sharply enough to get her to pause and give me a suspicious side-glance. Truthfully, Mrs. Mills's gush of praise had nauseated me. Ironically, I thought I'd end up in her office, complaining of stomachaches.

"I didn't know what to anticipate, Gish. I don't talk to her that much. What do you mean?"

"I know your winning wasn't as big a surprise as you made it seem to everyone," I said, before her usual crowd of admirers could join us and compete to lavish the best compliment, win the most favor.

"What are you saying, Gish?"

"You expected you would win, Gloria, especially when you read your essay aloud to Daddy and he said it was the cleverest explanation of the importance of ambition he had ever heard. Am I right?"

She smiled. "Yes and no."

"How can it be yes and no?" I demanded. "Well?" Her Buddha-like smile wouldn't wash me away this time.

"Yes, I was confident, even though dads are far from objective."

"Ours is. Brutal truth, you call it. You said that was what made him a successful investment adviser. You said it spills over to our daily lives."

"Good grief, Gish. Do you memorize everything I say and have said?"

I didn't answer. She knew that I did.

"Look. If you convince yourself it might not happen for whatever reason, reasons you can't imagine or control, Gish, you'll enjoy it more when it does, no matter what it is, and that includes romantic love."

"I don't have to convince myself it won't happen," I muttered, a little bitterly, maybe because what she said sounded so logical and true. "I have sacks of disappointments to carry around."

She laughed. "It's not always bad to be disappointed," she said.

"Huh? How can it not be?"

She tilted her head just a little to the right, as if she was forcing a secret thought to leak, and said, "If you weren't disappointed, then you didn't care. You don't ever want to be like those who don't care one way or another. They're nowhere people."

"Nowhere?"

"That's where they'll go," she said.

I shook my head.

"What?"

"You have an answer for everything, Gloria."

"Not everything," she said, her smile fading so quickly that I felt my heartbeat quicken. "There are lots of things that confuse me, especially things about myself."

"About yourself? What?" I asked.

I had really never heard this self-concern, this note of pessimism. I was too skeptical about Gloria ever being really unhappy or unsatisfied to believe her. What could be wrong with someone so beautiful, intelligent, and admired? I'd readily confess that a part of me had always wanted her to be sad, but the closer that came to being true, the more frightened of it I became. It was like Daddy always warned, "Be careful of what you wish for. You may get it."

"Tell me what you mean!"

"I'll tell you when I figure it out myself," she said, remaining mysterious. Other girls began to surround us, showering Gloria with their compliments. I fell back, outside the nauseating circle.

Would she ever tell me what bothered her? Would she ever need me? I couldn't even imagine it. Despite my jealousy and being incapable of wishing she would need me more than I needed her, at least once, I placed her far above my mother's wall of celebrities. Maybe that was because I knew Mother expected Gloria would become one, but she was already and probably always would be my personal celebrity in every way. Her picture belonged on that wall of the famous. Mother even should have had her sign her name on the wall of autographs so that whoever bought our home in years to come would have it, too, because Gloria was bound to do something great.

If Mother had insisted on Gloria writing on the wall, it would certainly not have been a surprise to me, and, I ventured to guess, not to Gloria, either. Mother was like most everyone when it came to celebrities. Yes, she was over-the-top with it, but even Gloria now believed that we viewed our celebrities as so superior to us. When I tried to be skeptical, critical of Mother, she defended her.

"Don't blame her too much, Gish. She's reflecting something rampant in our society, maybe every society. If we're lucky to actually meet a celebrity, we cherish their words and maybe a smile cast at us, and lock it all so well in our memories that decades from the moment, we will describe the moment as if it had just happened. It becomes one of those immortal minutes, Gish. Mother taught us that early with her constant adoration of the names on the wall and the way she valued every fact she had learned about this star or that, no matter how old. For Mother, we live where gods once strolled. We can't fault her for wanting something special for us all."

Gloria could convince me of anything, I thought. And she could change my mind about something in an instant. And all that time, she never realized that I was creating my own wall of celebrity with just one face, one signature, and one set of biographical facts. I was worshipping my sister. Of course, I would cherish and memorize practically every word she said, every confession she made about her own feelings, and especially her romantic ones. It would be an honor to be so trusted, to have her trust me more than she trusted our parents.

Back then, I thought I would never live as deeply, enjoy any pleasure, suffer any disappointment, or dream any dream as well as Gloria would anyway. Maybe she knew that. Maybe she encouraged me to believe it, although she would never confess to such a thing. I suspected that my sister enjoyed her sense of control, especially over me. I loved my suspicions, especially of my perfect sister. And yet I knew in my heart that, like Daddy had said, I should be careful about what I wished for regarding her. I might get my wish, and then I might be very unhappy I had. How could I go on anyway without total trust in her, and in what she had pledged to me, especially about romance?

The night of her first date with Lee Aaron, I had tried to keep awake so I could hear her come home. Mother told me to go to bed just after eleven. The next day school was closed for teachers' meetings. She found me asleep in the big cushion easy chair in the living room where I had been waiting for Gloria and shook me awake. She and Daddy had just returned from their dinner date. Although I wondered if our parents had given Gloria a curfew time, I was afraid to ask, in case she had already violated it.

"Go to bed," Mother said. "Don't you know enough to do that yourself when you're tired? Do you have to have your sister here to remind you when to go to sleep, when to brush your teeth?"

She looked at my father, who, with his disapproving scowl, seconded her unhappiness with me. When had he ever done otherwise?

Without replying, I hurried up to my room, washed, and changed into my pajamas. It was eleven thirty by then. Twice I had dozed off in bed. When I awoke the second time, I saw it was nearly twelve fifteen. My first thought was that Gloria had come home and was either in bed or getting ready to go to sleep herself. I was so disappointed. I rose and peered into her room and was cheered. Her bed was untouched, and the lights were off.

Surely, though, Daddy had given her midnight, the Cinderella hour, as a time to be home, I thought, and returned to my room. Would he be waiting up for her, yell at her, and send her directly to bed? Just before twelve thirty, I heard her rushing up the stairs. I hadn't heard anyone sound angry, but I held my breath. Then I saw my door open slightly, and Gloria peeked into my room.

"Hi," I said, and quickly sat up.

"Good. You're still awake," she whispered, closed the door, and hurried to sit on my bed.

"Did Mother and Daddy say you could stay out this late?" I asked, eyeing the door.

"They didn't give me a specific time," she said.

"Really? You could come home whenever you wanted?"

"They trust me to do the right thing," she said with a smile. I had never heard her say something like that with such self-satisfaction. It was as if she was successfully taking advantage of them.

"Well, how was it?"

"I unexpectedly had a very good time. Everyone from our school who was at the game, too, paid us a lot of attention. Even the coach came over to us to kid me especially."

"Especially you? Why? What did he say?"

"'Be sure you keep my team captain on the straight and narrow.'"

"What did that mean?"

"Under it all, I think he means keep him from doing anything wrong that would damage his sports reputation. When he saw the look on my face, he said something about hurting his jump shot. Everyone laughed, but I could feel the way they looked at me changed," she added.

"Why?"

"I wasn't the celebrity for a change. Lee was, and I liked it, liked people paying attention to me because I was with him and not vice versa."

I sat there with my mouth open, looking stupid, I was sure. How could she ever be tired of being the celebrity or prefer that someone else be?

"I've never learned so much about basketball strategy," she continued. "It was important to Lee that I understand everything. I don't think he believed I'd enjoy that, but I did."

I grimaced. "Sports? Didn't you talk about something else?"

"Not there. The game was quite exciting. It will be a tough one next Friday."

"Well, what happened afterward?" I asked impatiently.

"Afterward, we escaped."

"Escaped? From what?"

"All the others. He told everyone we were going to Nat Levine's in Rancho Mirage for pizza and then he made a turn and said we were going to a hole in the wall he had found off Country Club Drive. There was no one else there our age. It wasn't anything spectacular, but it was special, know what I mean?"

"No," I said, getting more and more frustrated. "Why was it special to go where no one knows you?"

"There was no one to take his attention from me or mine from him. We were actually ignored. No one there knew either of us."

"So?" I said, still not fully understanding why being with a bunch of strangers was so great.

"When you're alone like that and there's no one there to interrupt you, you can get to know someone for real. I mean . . ." She looked up at the ceiling as if she was searching there for the right words. "You feel more authentic."

I shook my head. Couldn't she say it simply?

"There wasn't a crowd of his friends around us. Neither he nor

I was afraid someone would overhear us. You're usually not honest when you first meet someone like this."

"Why not?"

She looked at me as if she was going to share a great secret just the way we might in the casita. "You hold back because you're afraid you'll discourage each other. You might say something that offends him or gets him to think you're weird or something, and everything stops before it even gets a chance to begin. You have to know more about someone before you share the truth, Gish. Like I said, trust takes time to develop, and if you're impatient, you could drive away someone you really like. I read somewhere that most first dates never see a second. He started it, though. I mean being boldly honest."

"How?"

"He told me that his parents, especially his father, are putting a lot of pressure on him. He took a leap of faith."

"What do you mean? What leap?"

"He could have been worried I'd tell Mother or Daddy what he had said and it would get back to his father, and then . . . who knows what. They'd surely frown on our continuing to go out."

"What is he pressuring him to do?"

"Be an outstanding basketball player."

"But he is."

"More than he is, especially this Friday. His father wants him to get a basketball scholarship to Michigan State, his alma mater. He said his father has a scout from the college coming to watch him play this coming Friday. His grades are okay, but they're not . . ."

"Like yours?"

"No. Not that he isn't very intelligent. He is," she quickly added. "But he might not get accepted if he doesn't win the basketball scholarship. I mean, he'll get into many other colleges but maybe not that one. He's very worried about it. Boys want to please their fathers more. I felt sorry for him. He's afraid he'll disappoint his teammates by hogging the ball or something just so he looks more spectacular."

I thought a moment. This didn't sound like as exciting a date to me as she was portraying it to be. She sat through a basketball game she surely didn't really care about one way or another and then went to some restaurant where no one knew her or him and heard him complain about his life. Why was she trying to convince me that this was a good date?

"You said he was boldly honest first. So what did you confess to him that was so honest?"

For a moment, I thought she wasn't going to tell me. She actually looked at the door as if she was afraid Mother was eavesdropping on us, something we both often had suspected.

"I told him I really wasn't looking forward to going to college."

"What? Why not?"

She shrugged. "Not right away, at least. I was thinking about traveling for at least a year."

"Instead of college?"

"I would enjoy a break. Everyone, especially Daddy, expects so much of me. I can't have a bad day. Ever. A year without doing anything important and having people fawn over what I achieve would be nice."

"But a year? Traveling? Where?"

"Europe, probably. Backpacking. That's our secret," she quickly added, and then grimaced. "I'll probably go to college anyway. I don't know if I have the courage to tell them, tell Daddy what I'd really like to do. Remember when I got that eighty-five on a math exam in the seventh grade and I was crying? I couldn't help it."

"I was happy to get an eighty-five."

"It was far from the end of the world, but I could imagine Daddy's face when he saw it."

"You got ninety-eights after that."

"Yeah, but the eighty-five just didn't disappear, at least for quite a while. It made me work harder and harder."

I stared at her a moment. I was the one who was supposed to feel the pressure because of her, not her. I thought it came easily for her.

"It doesn't make a difference now, Gloria. You'll win every scholarship you want," I said. "Won't that be exciting?"

"To tell you the truth, I worry I might be taking it away from someone who really needs it. We can afford my full tuition at Yale. Sorry. Didn't mean to leave you on a note of depression and sadness."

She had started to get up when I reached out quickly and seized her wrist. "That's it? That's all you're going to tell me about your date?"

"Aren't you tired?"

"No. I mean, yes, but you promised to tell me everything, Gloria."

I hated that I sounded like I was whining, but I was.

She sat again and took a deep breath. "We were having such a good conversation at the restaurant, we decided to keep talking and went to the school parking lot."

"The school? Why there?"

"No one is there that time of night, so it was quite private."

"And?"

I held my breath. It was important for it to be private. What did she do?

"We kissed eventually. He's actually a little shy," she said. "Or maybe pretends to be. Some boys have clever techniques to catch you off guard, especially someone as suave as Lee Aaron."

"I don't know how or why you know so much about boys. This is your first real date, Gloria."

"You have some built-in alarms. All women do. You'll see. The trick is to pay attention to them, or want to."

Whether or not Lee was using a technique on her wasn't that important to me. She was hesitating. I knew there was much more to tell.

"So? Then what happened? Was it a romantic kiss? Like we read in *Love's Secret Door*?"

She nodded. "Not the first time, but the second and third kiss were."

"Second and third? What else did you do? You didn't just kiss, did you?"

"I let him run his hand over my breasts. He kissed me on the neck and started to unbutton my shirt, but . . ."

"But what?" I asked breathlessly.

"I wanted to do more. I really did, Gish, but I thought he might get the wrong idea about me."

"Which was what?" I asked, the disappointment surging.

"That I was too easy. It was only our first date. I don't think most boys expect to score on the first date. Besides, Daddy's right. The best things in life are those that take time to happen. That especially goes for how you behave with a boy you like."

This sounded boring, too much like some science experiment or one of her philosophical ponderings. What about the romance, the passion? Wasn't it supposed to be overwhelming? In so many of the stories we read together, the woman enjoyed losing control.

"How long do you expect it to take with Lee Aaron? How many dates?"

"I don't know. You don't mark a calendar or anything. It's not the same for every girl. I told you. You let things take their natural course, if they're meant to."

"But you think it's going to happen? And with him, don't you?"

"Maybe."

"Maybe?"

"Why are you so disappointed?"

I didn't answer. "How will you know? What will happen next time? How close did you really come this time? How could it be maybe with Lee Aaron?"

"It's late. I'm so tired. Really."

She rose.

"So you're definitely going to see him again?" I asked quickly.

She smiled. "Tomorrow night, or I should say tonight," she said. "We're going to babysit his six-year-old little brother because his parents are going to the same charity affair Mother and Daddy are attending. I think they're sitting at the same table. I imagine we might be the topic for their discussion. Again."

She stood there looking like she might want to keep talking.

"You got very excited, didn't you?" I demanded. I would have something more before she left. "Like you and I read in that novel you said had the most detailed sex. I know what to expect, and I believe you did, too."

She kept her eyes down. I thought she wouldn't say anything else, but then she looked up and surprised me. "Excited more than I thought I would be," she admitted. "Almost too much. Which was what surprised me the most about myself."

"What does that mean? What else really happened, Gloria?"

"We'll talk tomorrow. I'm falling asleep on my feet. It was emotionally exhausting," she added. "Promise."

I watched her leave and lay back on the pillow. When I closed my eyes, I saw Lee Aaron bringing his lips to mine, kissing me the way the kiss was described in *Love's Secret Door*, a kiss just hard enough to reach down through you and feel like lips on your nipples and a warm hand moving down your stomach. Gloria had read the words aloud in the casita, and then she had paused and said, "It makes you think it's a wave goodbye."

"A wave goodbye?"

"To your virginity," she had said.

I know my face was full of surprise and delight. We both laughed.

But we were younger then. Scenes like those in that novel seemed years away for the both of us. Now, because of Gloria's experience tonight and the way she was acting, I believed it surely would happen to her sooner and with the boy I would most like to wave that goodbye with.

As I lay there, I looked at the thin light go out under the door. The excitement she had stirred in me wasn't dissipating. If anything, my fantasy was more vivid. It was truly as though I had been there and felt Lee's hand on my breasts, too. I wanted his hands to move all over me. I wanted to kiss him harder. I wouldn't have stopped him when he started to unbutton *my* shirt. Now I could vividly see him doing it and feel him touch me, his fingers over my nipples, his lips pressing harder.

My moan shocked me. Had anyone heard it? I waited and then turned on my side and embraced my pillow. I should have had her describe how they had said good night, and right outside my window, too.

I could easily imagine it.

"I had a really good time," he said, and she said she did, too. They held tightly to each other's hands, especially Lee holding on to hers. "I've got to go in," she said. "I'll see you tomorrow." He let go but then seized her to kiss her good night again. She laughed and hurried out, pausing at the front door. The smile they gave each other was filled with sexual promise.

It was easy to envision. That's the way it would have been for me. It was truly as if I was there.

The flow of sexual tension and desire rushed through my body. I tossed and turned and embraced my oversize soft pillows. I was embracing Lee, moving my body rhythmically against him and feeling his breath warm and quicken with mine. Was Gloria doing the same thing next door in her room? Did I imagine her moans synchronizing with mine? Did we both gasp at the same time as the rush built to a crescendo? Would she admit to it if I asked her tomorrow? I would not confess. I couldn't fool Gloria. She would know I wasn't simply curious. She would know how jealous I was.

For now, I fell asleep content with the imagined moments of love. I had successfully slipped into one of Gloria's and my forbidden novels.

At breakfast, Mother and Daddy had more questions for Gloria than I had about her date, but none to do with sex, of course. They were indeed going to sit with Lee's parents at the charity event, and I could see that Mother wanted to hear positive things about Lee Aaron.

"I spoke to Mary Aaron last night," she said. "She never liked the girl he was going with. She said she was quite vapid."

Gloria just shrugged. "I don't know her that well, Mother. She's not unhappy with their breakup, right, Gish?"

"Right," I said, but Mother gave me little more than a glance. Daddy kept eating as if none of us was there.

"Anyway, she knows your accomplishments. She's quite happy Lee asked you out. I told you that last night, didn't I, Alan?"

"What?" Daddy looked up. "Oh, yes, yes, you did."

"Well, it's nice you two got along. First dates are very important," Mother said.

And like most everything else Gloria did, Mother turned it into a lesson for me.

"It's very necessary," she said, looking at me now, "that you are careful about the company you keep, especially the boys. You're both at a very vulnerable age. Fortunately, your sister is very particular. We hope you will be, too. You must always remember that a child is like a family ambassador. Whatever she does reflects on the respect her family has in the community. Gloria is quite aware of that."

Gloria, Gloria, Gloria, I thought as the blood raced to my cheeks. What had I done to deserve even the suggestion of a warning?

"How do you know Lee Aaron's so good?" I asked, without looking at Gloria, who I knew was surprised at my question. She was probably afraid I'd just burst out with some of what she had told me. "Just because his parents have money and he's good at basketball?"

"It has to do with upbringing," Mother snapped. "We know how the Aarons have brought him up. We've been friends with them for years." She looked at Daddy for reinforcement.

"If he's not a good boy, Gloria will know first, and if I know Gloria, she'll give him his walking papers," Daddy said, smiling.

Gloria had her eyes down during Mother's comments to me. She looked up at all of us after Daddy's statement and gave a little laugh.

"It's only one date," she said, glancing at me.

"Yes, well, Lee is a nice boy," Mother said. She looked at me and then turned to Gloria and said, "But if he brings anyone around to date your sister, you make sure he's just as respectful a young man."

Brings anyone around? And if he did, Gloria had to approve? Now Gloria would be choosing my boyfriends besides most everything else in my life, all with Mother's blessing and encouragement.

"I'm not going on any arranged double dates. I'll go on my own date," I said defiantly.

"Not until you're older," Mother said. "Don't dare accept any invitations on your own."

"But I'm not that much younger than Gloria, and you just said if Gloria and Lee want to have a double date—"

"That's because your sister will be there," she said.

"Holding my hand? You think I'm an idiot," I said, tears welling up. I threw my napkin on the table. "She's doesn't know everything."

I leaped up and rushed out of the breakfast nook, defying my father's call to come right back. I kept walking fast until I reached the pool and then flopped onto a lounge chair and watched the water rushing over the built-in hot tub and into the pool itself. It suddenly occurred to me that I wasn't angry about again being treated like a child. I was too used to that by now; I was clearly and simply just jealous, but I was bringing jealousy to a new and even frightening height. I was wishing bad things would happen to my sister, including that something would mar her angelic beauty.

"Hey, silly," I heard. Gloria hurried to join me. "Why are you so angry? It's better than you think."

"What? How is what just happened better than I think? She just talked to me like I was five again. In fact, she always talks to me that way, and Daddy doesn't stop her."

Gloria sat on the lounge chair next to me. "You are not thinking clearly. Push the anger out. This is a great opportunity."

"Huh? How?"

"Maybe Mother would stop you from going out on a date with someone you liked, but now you can, silly goose."

"What do you mean?"

"I'm not going to choose who you should date on a double date, and neither is Lee. You tell me who you'd like to date, and Lee will invite him to join us. Everyone wants to be with Lee. I know you're shy, but there must be someone you like or think you would like. Wait, I know. After you decide on someone, you can come with me tonight to Lee's house. It'll be like our own private party."

I sat up. Being offered such an opportunity was so unexpected and maybe even more enraging. Everything I would do would still be through her first.

"I don't know who I'd want, and what if he came just because you or Lee asked him to? How would I look then? I'd be like that girl in the play we both had to read in class, Laura in *The Glass Menagerie* . . . a cripple who needs her brother to find her a boyfriend."

"Don't look at it like that. We can both have fun. And besides, even if that was true, you'll change his mind quickly. He'll be happy he came because of you."

"I don't know," I said skeptically.

Why would any boy be so won over by me? What made her so confident about it? She sounded so sincere, but Gloria would do anything to make things pleasant at our house again. If she were the weather girl, it would never rain.

"Well, think about it instead of pouting. I'll call Lee as soon as you think of someone. We'll do our hair and nails and have fun deciding what to wear. It will just be a date, but we'll make it seem more like the prom. Okay?"

"I don't know who to suggest," I said again. I couldn't think past Lee Aaron. Who would even come close?

We both turned as Nick O'Sullivan came around the corner of the pool house. Had he heard our conversation? He paused and stared at us a moment with a look of disapproval. He was carrying a hose and a rake and resembled some medieval soldier. After a moment, he walked to the rear of the property.

I lay back again. I wanted to fall into a pout, but her suggestions did excite me.

Maybe going on a double date tonight was a good idea. I wasn't sure whom I'd choose, but it would still be like I was on a date with Lee, too.

"Let's go through some boys," Gloria suggested. "Of course, it has to be someone you agree to, but maybe I can help. And if we think of someone and I call Lee, he'll be honest in his opinion."

I know he will, I thought, *but to please you, not me.*

She leaned over to squeeze my hand. "Let's go to the casita and think of some boys, and I'll tell you what I promised to tell you about my date last night, the rest of it."

"Really? There was more?"

"Yes. Lots. Come on," she said, rising and reaching for my hand. "We've got to scare away the ghost first. Well?"

Lots?

I took her hand, and we went running and laughing toward the casita. The sadness was gone with the anger, too, and in its place was new excitement. I felt like I was in one of those rafts going down the rapids like we had done in Jackson Hole, Wyoming, two years ago on a family vacation. Fear turned into exhilaration and thrill.

I wondered if being so sad and then so happy in an instant would eventually drive me mad.

Maybe in the end, that was exactly what happened to Gloria.

Maybe all this time she was in a raft bouncing over raging waters that I never realized were flowing just below both of us.

But especially below her.

chapter five

I couldn't come right out and say it, but it was hard to think of anyone I'd like to be with other than Lee Aaron. I thought it was going to be a waste of time to try to come up with anyone nearly as exciting. Ours was a private school with only four hundred students in grades nine through twelve, with an almost two-to-one female-to-male population. There were some good-looking boys and some boys I enjoyed talking to, but no one who brought me fantasies the way Lee did now. Perhaps that was solely because he was becoming Gloria's boyfriend. Sometimes I felt like a sleepwalker on the beach, stepping carefully into the imprinted footsteps Gloria had left behind.

I should try really hard to think of someone else, I thought. *I should break away and find myself, make my own choices and have my own dreams.* Was I afraid? Maybe I was deliberately keeping myself in Gloria's shadow because it felt safer to do so. Having my own opinions and likes and dislikes wasn't easier just because I was a teenager now. On the contrary, it was more like becoming a trapeze artist working without a net, because my words had more consequences. How often had I kept my opinions to myself because I was afraid they would be contrasted with Gloria's? I remembered when I was in sixth grade and had groaned when we were assigned more homework for the weekend. Mrs. Steiner stopped talking and glared at me. The whole class held their breath, and she said, "Your sister would never do that."

Was there any blood left in my face? I never told Gloria about it, but someone else did, and she came into my room that night to assure me that what Mrs. Steiner had said was unfair, even stupid. I pretended it didn't bother me, but it was truly a scar, a wound inflicted on whatever independence and self-respect I had managed to have living and breathing in her shadow.

"Okay," Gloria said when we were in the casita and lying beside each other. "Let's think about this rationally."

"What does that mean?" I knew what it meant, but I didn't think it was anything romantic or sexy.

"Let's start with this question. You're absolutely, positively sure there is no particular boy you would like to be with, someone you have been thinking about but you were afraid to say, even to me?"

I was silent, so she reached over to tickle my ribs.

"Come on. Confess. Secrets are safe in the playhouse."

How should I put this? I wondered. The last thing I wanted her to know was that I wished Lee Aaron was more interested in me than in her. I didn't even want to tell myself that. Envying Gloria for anything only led to more self-pity, and I was starting to drown in it.

"Not like you do with Lee. Most of the boys in my class are quite juvenile, and usually, unless I'm with you, senior boys don't talk to me."

"What about Stanley Bender? He's kind of cute, always dresses very nicely, and I think he's the smartest student in your class."

"He is, but he has terrible bad breath. When he comes near me, I cringe."

"Oh. Someone should tell him, slip a note in his locker or something."

"He's not that important to me. Or to any of the girls, for that matter."

"No one else, then, even a little bit?"

"No one in particular. The boys who show interest in me don't seem sincerely interested in me."

That was a nice way of saying they really wanted to talk to and be near her. If she understood, she blinked it away.

"Well, maybe we should look at it from a different point of view, then," she said. "Let's consider who would best fit on a double date with Lee and me and be someone you might become interested in and who might be interested in you once you got to know each other better."

"What does that mean? Fit?"

"If there's a boy you might get to like and he's close with Lee, we'll all have a better chance at getting along and having a good time. Double dates are probably the most risky because there are four people involved, four different personalities with each having his and her likes and dislikes."

"Wise old Gloria," I said a little bitterly.

She ignored it, or maybe she was so deep in thought she hadn't heard me. She nodded her head, agreeing with herself, her own new thought. "I also think you should have your first date with someone who is not so into himself that he'll treat you badly or, worse, go too fast for you. Someone who isn't insensitive or uncaring."

"From the little you told me last night, Lee wasn't exactly keeping to the speed limits," I said a little sharply.

Gloria laughed. "That's very good, Gish. Now I'm worried you might run right over most of the boys."

We were both quiet, me because I didn't know what to say and Gloria because she was in deep thought, maybe reliving last night. I was still waiting for more intimate details.

Outside, Mr. O'Sullivan and his team had begun to mow the grass. It sounded like an army of bees. We could hear Mr. O'Sullivan shout angrily from time to time. I wasn't sure if he really took that much pride in how our grounds looked or if he was just afraid of Mother.

I always thought he worked more for our mother than our father anyway. Daddy wasn't as anal about our grounds, but Mother had been talking more and more about holding charity events here, very expensive ones. She wasn't convinced yet about which charitable organization she wanted to launch on our property. From the way she and Daddy talked about it, I didn't think the organization in most desperate need was her top priority. Of course, her event would be headlined with some celebrity or even celebrities Daddy or she could attract with the help of some very wealthy people who had access to them.

"If we're going to charge some of the numbers I'm thinking of charging for a ticket," Mother had said, "then we'll need very special people to attract everyone. Maybe we'll do yearly events at Cameo, events everyone will look forward to attending. We do have one of the most, if not *the* most, beautiful properties in the old movie colony. People look up to us, expect us to do more for the community, Alan."

Maybe she really thought she and Daddy should sign the wall of autographs.

Yet despite all that Mother did to make us important, it was Gloria, I thought, who brought us the most attention. Just last week, one of the more prestigious art galleries in the Coachella Valley had taken her latest pastel to sell. The *Desert Sun* newspaper featured it in an article about local talent. It was the portrait of a girl in a ballet costume sitting on a sofa with one leg folded under the other. The girl didn't look more than ten years old and was pretty, but there was an adult-like expression on her face. When I asked Gloria if she was supposed to be sad or just thoughtful, she said, "Sometimes they're one and the same."

I had no idea what she meant, but I often let something Gloria said go by because I didn't want to look dumb. Most of the time when she said something so deep, I thought she wasn't saying it to me anyway. She was saying it to herself.

Meanwhile, the longer we lay there trying to think of a boy who would be a good date for me, the sadder I was becoming. It made me seem so pathetic. I often felt like an outsider at home, and now I was feeling like an outsider at school. Gloria's shadow was simply too wide and deep. Rarely was the light on me. Maybe I didn't really exist. Perhaps I was a figment of her imagination. She'd blink and I'd be gone. That's how I really felt most of the time. It was easy to blame my parents or even Gloria. How could I blame myself? What had I done besides being born unwanted?

"What do you think of Bobby Sacks?" she suddenly asked.

"Bobby Sacks?"

"He's not really a bad-looking boy, and he's fun to be with. Lee adores him. Most important," she said, turning to me, "he really is shy when it comes to girls, despite how aggressive he is on the basketball court. He blushes like a fresh rose whenever I talk to him."

That's you, I thought. What boy wouldn't? *The goddess had noticed me, opened her wings so I could look upon her.* How many of the boys at school had slept with her in their fantasies last night? How many had envisioned her naked or had brushed against her in the hallway, thrilled with the touch? Was she that oblivious to the difference between us?

"I certainly don't think he'd be one to take advantage of you."

Was that the most important consideration? Right now, I was wondering if I might enjoy being the victim. Whatever happened, I could blame it on her. This was really all her idea, wasn't it? My great, wise older sister would be at fault. Maybe then, finally then, my parents would sympathize more with me, and she would be the one who had given Mother premature gray hairs.

"What do you think?" she pursued when I hadn't spoken for almost a minute.

"I'm thinking."

Bobby Sacks was one of the starting five on the basketball team. He was six foot one with hair the color of straw that looked like an eagle had splattered it on his head while on the way to build a nest. His best feature was his greenish-blue eyes. I had seen some games and knew that as a basketball player, his best feature was the springs in his legs. From a standing position, with his long arms and big hands, he could hover above the basket, pull down rebounds, and block shots. He walked like his upper body had recently been attached, the bottom half of him appearing to be slightly ahead of the rest of him. But Gloria was right: he did have a nice smile and was always congenial because of his bubbly personality. Off the court, he was almost as popular as he was on the court, too.

In fact, when I really thought about it, she had made what she called a logical suggestion. Next to Lee, there was no other senior boy quite as popular and well liked as Bobby Sacks. He did have a girlfriend from time to time but, as far as I could tell, he'd had no serious relationship. Although I saw him looking at Gloria, just like every other boy in the school, I never caught him looking at me.

"Isn't he dating Eileen Cauthers?"

"He double-dated with her when Lee was going with Kaylee, because she is Kaylee's best friend, so you can figure that out. He's not seeing anyone now," Gloria said.

"He went out with someone just because she was Lee's old girlfriend's best friend? He does whatever would make Lee happy?"

"They're birds of a feather," she said.

"So now he'll go out with me because I'm your sister and Lee's dating you?"

"Honestly? Maybe at the very start, but he'll be happy about it once he meets you. I think he's nice," she sang, dangling her words like bait.

I didn't say anything.

She turned to me. "Should I call Lee and see what he thinks?"

"You were going to tell me more about your date last night. You promised."

"I will. Let's do this first. Okay?"

"I guess," I said.

She laughed. "Don't be so enthusiastic."

"Well, I don't know if I want to be with him," I snapped back at her. "We've hardly said two words to each other this year, maybe ever. He might even say he never knew you had a sister."

Gloria always had that moment of pause before she responded to anything or anyone unpleasant. I could see her holding her breath, and I could read her eyes. The seconds of hesitation ticked away, and whatever monster of rage had roared calmed to settle back in its own pool of frustration. If she wanted me to be like her in any way, in anything, that would be my choice over her high grades, maybe even her exceptional good looks. She always clamped down on my anger, especially when it involved Mother. "Anger is the quickest way to lose control of yourself and be at the mercy of mistakes," she told me. Lady Jesus and Miss Buddha rolled into one. How was I ever going to be like that?

"Don't worry about it so much, Gish. It's just a first date. You'll be with us," she said. "Neither Lee nor I would let something unpleasant happen. If it works out, it works out. If not, no terrible loss. Okay?"

"How do you know Lee wouldn't let something unpleasant happen? How do you know so much about him? You went out only once with him."

She shrugged. "I just know. I never analyze why."

"Um," I grunted. Unlike her, I never stopped analyzing myself. Obviously, she was better off the way she was.

"So?"

"Okay," I said.

She rose and took her cell phone out of her pocket. As she called, she wandered out of the bedroom. "Hi," I heard her say, and then her voice grew lower until I realized she had stepped out of the casita altogether.

A part of me wanted to be in total rebellion and just run out of the casita and back to the pool lounge to pout. What was I doing? Exactly what I'd said I wouldn't do. I had told myself I wasn't going to let Gloria choose whom I should care for. There was so little I did for myself as it was. She had been on top of my studies, buying my clothes, and looking after my needs from the time we were nine and ten to now. Whatever I wanted to do, she would do, but her way. She was the one who had turned the casita into our private place, and she was the one who decided what we would talk about secretly. She was the one who knew how to dance and showed me some steps. She knew the popular music. She created the word games we played, and when we went anywhere, she led the way, chose the destination, even if it was somewhere I wanted us to go, something I wanted us to do. It wasn't that she could read my thoughts; she always seemed to find a better reason to do what I wanted.

Who, I wondered, does she see when she looks at me? A total fool, just like Mother sees? I was so dwarfed by her that our parents just assumed I needed to be led along with everything and assumed I'd be the one to create the problems children caused for their parents. And all the while, Mother especially expected me to be grateful I had such a sister. According to her, in every other family, practically, the blind led the blind. But not in ours. We had Gloria.

Gloria, Gloria, Gloria.

"He's so excited," she said, returning. "I almost didn't get everything out before he said so. And he's so looking forward to being with you, too."

"He is? Why?"

"He said he's always wondered about you. He thinks you're very mysterious because you're so quiet in school, looking so thoughtful all the time."

I smirked skeptically. What else could I be but quiet and thoughtful with my sister often on everyone else's lips? What was

Gloria wearing? Did you notice she changed her lipstick? Was Gloria going to do this or that?

"He does! And he says he couldn't think of a girl more perfect for Bobby. He agrees. Bobby is very shy, and an overpowering girl frightens him."

"How does he know I won't be one of those?"

She widened her smile. "That's good, Gish."

"Does he think I'm just like you?" I asked.

"Of course not," she said, but weakly.

My suspicions grew. "What happened last night when Lee began to unbutton your blouse?"

She smiled, nodded, and lay next to me again. "I wasn't honest about it when I described what happened. I think I was still a little dazed myself, and if I talked about it any more, I'd never sleep."

"What really happened?" I asked breathlessly.

"I let him unbutton it completely, and . . ."

"And?" She was taking too long. I almost couldn't get out the word.

"I let him slip it off me."

"You were just in your bra?"

"It's one thing to read about it and another to do it yourself," she said, looking now as if she was talking to herself and not to me.

"Do what?"

She was quiet.

"What, Gloria? You said you would tell me everything."

"I let him unclip my bra. My heart was pounding. He gently slipped the straps down my arms and then brought his lips to my breasts."

I just stared at her a moment, the image of him moving his lips over her breasts filling me with more excitement than I had experienced last night in my imagination. This was real.

"I thought you said he was bashful."

"I said maybe, maybe it was his technique."

"Was it?"

"I didn't care at the moment."

"What else happened?"

"I was sliding back on the seat, and he was moving between my legs, and then . . ."

"Then what?"

"I just stopped it."

"How?"

"I put my hand on his chest and told him it was time to take me home. The rest was as I told you, only I didn't add those details."

"Was he angry? There were those men in those books who were so angry about being teased. Remember? We talked about it."

"Probably. He didn't act like he had been teased. He was respectful of my wishes, more than I was, actually."

"I don't understand. More than you were?"

"I was discovering more about myself than I was about him, Gish. That's the . . . way it is. That's when you're most vulnerable."

"I'm not sure I fully understand."

"You can't be sure you'll always be in control. Maybe I didn't want to be. That's the part of myself I hadn't met before last night. I was a little frightened, but it's a different kind of fear. I . . ."

"What?"

"Enjoyed it."

I stared at her. There was so much about what she was saying that I really didn't understand. Was my perfect, always-in-control sister telling me she could fall?

"It's like the thrill of getting too close to the edge of the cliff."

"What stopped you from going over?"

"I'm not sure. It wasn't simply because it was dangerous or would damage my reputation to have what would have been unprotected sex, I think. I'm not sure. But I will be," she said quickly. She sat up. "Now, let's go to your room first and see what you should wear tonight."

I wanted to confess that what she had just described had gotten me quite excited. I felt so frustrated now that I wished I hadn't asked her to keep describing it in the first place. There were too many unfinished sentences. And questions about myself, too. Would I have put my hand on his chest to say "stop"? Was I exactly who Mother thought I was, the weaker, dumber child?

She got off the bed.

I took a deep breath and stood, too. "Do we tell Mother now that I'm going with you or wait?"

"Let's wait to see if she figures it out," Gloria said.

"What?"

Tease Mother? My sister was full of wonder and surprise. Why should anyone be amazed at how much I envied and loved her?

And hated her, too.

Maybe *hate* was too strong a word. It was too easy a word so quickly seized to explain your feelings. What I hated really wasn't Gloria. It was what Gloria made me think of myself. Why had nature made us so different? We should have been born twins.

"Don't worry about it right now. We have more important decisions to make. Come on," she said, reaching for my hand.

We rushed out of the casita, winding our way around the grounds workers. I saw Mr. O'Sullivan turn to look at us with a cold smirk running through his face. We knew so little about him besides the fact that he had separated from his wife years ago and had a son he rarely saw. Perhaps he wished the opposite of Daddy, wished his wife had given birth to a daughter or daughters. Girls were supposed to be closer to their fathers. He would have seen more of them than he saw of his son.

I wasn't sure if I should feel more afraid of him than sorry for him, but this was Cameo, after all, and, like a movie, you explore an emotion and never really go too far below the surface with the characters around you. In a short time, you'll see *The End.* They will be gone, and you'll become someone else with some other people. A new film will have begun.

To do otherwise was nice, maybe, but very dangerous. I don't know how I knew that; I just did. Maybe I was more like Gloria than I thought.

We burst into the house and hurried up the stairs. Behind us, Mother shouted about how roughly we treated her precious doors and floors and how hard we pounded those stairs that Fred Astaire himself had danced down.

What I heard clearly was "Gloria, keep your sister from breaking anything. I warned her not to run in the house."

Gloria ran faster. Our laughter swept us away. I was beginning to think she was even more excited about this double date than I was.

We went right to my room, and Gloria shoved open the closet's sliding doors to consider my clothes, quickly sifting through the garments. Then she paused and shook her head.

"What?"

"I never realized how conservative your clothes are," she said.

"You helped buy most of them." Did she deliberately want me to look plainer than she looked?

"I know. It's my fault. I should have been foreseeing a night like tonight." She slid the closet closed. "Let's go look at what I have that might work for you."

I followed her like someone who just had been brought from

life as an Amish girl or something into the modern world. Once again, we, or I should really say she, considered what was hanging before us. She reached in and took out a white blazer over a pink blouse. She placed it on her bed and opened a drawer to take out a skirt, which she put with the blazer and the blouse.

"Remember this? I've worn it only once. This is called a tribal skirt because of the traditional tribal print. It's sexy and a little elegant, too. Makes the statement we want," she concluded.

"What statement?"

She threw her head back and raised her hand dramatically. "I'm a young woman of quality, Evelyn John's daughter."

We both laughed. Gloria didn't often satirize Mother. I looked at the skirt and held it up against me.

"Won't it be tight? You're narrower in the waist and hips."

"Let's see," she said. "You've lost a few pounds. C'mon, try it on. You have the hair for this outfit, too," she said. "We'll brush it down so you look a little . . ."

"A little what?"

"Wild. Miss Temptation herself."

I squinted. Me?

"Come on," she urged.

She put on some music and began to dance around me. I hurriedly took off my clothes and put on the outfit. She was right about the skirt. It fit. It was short, a good four inches above the knees. We were almost the same height, with my being just an inch or so taller.

"I love it," she said. "Makes you look older, more sophisticated."

"Does it?"

I studied myself. Was she right? I wondered what Lee would think of it.

She took my hand, and we danced, me really trying to keep up with her. She was a great dancer. What *wasn't* she great at?

"We'll wear out the basketball players. They won't keep up with the John sisters."

John sisters, I thought. Funny how we never talked about ourselves that way.

"What will you wear?"

She spun around and returned to her closet.

"I've been looking for a reason to wear this," she said, plucking out a floral-print minidress. She had the hair bun and the legs for it. "I'll borrow some of your colorful wristbands. I have the perfect boots for it, too. What do you think?"

"I always liked that dress and wondered why you haven't worn it."

"Mother."

"Mother?"

She stiffened her posture and glared at me. "You save your clothes to make them more special when you wear them," she said, imitating Mother again.

We both laughed, and loudly, too.

"Okay," she said, "let's play with makeup. We haven't done that in ages."

I followed her to her vanity table.

"Take off the clothes, silly. We don't want to mess anything up until we're at Lee's house."

"What's that mean? How will we mess them up at Lee's house?"

"I don't know. It sounds good, though, doesn't it?"

I laughed nervously and took off the clothes. We sat beside each other in our bras and panties. I felt a small trembling start at the base of my stomach. She was so calm and intent on the makeup. Could I be almost as pretty as she was?

"What are you two doing?" we heard, and turned. "And turn that music down."

Gloria reached over to lower the volume. Mother had come up to get herself prepared for the charity ball. Even when she had her hair done, it took her a minimum of two hours to get ready to go out. I was suddenly afraid that after all this, she would forbid my going.

"You predicted it, Mother," Gloria said.

"Predicted what?" she asked, her eyelids narrowed suspiciously.

"We're going to Lee's house to babysit his brother, and Lee and I thought of the perfect boy for Gish to meet, Bobby Sacks. He's the center on the team."

"Sacks?" She squinted. "What does that family do?"

"They own one of the biggest plumbing companies in the desert."

"Plumbing."

"They've done most of ours, Mother."

"Oh." She stood there thinking. "Remember. Your sister has been only to chaperoned school parties," she said. She turned to me. "You behave yourself, and absolutely listen to your sister," she said.

I simply stared back at her.

"It will be fine, Mother," Gloria said. "You have a good time tonight."

"Yes, thank you. I'm trying a new foundation Theresa Simpson suggested."

"Watch your allergies, Mother," Gloria warned.

Mother smiled. "Yes," she said. "You're so smart to remind me."

When she walked off, it felt like all the air was returning to the room.

"Did Mother ever tell you how she and Daddy met?" I asked.

"No, I don't think so. You?"

"If she didn't tell you, she wouldn't have told me."

"Maybe they met at the movies," Gloria said, with that impish grin on her face again.

Suddenly, I felt closer to her. Maybe she really didn't like the way Mother treated me in contrast with how she treated her. Maybe . . . maybe deep inside, Gloria didn't like our mother at all.

When we were ready, we both went to the doorway of Mother and Daddy's bedroom. She was still at her vanity table but not doing anything more than staring at herself. We stood for a good thirty seconds or so in the doorway since Gloria had knocked on the opened door. We looked at each other.

"Mother?" Gloria said. "If you have a minute," she added, and Mother finally turned to us. "How do we look?"

Mother looked at us and nodded. She didn't smile. "Cherish these days," she said. "You never think about aging. You're like in a bubble, and then one day, the bubble pops."

"You don't look anywhere near your age, Mother," Gloria said.

"Mirrors have a different opinion." She looked at us again, nodding and almost smiling this time. "You've done a good job with her, Gloria. You both look very nice."

"Thank you," Gloria said.

"Behave yourselves, and be sure you're home by midnight at the latest," she said, turning back to look at herself again.

Why hadn't she told Gloria that last night? Did she think I could or would keep her out later?

"Have a good time, Mother," I said.

She turned and looked at me as if she really had just realized I was there, too. "Thank you, Gish," she said. "You just listen to your sister and you'll be fine."

"'Night," Gloria called, taking my hand and starting us to the stairway.

When we were downstairs, we stopped at the living-room doorway and saw Daddy sitting there, dressed way ahead of Mother as usual, reading a file from his office. He looked up, surprised.

"You're both going out?"

"Yes, Daddy," Gloria said. Mother had obviously not told him. "A friend of Lee's is coming over to help us babysit."

He nodded. "You two look very nice. I guess I had better catch up. You two will be off and married before I change clothes."

Gloria laughed. I was more surprised than amused. Could this be something, this double date? They always thought of Gloria as grown-up, but finally, they did me, too?

"Be careful out there," he said. "Both of you." He looked at his file again.

Just for a moment, I felt as if I had a real father.

Gloria tugged me again, and we were out of the house. She paused after we got into her car.

"Something wrong?" I asked when she didn't start the engine.

"No. But don't worry about that midnight thing. We're not Cinderellas," she said with glee.

Was this really my sister?

When we lunged forward, I thought I had just gotten into a roller-coaster car.

chapter six

We did have a remarkable and beautiful home, but if anyone asked me which house I'd rather live in, I'd choose the Aarons' house over ours. First off, it wasn't a museum; it looked more like a home. There were no walls covered in plaques, movie posters, and celebrity photos, just some nicely framed pictures of family. Although we would, of course, respect everything that was in the Aarons' house, we weren't afraid to touch an artifact or smudge an autograph. There were none on walls, of course, but there were a few sport celebrity photos signed and framed, signed to Lee.

Second and probably more important, this was a first-time home. The Aarons had built it, and until they sold it, they would be the only people who had lived in it. There were no ghosts, no spirits, and no strange echoes.

A house is almost a family's second skin. Its walls absorb all the laughter and tears, the conversations and arguments. The flickering shadows of birthday candles sink in just below the surface. Mother had convinced me that houses bank all the memories and even soak up thoughts and dreams. But I truly did come to believe that if you pressed your palm against your bedroom wall and closed your eyes and listened really hard, you could hear your childhood conversations with dolls and toys. Your house was supposed to capture your family's identity, its essence, which was why when you were away from it for a long period, you felt such joy in your heart when you returned.

That was my third reason for wanting to live in the Aarons' home rather than my way more valuable and famous property. My mother's celebrity spirits had taken all this away, all that ordinary families enjoyed. Gloria and I could attribute special personal joy to the playhouse casita, we could play and sleep and dream in our rooms, but ever present and standing between us and our past, our family's identity, were Mother's famous ghosts. Their laughter would always be louder, as well as their music. Whenever anyone walked by or drove by and gazed upon our home, they wouldn't think of the Johns and those two little girls who grew up there; they'd think of Clark Gable and Rita Hayworth, Cary Grant and Mary Pickford.

The Aarons' house had something else we didn't have: it had spectacular views of the Coachella Valley. The house had big rectangular picture windows so that anyone in either the dining room or the living room could look down at the valley and enjoy all the activity. At night when we were there, the car lights going in all directions were dazzling. We could even see the airport and planes coming in and taking off. It looked like a toy, make-believe world.

It was a long ranch-style home, and although it didn't have the property Cameo did, it had enough of a backyard to have a nice-sized heart-shaped pool and a hot tub, with a large patio. Lee's father had built him about half a basketball court off to the right. There were homes above it, but the mountain turned in such a way as to shelter and provide the Aarons privacy.

Unlike ours, with its vintage pieces making some of the rooms practically rebuilt movie sets, the Aarons' house was furnished in an ultra-modern style, which according to Gloria was more like that of a Scandinavian home. It had a clean, sparse look, with lots of space between furniture and walls. The lights were brighter. The floors were hardwood, with large area rugs. The framed artwork consisted of prints by the modern artists Lee's mother favored. There were a number that were simple black-and-white. Mother would say they belonged in a showroom and had no class.

Bobby was already there when we arrived. Gloria knew it was his car because of the bumper sticker that read *Take Care: Fragile Basket Dunker Driving.*

"We're a little early, and he's here already. Anxious to meet you, I bet," she said.

I said nothing.

Before we left Cameo, I had told myself not to do anything that would encourage his affections for me, no matter how nice he was and how attentive. Deep inside my heart and with every beat, I kept alive the hope that Lee would take a closer look at me and suddenly, as if hit by that love lightning Gloria ridiculed in our private talks, he would direct all his attention to me. Gloria would see that and decide that I'd make him a better girlfriend than she would.

Despite her vivid description of how she had courted passion almost to the point of no return on their first date, I thought I had sensed an indifference floating just below the surface, an unvoiced admission that when it came down to it, when her sexual thirst was taking her over, whom she was with wasn't as important as what she was thinking of doing. She left me thinking that it could have been with any boy.

Perhaps I was deluding myself, telling myself this fiction to make myself feel better and more hopeful. I was nurturing my wishful thinking, letting my fantasies overshadow reality. Gloria would tire of him, and I'd be there. The transition to me would be so smooth that no one would even notice. After all, he would still be with one of the John sisters.

Both boys greeted us at the door, and almost immediately, little Adam pushed himself between their legs to show us his new fire truck. He was cute, with the same shade of hair as Lee and the same beautiful eyes. As Lee, with Bobby at his side, showed us the house and property, Adam tried to get Gloria and me interested in his favorite toys.

"It squirts water and has a siren!" he exclaimed, without even learning who we were. "You can try it after I fill the tank."

"Hey, Adam, c'mon. Let them come in and see the house first," Lee told him, and obviously put some pressure on his shoulders to get him to retreat. Adam squirmed to get out of his grip but stepped back.

"We'll try it soon," Gloria promised him. "Hi," she said to Lee.

The brightness in his eyes when he looked at her fanned my disappointment. For too long a moment, they stared at each other, as if there was no one else there. Gloria came to life first.

"You guys know my sister, Gish," she said, directing herself more to Bobby, who had what I thought was a wide, silly grin on his face.

His hair was as disheveled as ever, and it looked like he had buttoned his flannel shirt incorrectly. I had the urge to reach out and unbutton it and button it back up.

"Sure do," he said.

I couldn't help my skeptical smirk through my polite smile. I did recall he had last spoken to me a year ago. It was just a "Hey," mainly to get me out of his way on the lunch line.

"Maybe we'll get him drunk or something so he passes out early," Lee kidded, and nodded at Adam, who was right on our heels.

We toured the house and grounds, pausing at the pool to look at the view. From there as well as the living room and dining room, we could look down on the lights and the traffic. Everything was far enough away to be silent, with only the occasional loud motorcycle revving up as it made a turn. Above us, toward the darkness at the peak of the hill, stars and the moon were blazing. A cooler breeze circled us.

"It's beautiful up here," Gloria said. "We have no views at Cameo."

"I heard it's still a pretty neat place," Bobby said. Beside me tonight, he looked taller than he did at school.

"It's neat, all right," Gloria said. "Last week, Mother stabbed a gum wrapper with a sword Errol Flynn used in *The Charge of the Light Brigade.*"

"Really?" Bobby asked. Gloria had said it so seriously that for a second, I believed it, too. After a moment, he added, "Who's Errol Flynn?"

"A ghost who visits from time to time," Gloria said.

I laughed, finally relaxing a little. Gloria's satirizing our home and Mother's obsession with keeping it pristine was surprising, especially in front of someone outside our family. But it was also refreshing. How quickly she could become so comfortable with everything, while I, wrapped as tightly as a ball of string, had entered Lee's house holding my breath and was still too nervous to speak. My heart was pounding so hard and fast I was sure everyone would soon hear it.

"You followin' our games?" Bobby asked me. I realized that if I said no, that would be the end of our conversation all night.

"Of course," I said. I looked at Lee. He was looking at me, his eyes full of interest, smiling in such an approving way. All our attention to how we dressed and made up our faces seemed justified, maybe especially for me. At least, at this moment I thought so.

"Bobby pulled down the most rebounds ever for our team already this year," Lee said. "Broke a record."

"Lee and me been playin' together since the fourth grade, right, Lee?"

"Something like that."

"Look at this," Adam said, shoving himself between Gloria and me. It was a pair of binoculars.

Gloria kneeled and took them from him. She inspected them as if she knew binoculars, looked through them at the world below, and nodded. "This is a good pair," she said.

"Look at the moon," he said, and she did.

"Wow. Check it out, Gish."

I did. "Fantastic," I said, and then handed the binoculars to Bobby, who looked like he might grab them out of my hands if I didn't.

"I got us a pizza for later," Lee said. "After you-know-who gets tucked in."

"I wanna stay up late," Adam said, not missing a word. There was little doubt in my mind that he would grow up as handsome as his brother. Maybe I was born too soon.

"Then how am I going to read you a story? I'll be too sleepy," Gloria told him.

His eyes widened with delight and surprise. "What story?"

She looked at Lee.

"The new one," he said. "The one about the bee. He's infatuated with bees," he told us.

"Well, I'd like to read that, too," Gloria said. "I love watching bees work."

"You do?" Adam asked. He looked at me for confirmation, and I nodded to verify it.

"You have to wash up and brush your teeth first," Lee told him. "I'll do that with you, and then Gloria will come into your room to read, but you have to be in bed first."

He still looked at us suspiciously.

Lee took his hand. "Why don't you get the ladies something to drink and turn on some music, Legs?" he told Bobby.

"Legs?" Gloria said.

"It's a joke between us. He's Legs; I'm Hands."

"Together we make one helluva basketball player," Bobby finished.

Gloria and I followed him, Lee, and Adam into the house. We went into the living room. Adam looked at Gloria, still quite distrusting. I had the feeling Lee had done similar things when he had brought Kaylee Donald here and who knew who else.

"You coming to read to me?" Adam asked her.

"I promise. I'll come as soon as your brother shouts for me," Gloria said, raising her right hand. That seemed to impress him.

"Ladies," Bobby said, rubbing his hands together as soon as Lee took Adam off to get ready for bed. "Something hard or soft?"

"I'm driving, Bobby."

"Right, right. What about you, Gish? You're not driving."

"Neither of us drinks hard, Bobby."

"Yeah, I don't, either, really. I was thinking more of a beer. Lee will want one."

Gloria looked at me. It was my decision to make.

"If you and Lee are having one, I guess I will," I said.

"I'll take anything soft. I have to read a story to a six-year-old."

Bobby was obviously not sure she was joking. He waited for her to smile. "Oh, yeah, yeah. Lee's parents drink something called mineral water. No alcohol," Bobby said.

"Fine," Gloria said.

Gloria and I sat on the left side of the reddish-brown leather sectional and watched Bobby at the bar. He looked like a research scientist taking great care with the pouring of chemicals into glasses.

Gloria grinned. "He's cute," she whispered.

Cute? I thought. Goofy was more like it to me.

He brought our drinks over on a tray and set it down carefully on the light brown coffee table.

"So what'd ya think of the game in Indio?" he asked Gloria.

"I think they'll be a challenge. That left guard has quite the jump shot. Almost unstoppable."

He nodded and looked at me. "You didn't see the game?"

"No."

He handed me my beer and Gloria her drink. Then he sat across from us.

"Oh," he said, his eyebrows looking like they wanted to jump off his face. "I forgot to put on music. What'cha want to hear?"

"Do they have any Ed Sheeran?" Gloria asked.

"Who's he play for, the Knicks?" Bobby joked, and started to sift through what looked like a pile of old CDs.

"Does Lee have Apple TV?"

"Yeah," Bobby said. He reached for the remote.

"Gish can find good music for us," Gloria said. "She's good at it."

I knew what she was doing. In a little while, I'd be alone with him. She was pushing to get us closer, talk more, and then who knew?

"Oh, yeah? Great."

"She can tell you all about the latest stuff," Gloria said. "Gish, better than anyone I know, can catch you up on what's happening in the music world."

I glanced at her. We both knew she had just described herself, not me.

"I'd like that," Bobby said. "I don't watch much more than sports. My mother calls me a 'one-trick pony.'" He thought a moment and then added, "I think she's just kiddin'." He widened his smile. "My dad says if that trick does it, good enough anyway."

"How do you feel about that?" Gloria asked him. She could pull a pointed, stinging question seemingly out of the air like a magician finding a coin behind your ear.

He shrugged, probably giving it the most thought he ever had. "I'm okay. Doesn't bother me. Only thing that bothers me is a ref calling a fifth foul on me."

He laughed at his own joke, his upper body shaking.

I sipped my beer and concentrated on getting the music for us while I wondered if there was enough time in this century to catch him up on what was happening off the basketball court. Once the music started, I felt myself relax. I rarely drank beer. Daddy liked some beer from Belgium, but I wasn't crazy about it. Gloria had once said she liked it, and Daddy had begun to talk about a trip he and Mother had taken through Belgium and France before we were born.

It was always like that. Gloria would say something he liked, and then he would talk to her, tell her things as if I wasn't even there. She always had the right questions to ask and somehow, as if she had been along on the trip or part of what Daddy had experienced, told him even more about whatever he was explaining or had seen.

"I'd swear," he'd say proudly, "your mother gave birth to a walking encyclopedia."

He probably thought I was a blank notebook.

When the music moved on to David Bowie, Gloria got up and started to dance, pulling Bobby to get up and join her. He looked at me and did. How someone who was so graceful and athletic on a basketball court was so awkward and gawky when dancing amazed me. Gloria tugged on me. I knew what she was after, but I had to get up. She started to move more and more to the side so that Bobby and I were dancing together. Out of the corner of my eye, I saw Lee reappear and gesture to her. She winked at me.

"I'll get him to sleep, and we'll be back," she promised, probably because I had this desperate look on my face. She left to follow Lee to Adam's bedroom.

"You're a great dancer," Bobby said. "I guess I need more practice."

"Try to go with the beat," I told him, frustrated with how silly he made me feel.

He turned serious and concentrated. Every once in a while, he took another long sip of his beer. I was beginning to feel foolish and was about to sit when Lee reappeared and stood there looking at us, looking, I thought, mainly at me.

"No one's gotten him up like that for anything but a jump ball," he said, nodding at Bobby.

"Hey. This ain't easy, Hands."

"Sure it is," Lee said, and filled my heart with a rush of excitement when he stepped in front of Bobby and began to dance with me. Bobby opened another beer and sat to watch us.

"She'll get Adam asleep faster if I'm not there," he explained.

My mind was reeling with possibilities. Why would he leave Gloria, no matter what? Did he really want to be out here with me? Maybe I hadn't been imagining things when I saw the intensity in how he first had looked at me. Wishful thinking was blossoming.

The music slowed. I thought he'd sit and drink, but he pulled me to him, and we danced closer.

"Lookin' good," Bobby said.

"Just giving you lessons, Legs."

I could barely feel my legs moving. His warm breath caressed my cheek. I thought he was going to pull me closer, but he had moved us closer to Bobby and suddenly grabbed his hand and tugged him to stand up and take his place. Bobby embraced me as if he was afraid he was going to fall off the edge of the earth. Lee laughed and backed away. My heart felt like it had slammed shut.

"Keep goin', Legs. You need the practice."

"Ha, ha," Bobby said. He continued to hold me too tightly, clumsily. I was sure I looked more like someone in pain than someone enjoying the music. The excitement that had built up in my body flowed out and followed Lee back down the hallway. I practically could see it pour after him.

"I need a fresh beer," I said, and broke away from Bobby.

"Sure, but did you finish that one?"

I just looked at him. No, I hadn't even finished half of it, but he saw the look on my face and hurried behind the bar. He opened the refrigerator as I sat and occasionally glanced at the hallway. Bobby returned with another beer and flopped into the chair across from me again. I took a long, hard sip of this one. I was really forcing myself to drink it. I wondered if I could switch to vodka.

"Dancing's hard," Bobby said. "But it's good exercise, huh?"

"Hmm," I said. I sipped my beer. Where were they? How long was Gloria going to leave me alone with Mr. Leggo?

As if he had been given a list of questions to use on a first date, he began to ask. "What's your favorite subject? Mine's study hall," he added quickly, and laughed.

"Aren't you going to college?"

"Yeah, I got somethin' of a scholarship to State for basketball. Lee got the same one, but he's tryin' for somethin' else."

"They won't let you play if you don't pass your courses, will they?"

He shrugged. "I pass, sometimes just pass, but Coach says I have a shot at the NBA. Make more money than the class geniuses. Except Gloria, of course. She'll probably become a rocket scientist or somethin'. You smart as her? Probably runs in the family or somethin', huh?"

How smart could I be if I'm sitting here with you? I thought.

"I do all right."

"Hey. Me too." He glanced at the hallway.

I had a feeling Gloria wouldn't be out with Lee to join us for quite a while. Silence was roaring in my ears. Truthfully, I felt like screaming. His stupid grin was grinding away at the grip I had on myself.

"You want some chips or somethin' until we have the pizza?" he asked.

"You know what I would really like?" I said. "My father's favorite drink. Think you could mix it?"

"Drink? Sure. What is it?"

"Vodka and cranberry juice. Do they have any cranberry juice back there?"

"Oh. I don't know. I'll look," he said, and leaped out of the chair. He opened the refrigerator and looked back at me. "Yeah, they do."

He took out the bottle and put it on the bar counter. Then he studied the bottles of liquor as if he had just learned how to read English.

"The third bottle from the left," I said.

"Oh, yeah, right. Vodka." He opened it and then looked confused.

"Put in three shots," I said.

"Three shots? Right."

He did and then reached for the cranberry juice and looked to me. I nodded, and he poured it and stirred. He had used the wrong glass, a beer mug, but I didn't want to stop him. He brought it over and stood waiting to see what I thought when I had sipped it. I could feel the pleasant heat in my chest. The tension softened.

"Good," I said, taking another long sip. He was standing there staring at me as if he expected me to explode or something. "Don't you like vodka?"

He shook his head. “Naw. I just drink beer. Coach is pretty firm about our drinkin’ and smokin’. He’d throw me off the team no matter what.”

“Maybe he’s the one who’s a one-trick pony,” I said. It was the first time I really smiled and laughed, but I felt more at ease, especially after another long sip. I was probably drinking too quickly. I was already three-quarters done.

“Huh?”

I drank some more, just about emptying it, and then, more out of boredom than anything, got up and started to dance to another David Bowie song. When I closed my eyes, I imagined dancing with Lee again. I could dance better than Gloria, I thought, and moved faster. Bobby watched me with his mouth slightly open. He took another long gulp of his beer, like someone working up his courage, and began to dance. I drank as I moved, totally emptying my beer mug of vodka and cranberry in one sip.

I handed him the glass.

“You want more?”

“The night’s young,” I said, and laughed.

“Yeah,” he said, and hurried back to the bar to make the same drink. I danced on. No one was coming down that hallway soon. I didn’t have to work hard at imagining why not. After I was half finished with my second vodka, I got into a laughing jag watching Bobby try to dance. Rather than get insulted, he laughed as hard himself. He drank two more beers, and then I suddenly felt my stomach churn threateningly.

I stopped drinking and looked at him, hoping he would understand, but he kept dancing and drinking. I knew what was about to happen, so I rushed past him and out the patio door. I made it to the side of the property that was fenced in because the hill had a steep drop at that point.

There I stood retching.

Bobby, terrified at what was happening, stood in the patio doorway and called for Lee and Gloria. After what felt like I had emptied out my stomach and all my other organs, I sat hard on the ground, still feeling sick. I fell over on my side, embraced myself, and groaned. I was so out of it that I didn't realize Lee had come rushing out and had scooped me up to carry me back into the house and to the powder room. I had soiled the front of my blouse. My chest felt soaked.

"I'll take care of her," I heard Gloria say. "Maybe you can get me one of your sweatshirts or something," she told Lee.

After he and Bobby had left, she stripped off my blouse and my bra and began washing me down. I had my eyes closed the whole time and didn't realize what was happening. There was a knock on the door. Lee handed Gloria one of his basketball team sweatshirts, and after she dried me, she pulled it over my head and on.

"Let's put her in my room for a while," I heard Lee say outside the door.

"Okay," Gloria said, and brought me to the door. They guided me, practically carried me, through the hallway to his bedroom, where I was sat on his bed, and then Gloria gently guided me back so my head was on the pillow. I felt her lift my legs after she had removed my shoes. Maybe I passed out after that. All I remembered was waking and hearing voices in the hallway.

"Gloria?" I called, and she and Lee, with Bobby right behind, came quickly.

"What happened?"

"You drank way too much, Gish, and got sick all over yourself."

She didn't sound angry, just factual. That was Gloria, always in firm control.

"I have a headache," I moaned.

"I'll get some Tylenol," Lee said, and hurried out.

"Hey, I'm sorry," Bobby said. He was standing in the doorway. "I guess I gave you too much. Gloria says I did. Sorry."

I didn't answer. I wasn't in the mood to tell the truth. Lee returned with the pills, and I took two.

"What do you think?" Lee asked Gloria.

"I'll take the long way home. Try to make it seem like she's just tired. I'll tell them she spilled some soft drink on her blouse. My mother doesn't do our laundry. You hear what I'm saying, Gish?"

I nodded.

"Hey, I thought she could drink," Bobby said. "She seemed to know how to make it and everythin'."

"Forget it," Lee told him. "This never happened."

Gloria urged me to stand. The room spun. She put her arm around me.

"Let me," Lee said, and embraced me firmly. "A little walking first will help."

I looked into his eyes and smiled as I let my body lean into his, my head on his shoulder. We started out.

"I'll get everything together," Gloria said.

I walked where Lee led. Bobby was mumbling something behind us, and then that stopped when we were out in the back of the house again. We had made a small circle. I felt Lee's fingers move hair away from my face gently.

"Maybe you should walk me home," I said.

He laughed. "You'll be worse in the morning," he warned. "Hide out."

"Will you come to see how I am?"

"I'd better do nothing to create any suspicion, but I'll be around."

"Good," I said. "Good."

We circled back through the house and met Gloria at the front door.

"She'll sleep for sure," Lee said.

Gloria opened the door, and Lee brought me to the car. Bobby rushed out to open the door and stood back as Lee gently placed me on the seat. He leaned over to fasten my seat belt, his neck and face so close to my lips that I couldn't help but brush him. He didn't seem to notice, but it sent an exciting chill around my breasts. Then he backed away.

"Sorry about all this," I heard him say before he closed the door.

Bobby brought his face to the window and mouthed, "I'm sorry."

"Rebutton your shirt," I said.

"What?"

I started to laugh, and then I closed my eyes. I kept them closed until Gloria got in and started the engine.

As we drove out, she said, "What the hell did you do, Gish?"

I wanted to respond with a question: *What did you do? Did you do it?*

But I was silent all the way down the hill to the main highway.

"He gave me too much vodka," I said.

"He said you told him how to make the drink, told him to put in three shots each time."

"I didn't think it was that much. I couldn't taste it."

"Whatever, you drank it too quickly anyway. We tried vodka together. You didn't like it that much."

"Daddy drinks it. I thought I could, too. Maybe I wanted to get drunk."

"Oh, Gish," she said. "Let's just concentrate on getting past the guards at the gate."

We drove on. All I could think about was Lee's face, my brush with a kiss, and the scent of him. I would dream about that, I thought.

But what would Gloria dream about? Would it be a hope or a memory?

chapter seven

Once the gate had opened, Gloria eased into our driveway as if she didn't want us to be noticed. She turned the headlights off quickly. We weren't home late. It was just after eleven. I had fallen asleep for most of the way and woke when I heard our gate opening. Since Miles surely had driven our parents to their charity event, there was no way to tell if they were already home. All the other cars were parked in the garage before the night had begun.

Gloria wasn't moving. She sat there staring at the front entrance.

"What?" I asked. "Why are we just sitting here?"

"If they're home from their event, don't look directly at Mother or Daddy when we enter. They still could be up and waiting for us in the living room. Assume they are. You keep walking to the stairs.

I'll stop to talk to them. The less they see of you, the more they'll believe what I tell them."

"I look that bad?"

"Yes," she said.

"How can you lie and look at Daddy directly? Daddy's got a built-in lie detector. You're the one who told me about it."

"Not when it comes to me," she said. She didn't sound like someone bragging. It was colder, more like a simple statement of obvious fact. "He's blinded by what he wants to see, Gish. He has me on a pedestal so high up that when and if I fall, I'll surely break my neck. And shatter him as well," she added. "I should have been more of a screw-up. Everything would be easier," she muttered.

"What? Why would it be easier?"

"Angels never need forgiveness."

"Huh?"

"Let's go, Gish. Carry your bundled blouse and bra in that towel close to your body, and keep your head down."

She got out and closed the door ever so softly. The way she was behaving made it seem like I was about to run through a raging fire. After I got out, she stepped up to me and put her hand on the middle of my back firmly. It was as if she thought she had to push me into my own house. I took a deep breath and moved as quickly as I could. Gloria opened the door and stepped back so I could enter and head immediately for the stairway. She was right about them waiting up for us. As soon as she heard the door open, Mother called out, "We're in here."

Gloria moved to my right side, using her body to block me from view as we reached the living-room doorway. I rushed on by as she turned and stood in the doorway.

"Where's Gish?" Mother asked immediately. "Didn't I hear her come in, too?"

"She's tired and she's embarrassed, so she's going right up to bed," she replied.

I paused on the first step to listen.

"Embarrassed? Why?" Daddy instantly demanded.

"She spilled almost a full glass of Coke on herself. Her blouse was soaked, so I borrowed one of Lee's team sweatshirts for her."

"Oh, dear God!" Mother exclaimed. "We just got home. The Aarons surely got home ahead of us. Their house is closer to the Palm Springs Convention Center where the event occurred. Did they see this fiasco? Did she ruin their furniture, a rug, what?" she asked, her voice on the verge of hysteria. A demerit for the John family?

"No, Mother. It just spilled on her clothes. We left before they had returned. It was no big deal."

"Of course it was a big deal. I'm sure it spoiled the night for you. I knew it was a mistake to let you plan anything like this with her. The girl's not ready to be social."

"It was just an accident, Mother. It had nothing to do with her being ready to be social, and why isn't she ready anyway? She's a junior in high school. She's been to school parties, charity events, and dinners. Gish knows how to behave in public. You taught her yourself, as well as me."

"I'm getting a headache. See that she gets the dirty clothes taken care of and gets to bed. Did she do anything else I'll hear about tomorrow?" Mother demanded.

"I doubt that you'll even hear about this. It was a simple accident," Gloria said more firmly. She started to turn away and stopped. "Actually, if you want to know the truth, Lee's friend is a bit clumsy. He moves like he's always on a basketball court. He bumped into her and caused the glass of Coke to spill on her."

"I don't understand. She was playing basketball with a Coke in her hand?"

"No. I meant . . ."

"Just let it go, Evelyn," Daddy said. "Gloria has it all under control."

"Thank God for that," Mother said.

I continued up the stairs and to my room. When I stepped in, I threw my soiled blouse and bra wrapped in a towel to the floor, where both fell out. Then I flopped face forward on the bed, that all-too-familiar ball of tension and disgust rolling around in my chest. I felt like pounding the bed and screaming. What had turned my mother against me at the start? Was it really only because I paled when I stood beside Gloria? Did she despise me while I was still in her womb? Was the need for my father to have a son so great that I could never be loved and appreciated, whether I was as smart and as beautiful as Gloria or not? How had she turned my having a perfect sister into a curse on me?

"Hey," I heard Gloria say. "It's okay. They believed me. Thanks to Mother, Daddy didn't get a chance to really listen and think about it. He barely turned away from watching the news."

"I heard everything she said. I don't care what she thinks. I hope she comes in here and smells my blouse, sees my bra, and gets a clump of gray hairs. In fact, maybe I'll invite her in when she comes up."

"Gish, calm down."

I felt her sit on the bed. She put her hand on my shoulder.

"Blame it on me. I shouldn't have left you alone so quickly and for so long. I'm sure you were nervous, and unfortunately, Bobby wasn't up to the task of being entertaining. I should have thought more about it."

I stopped sobbing, sucked in my breath, and turned over to look up at her. "Why were you gone so long anyway?"

She smiled. "When Bobby screamed for us, I never got dressed so fast."

"You were undressed?"

"Completely. So was Lee. It took quite a while to get his little brother asleep, but as soon as he was, we held hands and tiptoed out of his room and went to Lee's. We didn't even put on the lights. The moonlight was blazing by then. I thought the glow had turned us both into candles just waiting to be lit. Neither of us said a word. We just started to undress, slowly at first and then racing to get everything off, as if the only thing left standing between us and ecstasy was our clothes. Neither of us touched the other until we were both completely nude."

The whole time she spoke, I held my breath. "And then?"

"We embraced and kissed. It was just like in *The Lover's Knot*, that passage I read to you in the casita. Every part of my body came alive. When he started to kiss my neck and move down to my breasts, I thought my legs would melt. He knelt and kissed my stomach, holding me firmly, his hands on my rear and pressing me to him, to his lips.

"I just laid my head back as he moved down farther. I thought I was going to explode, Gish. Wave after wave of what felt like warm ocean tide rose up my body. I was completely submerged. I wanted to stop. This was only our second date, but I felt so helpless, and I enjoyed that feeling. I could hear nothing but the beating of my heart drowning out even the thought of restraint."

"That's exactly the way it was described in that novel," I said suspiciously. "Word for word."

"Yes," she said. "Yes, it was very accurate."

"And then?"

"Then he lifted me gently and easily. I was so limp and delightfully defenseless. I couldn't even think of resisting him. He brought me to his bed and lowered me so gracefully that I felt almost poured onto it. My arms were at my sides. I made no attempt to cover any part of myself. My whole body ached for him to touch me."

"The bed I slept on?" I said, more to myself than to her. At the moment, knowing I had been in that very place a short while after all this excited me even more. "That part sounds right out of the book, too."

"Exactly. For a long moment, he stood there looking down at me and telling me how beautiful I was. He wasn't rushing a moment of it, even though he obviously was pretty excited," she said, smiling. "He moved his hands an inch or so above me as if he was molding a statue the way I mold things out of clay. I anticipated his touch so much that it felt like a hot rolling ball traveling down my body. Finally, I reached for his hand and brought it to my breast, but he still didn't rush. He smiled calmly and opened the nighttable drawer and took out a condom."

"He had them right next to his bed?"

She nodded. "I know. Like a married man would. It flashed through my mind that I was obviously not the first naked girl in his bed. There was Kaylee, of course, and who knows who else, but I didn't let it bother me. He had just started to get on the bed and put himself between my legs when Bobby began to scream."

"You weren't there until then? You mean you were in Adam's room so long?"

"I had to read that whole children's book, but it didn't make him sleepy enough, so I started another. Lee had left for a while, because he thought his being there was keeping Adam awake. He returned and said he had danced with you and encouraged Bobby to do the same, and you were having a good time. He listened to me reading on and on. I think he almost fell asleep instead of his little brother," she said, smiling. "Finally, Adam's eyes stayed closed. He had fought it hard but gave in. We left as quietly as we could. I heard you laughing and sounding like you were having fun, just as Lee had described, so I imagined it was all going well enough."

"I'm sorry," I said. "I just fell into a laughing jag until my stomach exploded and I ruined everything."

"It's okay. Just go to sleep. We'll find a way to do it again."

"Bobby's dorky," I said. "I don't think I could do anything again with him."

"We'll think of someone else. It was almost a perfect night."

Almost for you, I thought.

She brushed back my hair and kissed my forehead before saying good night, just the way Mother should have. She looked so sorry for me, too. Gloria often felt somehow responsible for all that was missing in my life, and I let her. It was certainly a big part of the reason for her sharing her intimate experiences. Every time Daddy had kissed her and forgot about me, complimented her and bragged about her in front of people with my being present, she suffered a little, especially after she looked at my face. She had tried so hard to include me in every accolade she had received, whether it was to claim I was the model for her paintings or her telling me cryptically that I was what kept her sane and able to do what she had done.

"All I've ever wanted was to be a normal girl, Gish," she told me once. "The truth is, I envy you most of the time. I might look and act like I am happier than you, but I'm not as carefree. Many a night I've stayed up worrying about this exam or that. I've wished Daddy wasn't so proud of me. Sometimes I've had nightmares about it in which I failed and he died of disappointment, right then and there."

So that's what she meant just before when she said angels don't need forgiveness, I thought. Back then, I believed she had said all that to make me feel better, but lately I wondered if that was really how it truly was for her. It didn't make me feel any better, however. Maybe I didn't want it to be true. I used her to explain my own failures most of the time. Why try to keep up with her? Coast along and go along. She had enough popularity and attention for the both of us. *I'll lap up what she spills.* Who ever dreamed she'd be envious of that?

But suddenly, tonight I felt it was becoming different. Something was unfolding inside me. It was more than jealousy, too. It was more like I believed I was ready to be competitive. I had no idea why. Why did I suddenly have this self-confidence? If anything, I was a total screw-up tonight. She still had to protect me, look after me.

"'Night," she said. "Feel better."

She left my room. I rose to change into my pajamas and then stopped. Instead, I stripped from the waist down and kept Lee Aaron's sweatshirt on. I pressed it against my breasts and brought it to my face. The scent of him was there. The material felt sensuous against my stiffened nipples. I embraced myself and lay against the pillow.

She had almost made love to him, I thought, but I was sleeping with him. As sick as I still felt, I smiled and fell asleep with that warm satisfaction comfortably set on my face, especially on my lips.

Thanks to the descriptions of her romance she had promised she would give me, Gloria had successfully made me part of the lovemaking in Lee's bedroom. She had included me, despite how special last night was going to be for her. She made me feel like I was right beside her, only tonight, in my dreams, I gently pushed her away and really took her place.

Morning burst in with the clang of a pair of cymbals. I nearly screamed with frustration, surely the way Gloria had felt inside herself so close to ecstasy when Bobby had screamed for them. Images shattered for me, words crumbled, and kisses popped like soap bubbles. I groaned and turned over to look up at the rapidly disappearing shadow on the ceiling, shoved aside by the spoiling sunlight. I had forgotten to close my curtains.

Before I could get out of bed, Gloria came rushing into my room. She was still in her robe.

"Lee just texted me to see how you were," she said.

"Really?"

"He feels a little responsible, I think. Bobby is his best friend. He had agreed to matching you up. He thinks I'm upset about it."

"Oh."

Hoping for more of his personal concern for me, I lay back against the pillow. As hard as it might be for anyone to believe, I was enjoying this.

"How's your head?"

"Thumping a little; maybe more than a little."

If Lee called again, she might tell him.

"I'll get you some Tylenol. Take a good shower. You'll have to make an Academy Award–winning performance at breakfast for

Mother. Daddy knows what a hangover looks like, so what I suggest is you act apologetic but also angry at Bobby. That will cover up your dour appearance. I'll back you up about his clumsiness. Daddy's seen him play, so we can't make him too much the blunderer. Take your time coming down. I'll tell them how upset you still are."

"I am upset. I don't have to pretend."

"Lee will be over this afternoon."

"He will?"

"You have to give him back his shirt," she said. "Funny how you fell asleep still wearing it."

"I passed out."

"I guess so." She thought a moment and added, "We should wash it first."

"I'll do it," I said quickly, keeping the cover practically up to my neck, as if I was preventing her from ripping it off me.

I didn't think she suspected what pleasure wearing it had brought me. She left to get me the pills.

I didn't want to wash Lee's shirt and have his scent replaced with some soapy odor, turning it back into just a shirt. I didn't want to give it back. Maybe I'd pretend I forgot to wash it.

Gloria returned with the pills and a glass of water. "I'll get breakfast started," she said. "They haven't gotten up yet." She started to leave.

"He's not bringing Bobby around to apologize again and spend the day with us, is he?" I asked, grimacing.

"No," she said, and then smiled. "Bobby's not that terrible, Gish. He's just a little . . . goofy."

I watched her leave and then took off Lee's sweatshirt and folded it neatly before putting it in my bottom drawer. Maybe he wouldn't even ask for it. He was coming. The prospect of that gave me the energy to get up and dressed. The worst thing I could do was look as sour and unhappy as Gloria had described. I could go along with her plan at breakfast, but I'd drop that almost the moment Lee appeared. Or maybe sooner. What if I looked so bad that Mother thought I was sick and told me not to socialize with anyone? Besides, I wanted to look good for Lee, didn't I?

Now, I thought, *what to wear?*

When we had gone through my closet to find something for last night, Gloria had commented about how conservative my clothes were. We had to go to her closet. *Why don't I do that again?*

I waited until I heard her start down to get breakfast organized, and then I hurried into her room. As quickly as I could, I sifted through her dresses and pants outfits. I recalled one dress that had turned a lot of boys' heads. It was her black floral corset swing dress. I knew it fit me almost as well as it fit her. I had tried it on when she first bought it.

Why not? I thought, and hurried back to my room to shower quickly, brush my hair, put on the dress, and go down to breakfast. Mother and Daddy were already seated at the breakfast-nook table, and as usual, Daddy was into his morning paper. Mother was still in a ruby silk robe, her hair pinned up. I would never say it, even suggest it, but without her gobs and gobs of makeup, Mother was looking more her age, if not a bit older. If I even hinted at it, she'd only blame me.

Everyone turned to look at me when I had entered. Gloria's face wasn't just full of surprise; she looked upset. Her eyes swung toward the ceiling and then back at me, full of questions.

"Why are you dressed like that?" Mother demanded. "You're not going anywhere this early."

"No. I just thought I should try to brighten up the morning," I said.

Gloria poured Daddy his coffee. "We're having Swedish pancakes," she said, a little curtly, to me.

"What can I do to help?"

"Nothing. Just sit, Gish. Everything's on the table."

She turned and went to the pancakes, placing them on the serving tray.

"Sorry I took so long to get ready," I said.

Daddy snapped his paper, folded it, and served himself some pancakes.

"As I understand it," Mother said, with her hands clasped and her elbows on the table, "you did not have a very successful evening."

"I'm over it," I said, eyeing Gloria, who sat. "As you often say, Mother, don't dwell on what you can't change."

"Don't dwell, but learn from it. When you're holding a drink, no matter where you are, you have to be cognizant of everyone around you. It takes two to make an accident, especially socially. These sorts of things are far worse when you've been invited into someone's home. You know how I feel when someone spills something here."

"Your eyes become sharper than daggers," I said. I thought about how often I had been stabbed by them when I was a child.

"Yes, so you understand. I hope you've learned something."

"Something," I said, and forked some pancakes. "These look wonderful, Gloria."

"Our recipe," she said. "That little touch of lemon. It was Gish's idea," she quickly added.

"They're really good," Daddy said. "Maybe I'll invest in a restaurant and call it Gloria's Kitchen."

"Don't even think of it," Mother said.

Gloria's Kitchen? She just said it was my suggestion that made the pancakes better. Why not Gish's Kitchen?

The remainder of the breakfast went as I had expected. Mother went into a history of social blunders she had seen at various dinners and parties. Most of it was clearly the fault of a giddy woman "too concerned with how she looked to everyone rather than what was happening around her."

Blaming me, blaming me, blaming me, I fumed.

"All women worry about how they look to everyone else," I said, probably too curtly. "Don't you, Mother?"

Daddy's eyes widened as he looked up from his food at me and then at Mother.

"The trick is to know how to balance it," she said. "Whenever a man is involved, the blame somehow always falls on the woman."

"What a true burden it is to be a woman," I said, with an overly dramatic flair. It was a quote from *Love on the Loose*, one of the more recent titles Gloria and I had read together.

She stifled a laugh.

Mother looked at her and then at me. "I'm going to the charity flea market this afternoon," she said, mostly, I thought, for Gloria's benefit. "If you want to attend . . ."

"Oh, Lee Aaron's coming for lunch," Gloria said. "I thought we'd have something in the casita. He's still feeling bad about what Bobby did to Gish."

"I see," Mother said. She ate another Swedish pancake and then sat back. "Just so you two know, the first thing I did this morning after I woke was to call Mary Aaron, just to be sure they weren't upset with anything."

Gloria and I looked at each other nervously.

"Were they?" Gloria asked.

"On the contrary. She said Adam was quite taken with you. You read him a story, and he couldn't stop talking about it this morning. He woke them up to tell them. I would have thought Gish would have been the one to do that," she said, looking at me.

"Why?" I asked.

"You're closer to his age."

Daddy smirked. "Don't you remember when Gloria would read to Gish?" he asked her.

"Yes, of course I do."

"She was always good at it. I love hearing her read poetry," he said. "And I was never one for poetry. You used to read to me from movie scripts sometimes, Evelyn."

"I don't remember you ever reading to me when I was a child, Mother," I said. "I wonder why not."

"Your sister had more patience for that sort of thing."

"Sort of thing? You mean motherhood?"

The silence was like an explosion.

I laughed, surprised more than anyone else at my courage.

"Thank you for the preparation of a wonderful breakfast, Gloria," Mother said, then dabbed her lips and rose. "I have things to do before I go to the flea market."

We watched her leave. I looked at Daddy.

"You owe her an apology," he said.

"For what? Being born?"

He shook his head and returned to his paper.

After he left and Gloria and I began cleaning up, she pounced.

"You were supposed to come down angry, upset, but not at Mother. I needed you to cover up your hangover, Gish, not stir up suspicions."

"I didn't think I looked as bad as you predicted I would. Then I thought I would please everyone more by being brighter and joyful. You don't mind me wearing this, do you?"

"No," she said. "Oh, Gish. You and Mother . . . oil and water."

"Which one am I?"

She thought a moment, looked at the doorway, and laughed.

"You don't squeak," she said. We both laughed.

"We're really having lunch in the casita?"

"Yes. Let's plan that after we do this. And now you have me wondering about what I should wear."

"All women worry about how they look to others," I said, mimicking myself.

"You're a devil," she said, sounding jealous.

To my surprise, hangover and all, I felt more chipper and excited than I had in a month of mornings.

"You know," Gloria said later, when we were in her room deciding on what she should wear, "I always worried about whether or not you could stand up to it."

"It?"

"Life. People like Mother, boys like Bobby, all of it. I was afraid you weren't making any progress. You don't have many real friends, and I practically had to pull teeth to settle on a boy for last night. Admittedly, a mistake, but still . . . however," she went on as she moved her clothes from one side to another on the rack, "seeing you with Mother just now, I felt you've been growing up in secret. You're just one of those girls who one day simply . . ."

"What?"

"Blossom," she said.

I smiled. A compliment like that meant something when it came from Gloria. Would Lee Aaron see me the same way?

"Am I?"

"I think so. This," she said, and took out a black sweater dress with a white poplin frill hem. She put it on quickly and stood in front of her full-length mirror. "Remember when I bought it a few months ago? Mother said it was too risqué for school."

"I thought she was going to make you take it back."

She looks so sexy in it, I thought. *Gloria has more beautiful legs than I do*. What part of her *wasn't* shapely? I vowed then and there to lose another five pounds.

"I promised to wear it only at parties. Today's something of a party, right? Look at you." She took my hand to bring me closer so we could look at each other in the mirror. "The John sisters," she said. "We almost could be mistaken for twins."

"Yeah, right," I said. When I had impulsively gone to her closet and chosen the dress I was wearing, I dared to imagine Lee Aaron would think I looked better than she did, but now that we were standing together and looking at ourselves in the mirror, that idea fizzled. I felt more like a punctured balloon.

"Maybe I look stupid," I said. "I should change into something of my own."

"Oh, no. Actually, I'm glad you decided to come to breakfast the way you did, Gish. I wasn't looking forward to gray skies over Cameo when Lee arrived."

"Tell the truth, Gloria. He must have thought I was a real dummy to get so drunk last night."

"No. He really didn't blame you."

"Sure."

"He didn't."

She paused. My face was flush with skepticism.

"Check this out," she said, and reached for her cell phone.

She pressed on the apps and turned it so I could read Lee's message this morning. The one line that jumped out at me came near the end. *Your sister's kind of cute. Never realized it.*

"See? So stop blaming yourself. Forget about it."

Cute wasn't that much of a compliment. It was what you'd say about younger people, I thought, but for me, right now, it started small explosions of panic and excitement. I hoped I did look good.

"We'll make a fantastic picnic basket," Gloria said. "Daddy will probably go to his office as usual, so maybe we'll sneak some beer into it. For Lee, not for you," she quickly added. "Your stomach is probably still a little woozy. You didn't eat much at breakfast, but neither Daddy nor Mother noticed."

"I might be better by then."

"We'll see. Maybe we should set up the badminton net. You and I against Lee. Have to do something active with the school's best athlete. Sound like fun?"

"Yes," I said. *More than you know now*, I thought.

The early November day was unusually warm, even for the desert. We had stopped using the pool in early October, but it sure felt like a pool day today. She thought we'd definitely be more comfortable eating in the casita with some air-conditioning. It was that warm by late morning.

Just as she had suggested, we put up the badminton net. Mr. O'Sullivan watched us struggling with it, but he didn't come over to help us. He probably thought it wasn't worth his time and that everything we did with ours was frivolous.

Eventually, we got it up.

"We'll practice," Gloria said. "Unless you're too tired now."

"I'm not," I snapped. I seized a racket.

And I played better than I ever had. When I whipped another past her, we heard Lee as he was approaching.

"Maybe I should be on Gloria's side," he said. "Make it fair. She needs help."

I felt like I had just grown another inch. I had never heard anyone say that I did anything better than Gloria did.

"My sister is full of surprises today," she said.

He stepped up beside her and put his arm around her so that they were both looking at me.

"That's what I like," he said. "Surprise. I hope you both have one in store for me."

He was looking at me when he said it.

I wanted to look unaffected, as sophisticated as Gloria could look, did look, but it was as if all my fantasies were pouring out of my eyes and pooling at his feet.

chapter eight

I remember at that moment thinking that he really did belong on a movie magazine cover. He had that sparkle and glow about him that I saw in pictures of Mother's celebrities. She always said some people were simply photogenic. "They can't take a bad picture no matter how you surprise them." Lee was that sort of person.

I wondered if I was so infatuated with him only because Gloria seemed to be. I was thinking so hard about all this while I looked at him that I didn't see Gloria or anything else, for that matter, just him. After a moment, I realized Gloria was staring at me with an amused smile on her face. Was my infatuation with him so obvious? Did he see or sense it, too? He crossed over to my side after Gloria handed him a racket, his eyes so fixed on me that I couldn't move for a moment.

As I started away, he reached out to seize my arm.

"How are you feeling today, Gish? First hangover?" he asked, with an annoyingly amused smile. I hated being thought of as a younger girl, a naive and overly protected one as well.

"I'm fine. Don't get gray hairs and wrinkles over it," I said, and joined Gloria.

"I'm in great danger," he joked.

I looked at Gloria.

"Lee, let's play," she said.

"Right, boss."

He served the birdie, and I slammed it back so fast and hard he didn't have a chance of returning it.

"Whoa. Guess you are feeling fine," he said.

"Gish has a good return. Always," Gloria said.

"I'd better remember that," he said. He served again.

For the next twenty minutes or so, we had him running in every direction. We gave high fives to congratulate each other. He moaned and groaned about being victimized. His ego was a bit bruised. A few times, he really slammed it back, but overall, he couldn't keep up with us. Out of the corner of my eye, I saw Mr. O'Sullivan watching us with that familiar look of disapproval. Two spoiled rich girls.

"I think I'm outgunned," Lee finally conceded. "Can't beat the John sisters when they gang up on you."

"We have some beer in the casita and some lunch," Gloria told him. He took off his shirt and wiped his face with it.

"Better workout than basketball practice," he said.

"We have a shower in the casita if you want to use it," Gloria said.

I thought he was looking more at me. Maybe I was hoping. Seeing him shirtless revived the images I had conjured during Gloria's description of their lovemaking.

He nodded at the casita. "Let's check it out," he said. He circled around our net and tapped me on the rear with his racket.

"You're good," he said. "I think I was playing against you mostly."

"She's always been more athletic than I am," Gloria said as we started for the casita.

"I had no choice. My father wanted a boy he could wrestle," I told him.

"Yeah. Your father was a college wrestler, right?"

"Into the finals," Gloria said. "We have some trophies lost among the replicas of the Academy Awards," she added, surprising me. Her satirizing Mother could get back to his parents.

Lee laughed. "Yeah, I heard your house is like a movie museum. My mother raves about it."

"We'll take you on a personal tour if you want," Gloria promised.

Just before we went into the casita, I saw Mr. O'Sullivan watching us again from the doorway of the toolshed. I thought he looked very angry now, but maybe it was the play of the shadows. Maybe he was just old-fashioned and didn't approve of girls our age being alone with a boy like Lee.

"Wow, this is a nice hideaway," Lee said after we were inside. "A little house."

"That's what *casita* means," Gloria told him. "Small house."

"Oh, yeah." He nudged me. "Got to remember I'm with the class valedictorian."

He was joking, but I still sensed that he didn't like being told something he should have known or had forgotten. There was the sign of that arrogance Gloria had described. I think he was still a little annoyed at losing at badminton to girls, even though there were two of us.

"I never forget," I said. "Our mother would remind me if I did."

Gloria looked at me sharply. He caught the expression on her face.

"Just kidding. I'm sure you're all proud of her," he said, and continued to explore the casita.

"Do you want to take a shower?" Gloria asked him.

"I think I'm okay unless you two think I should," he said. "Maybe you both need one, too. Shower looks just big enough for the three of us," he said, with that impish smile that surely could make any girl's heart go pitter-patter.

The image of the three of us naked together brought a flush to my face. I glanced at Gloria.

"You're fine with us, right, Gish?" Gloria asked.

"Yes," I said, unable not to sound breathless.

"I'll put on some cool air, though," Gloria said.

"Okay," Lee said, still shirtless. "But don't say I didn't offer to wash your backs."

"I doubt you'd be satisfied with just that," Gloria said.

He laughed and went into the bedroom. "Wow, this looks like it was built for . . ." He turned to us. "Sleeping and other things. That bed does look like it belongs in a museum."

"If you talk to my mother, she'll tell you Rudolph Valentino slept in it," Gloria said.

"Who?"

"Better not talk to my mother."

"Why not?"

We looked at each other and laughed.

"It'll be the end of your basketball career," I said, encouraged by Gloria's humor.

"I don't get it. You two have too many secrets, the John sisters. And you're too good at badminton. You had my ass all over that lawn."

"Poor, poor basketball star," Gloria said, with a satirical face of sorrow. "You can rest while Gish and I set out the lunch. We made ham and cheese, cheese, and turkey and cheese sandwiches."

"I'll have one of those beers you mentioned, if I can."

"Gish will bring you one," Gloria said, and we went into the kitchen. She took a can out of the refrigerator and handed it to me. "You okay?"

"Yes, sure," I said. I imagined I still looked flushed from the badminton or more so from the suggestion of the three of us taking a shower together. That image was hanging at the forefront of my thoughts. I could envision him kissing her and then turning to kiss me while the warm water danced over our shoulders.

"I'll turn on the air."

When I returned to the bedroom, he was lying on the bed, shoeless, his hands behind his head, and smiling.

"Hog heaven," he said.

I handed him the can. "Want a glass?"

"Too civilized. Takes the man out of manly," he said, sitting up and ripping open the can. Some of the beer shot up and onto his chest. "Oh, shit."

"Some manly," I said.

I went into the bathroom and brought out a towel.

"Thanks. None of it fell on the bed."

"Lucky us."

He sipped his beer and looked at me in what I thought was a strange way. "You have a certain . . ."

"What?"

"Edginess," he said. "Like the look some players have when they're bearing down on me. I saw it out there playing badminton."

"Doesn't Gloria have it, too?"

He sipped some more beer. "No," he said. "At least, I haven't seen it yet, not like what's in your eyes."

I was going to say, *Not even last night?* But Gloria came in to tell us everything was on the table.

He put on his shirt and followed us. After we sat and began to eat, he turned to me and said, "Bobby called this morning. He's feeling so bad about last night that I think he'll do lousy in Friday's game. He's moping and moaning. You'd better call and forgive him. As a good school citizen," he added with a smile. "Right, Gloria?"

"Whatever Gish decides. It's her call," she said.

"I don't want him to feel bad, but I don't want to lead him on," I said.

"Fair enough," Lee said. He pulled his cell phone out of his pants pocket and looked at me with an amused smile of challenge.

"Call him," I said.

He made the call and handed the phone to me. "Thanks," he said. "Your school appreciates it."

I took the phone. "I'm not doing it for the school. I'm doing it for you," I told him.

He laughed and bit into his sandwich.

"Bobby, it's Gish," I said as soon as he answered. "I don't want you to blame yourself for last night. It was all my fault. No, my parents are fine with it. No, that's unnecessary, but if you really want to do something for me," I said, looking at Lee, "just win Friday night. Have a nice day."

I clicked off before he could say another word and then handed the phone back to Lee.

He looked at Gloria. "I thought you said she was shy."

"When she wants to be," Gloria said. "Lately, she doesn't."

"Well, that's fine with me. I think I struck gold at Cameo," Lee said.

Gloria's smile was strange, I thought. It was as if she was happy for me more than she was for herself.

"Let's have some music," she said while we were eating.

I rose and turned it on.

Lee talked about the upcoming game, repeating what he had told Gloria about a college scout coming to watch him play and how much his father was looking forward to it.

"Don't dwell on it, and you will do well," Gloria said. She sounded so stern. "We're supposed to be having fun right now anyway." She rose and started to dance. He laughed and joined her. Then Gloria reached for me.

"Hog heaven," Lee said when I started dancing, too, putting him between us.

After a few minutes, Gloria backed out and started to clean up. I turned to help her, but she pushed me back. "I'm fine. Wear him out," she said.

We moved back into the bedroom, where we had more space.

"You're good," Lee told me.

I knew I was showing off, but I couldn't help it. I cherished every little place I could go and be better at something than Gloria was. There weren't many and probably never would be.

She came in, and when she started to dance again, he retreated and flopped back on the bed to watch us.

"Giving up?" I asked.

"I need to save my strength and energy for Friday. Besides, I have the John sisters," he declared, "all to myself. Keep dancing. You're like pros."

He drank another beer and watched us. Gloria gave up first and dropped next to him. They both watched me until I realized they were. Embarrassed over how lost in the music and how I was exhibiting myself for him, I stopped and flopped on the other side of him.

"You're good, Gish. She's good."

"That's what I tell her."

"I thought you put on the air," I said, sitting up and fanning myself.

"Oh, I forgot."

Forgot? What was on her mind?

She rose to do it.

"You look like you need some," he said. He passed me his beer.

I looked at Gloria and then took it and had a long swallow before handing it back to him. When he offered it to Gloria, she shook her head. He handed the beer back to me and leaned over to kiss her. I watched them and took another sip of the beer. It was a long kiss.

He laughed and turned to me. "Sorry. Her lips are magnets."

She poked him playfully.

"Hopefully, only for me," he said.

"That works both ways."

"You know you have mine captured," he said.

My fantasies popped like soap bubbles.

He leaned over to kiss her again. Obviously, my being right on top of them didn't inhibit him. There were enough things to make me feel invisible at Cameo. I didn't need him adding to any. I started to stand up.

"Where are you going?" Gloria asked, pushing him aside.

"I thought I might turn on the hot tub."

"Great idea. Let us know when it's ready," Lee said.

"You don't have a suit, and my father's won't fit you," Gloria said.

He shrugged. "I'll go in wearing my briefs."

Gloria looked a little concerned.

"No one else is here except some of the help, and they'll be leaving soon," I said.

"Now, there's a real badminton player," Lee said.

"Okay," Gloria told me. "Go get it started, and get your bathing suit. Bring me my pink and blue two-piece, please. It's right at the top of the drawer."

"We could all skinny-dip," he said, smiling coyly.

"Not at Cameo."

"Didn't those famous movie stars do it?"

"Probably," Gloria said. "Mother never told us about that, though, and besides, secrets here are not well kept."

"Why not?"

"Gossiping ghosts," she said. "Get my suit, please, Gish."

I hurried out, looking like I was running from something for sure. I did see a few of the grounds workers leaving with Mr. O'Sullivan. He glanced back at me, still looking a little upset, and then kept going. I looked around. Daddy and Mother were gone. We were alone behind our walls, just Gloria and me and Lee, and that realization excited me.

When I went to my room and looked at my bathing suits, however, I decided they were all boring. Gloria had wanted me to bring her sexiest, but I knew she had a few like that, so I went to her dresser and tried on a gold two-piece. I still had a bigger bosom than she did. It was a tight and more revealing fit, but I kept it on, snapped up hers, and hurried to turn on the hot tub heater. I set out the towels and her suit on one of the chaises and opened two umbrellas, all the while anxiously watching the casita for signs of them coming out. They didn't for so long that the hot tub was already over one hundred degrees. I dozed for a while, and then when I saw they were still not out yet, I rose and went into the hot tub. The jets bubbled the water around me. I closed my eyes and fantasized again about that threesome shower.

I heard laughter and looked up to see them rushing toward the pool, Lee in his underwear and carrying his clothes like a football under his arm. Gloria saw her suit on the lounge chair.

"How is the water?" she asked.

"Great," I said.

"Took one of mine?"

"Is that all right?"

"Sure," she said. She glanced at Lee, scooped up her suit, and went into the pool house.

Lee dropped his clothes on a lounge chair and started for the hot tub. "If you look the other way," he said, "and don't tell your sister, I'll slip out of my underwear first. That way, I don't have to go home not wearing any."

"I think she might realize it."

"But too late," he said, winking.

I turned away and then sensed him right beside me. My heart felt like it was bubbling as hard as the water.

"Oh, this is great," he said. "Good idea, Gish."

He leaned back. I glanced at his nudity and then leaned back myself, trying to appear as cool and indifferent as I could. The last thing I wanted him to think was that I was too young for all this.

Gloria came out and joined us. "Well, well," she said, immediately realizing he was nude. "Aren't we going to be the cozy three?"

I studied her face, wondering if I could see whether she had gone past our reference to the famous "it" when they were in the casita without me. I wasn't sure. How was she supposed to look? Satisfied? Older? Embarrassed to be revealing it to me in front of him?

"A girl marks two days in her life," she once told me when we were having one of our intimate discussions, "when she has her first period and when she loses her virginity. Everything else surrounds those days."

I guess I fell into a pool of deep thought.

Suddenly, Lee nudged me, interpreting me wrong. "Don't look so serious. We're practically relatives now," he said, and both he and Gloria laughed.

Was that a confession?

"Hog heaven," he said, smiling and leaning back again with his eyes closed.

"You say that one more time, and you'll probably start squealing," I said.

He opened his eyes with surprise.

Gloria laughed. "Don't mess with her," Gloria warned. "There'll be nothing left of you."

"I'm beginning to think I might enjoy it," he said.

I looked at Gloria, expecting some indication of jealousy, but she appeared more pleased than annoyed. "My sister has always been underestimated," she said.

Lee looked at me and nodded. "Bet she has," he said. He moved closer to Gloria. "How about another beer?" he asked me.

"I think I might want one now, too," Gloria said.

"Okay."

I stepped out of the hot tub. Keeping an eye on Lee as I did, I caught the way he was studying me with what I thought was clear sexual interest, if not outright lust. Gloria's suit bottom had slipped over my rear cheeks to make it more of a thong. Those extra five pounds, I thought. I hated thinking like Mother, but it suddenly had become the most important thing in the world. I hurried back to the casita to get the beers.

When I entered, I looked into the bedroom. The bed comforter had been pulled back. The pillows were still indented. I couldn't help it; I went over and put my hand on the sheet, and maybe I imagined it, but it still felt warm, like it would if someone had just risen. It wasn't logical for it to still have the warmth of their bodies on that sheet, but the visions were floating around me: both of them naked and kissing and Lee moving over her.

I paused. Gloria had told me that girls sometimes bled when they made love for the first time, but just as often they didn't because they had broken their hymens in other ways. Using a tampon might have already broken mine. I ripped the comforter back farther, but there were no stains. Gloria wouldn't have let that happen anyway, I thought, but what did this really mean? Could they have been in here that long and not have done it? She had been willing to at his house. Why not here?

As I fixed the bed again, I had this sinking feeling that our casita was the one that had lost its virginity. It was suddenly no longer our special, secret place. Lee and she had stolen its innocence. All our childhood secrets had fled. I couldn't help feeling a little angry, or was that simply a lot of jealousy?

I got the cans of beer. As I emerged, I paused and looked at the pool and the hot tub. They were kissing. I reminded myself that he was nude. For a few moments, I stood there watching, mesmerized by how they turned and kissed with the water bubbling around them, his hands moving down from her shoulders and over her breasts. She had probably seen me and shifted away from him, splashing him. He splashed her back. I hurried across the lawn.

"Our heroine," Lee said, reaching out for a can. I handed the other to Gloria.

"You didn't get one for yourself?"

"No," I said. "Being cautious."

"Good. I don't want you to feel sick. We decided we're going for pizza tonight," she said. "Mario's in Palm Desert."

"Oh?"

"You're coming with us. And no Bobby," she quickly added.

"I don't have to go."

"Lee insisted," she said.

I looked at him.

He shrugged. "I want to be seen with the John sisters," he said. "Good for my image."

"What about mine?" I snapped back. I didn't know why I was struck with a bolt of anger, but I was. Was it simply jealousy? Their intimate kisses still floated before my eyes.

He started to laugh and stopped to look at Gloria first.

"Told you," she said. "She's good at comebacks."

"*Touché*," he said, raising his beer to toast me.

"I'm going to take a shower," I said.

"Now?"

"I was in there longer than you two," I said. I knew I sounded angrier than I wanted, but it was as if there was truly another me inside speaking. "Just feel like I need it. My skin itches."

"She's always been a little allergic to chlorine," Gloria told him.

"So have you," I snapped back at her, so sharply, in fact, that Lee looked a little puzzled, even frightened. He had yet to see any real tension between us. I regretted my tone almost the same moment I spoke.

"Right, but I'm not feeling it yet. I can just jump out and go under the shower here."

"I don't think there's any skin lotion in the pool house. Last time I looked."

"I'll be fine," Gloria said. "Don't worry, Gish."

Lee watched us go back and forth, his expression now becoming more deeply thoughtful. "Should I be worried about my skin itching?" he asked, to change the mood.

"You can use the outside shower," I said. "No one will see." I turned to Gloria. "You want me to bring anything when I return, chips or something?"

She looked at Lee, who shrugged.

"We're fine for now," she said.

"Actually, I have to head back in a while anyway," Lee said. Maybe he could feel how the mood had changed. I knew it had for me.

"Do you?" Gloria asked.

"A few chores. My mother asked me to pick up some groceries on my way home, and then," he said with a broad smile, "I have to get spiffed up for my double date. Don't I, Gish?"

I had no clever comeback. Was I part of a double date or just the infamous third wheel?

"Yes, you do," I said, and hurried off.

As I was entering the house, I heard their laughter. That bolt of anger returned. Maybe I shouldn't go with them, I thought, and then I was honest and admitted to myself that I was excited about it.

And whether I was honest about it or not, I was competing with Gloria in ways I never dreamed I would. I'd be back at her closet finding something to wear that would at least make him take some notice. I went to wash my hair and shower, still debating whether I should go with them. Was he toying with me? Was she still feeling guilty because of last night? Most important, was I making a fool of myself?

Where were you, Rita Hayworth, when I needed your romantic advise the most? I thought, and laughed aloud, loud enough to wake my mother's spirits.

I was drying my hair when Gloria came up. I didn't know how long she was standing there watching me, but when I turned, realizing she was, I had the feeling it had been a while. She had a swim towel around her and had her clothes in hand. She had probably left her bathing suit drying on a lounge chair.

"What?" I asked, turning off the blow dryer.

"You were great today," she said. "Lee was quite impressed."

"Did *it* happen in the casita?" I could see that my going right to the question displeased her. "You two were in there long enough."

"We were, but no."

"Why not?" I asked.

"He forgot his protection. Or, to put it more bluntly, he forgot to replenish what he had in his wallet, and I wouldn't take any chances. I'm not that close to my next period."

"Well . . . what did you do for so long?"

"Argued a little, and then I took off the edge for him."

I didn't say anything. My mind was reeling with the possibilities we had discussed during our intimate talks.

"Forget about it for now. Let's just have a good time tonight," she said. She started to turn to go to her room.

"Are you positive you want me to go, too? He'll replenish his protection as soon as he gets home, I'm sure, and that will only make things more difficult."

"What did I tell you about being too anxious, Gish? Besides, I want him to think of it as something more than what he's done with other girls. It's too special to become just another thing we do."

"But you thought . . . I mean, you made it sound like you really wanted it to happen."

"I'm not saying I don't. Don't worry about it," she said, smiling. "He'll be picking us up at seven."

"Mother's going to make a scene about it."

"Of course she is. This is Cameo," she said.

After a moment of amazement, I laughed. Scene? This was another surprising example of her making fun of our mother.

Something was happening.

To both of us.

Was it because of Lee?

Or was it inevitable, and the time had finally come?

"When you're ready, come into my room, and we'll shop for something for you to wear," she said.

After she left, I sat back and looked at myself in the vanity mirror.

Did she want me along because she really and truly wanted me to have fun, too?

Or did she want me along because she believed I could never be a threat?

I knew what I would want the answer to be, but I also knew that Gloria was a few miles beyond me. Since we were children, she had given birth to surprises. When she should have been angry at me, she felt sorry for me. Of course, I never expected she ever would be jealous of me. If on some rare occasion I did something better than she had, she would be annoyingly happy for me.

It was one thing to live in a house filled with celebrity ghosts but another to grow up wondering if you ever knew your sister.

And if you ever would.

chapter nine

Mother was quite surprised that Gloria wanted me along on her date with Lee again. When Gloria told her, she was immediately suspicious of our intentions but mostly of mine. She no longer could frighten or disturb me with those narrowed eyelids and slightly pressed-together puffed lips. I was far too used to her face turning into a blinding light and her questions being filled with accusations when it came to something I had done or wanted to do.

Anyone could read it on her face: if Gloria was to be the one who had inherited all that's good from her and my father, it followed that I would have been born lacking in intelligence and morality, at least to her way of thinking. It was as if Gloria had taken everything out of the bank and left nothing for me. I was especially incapable of respecting all that the John family had accomplished and owned. I was forever to be distrusted, doubted, and disbelieved.

As Gloria and I had finished dressing and we started down the stairs, I anticipated all this.

Right from the start of our preparations, I intended to make my appearance as close to Gloria's as I could. But I had trouble fitting into the pair of her designer jeans that I had always coveted. They were just a little too tight. I vowed again to lose weight, but before I could become depressed about it, she offered me one of her favorite T-shirts. It was black with a *Drama Queen* Renaissance meme graphic on the front. Short-sleeved with a crew neck, it was also a little tight, but, according to Gloria, "quite sexy" on me. I would wear it with my own black designer jeans and a lightweight black leather jacket.

"This would look great with it all," she said, and handed me the palm splash pink-multi topspin hat that she had recently bought. I tried it on in front of her mirror. "You look great, Gish. What fun."

I tried to imagine how Lee would react and then glanced at Gloria. She looked happy, like she really did want me to look good.

"Is this a setup?" I asked, having Mother's exact suspicions before Mother had a chance to voice them. "Who is Lee bringing to Mario's with us or having us meet there?"

Gloria laughed. "You're our mother's daughter, all right. He hasn't mentioned anyone, Gish, and I certainly didn't ask him to come up with another blind date. Scout's honor."

"What scouts? You were never in the scouts."

"We had a weekend with the Brownies once."

We both laughed.

"Besides," she said, "you heard him. He believes he'll look even more impressive with both of us hanging on his arms. I think you saw the raw ego on display today. He knows he's very good-looking and the most popular boy in our school. Sometimes I catch him posing, reflected in a hall glass display, and he loves when one of the girls in school asks him to do a selfie with her. You know the saying we've used to describe Mother, only we'll change it from 'she' to 'he.'"

"What saying? We have so many about Mother these days."

"There isn't a mirror he could pass."

"Right. Then why do you like him a lot? And don't say you're not sure you do, Gloria. I watched you together today." I practically leaped at her with the question.

She shrugged. "I suppose it's like taming a wild horse. I have this hope I can inject him with enough humility to become tolerable. For both of us and even himself."

"I don't care about his ego. Should I? Why do you care so much about him becoming tolerable anyway?" I asked after silence fell between us. She was looking at her eyebrows, but I was sure also thinking about my question. She turned back to me.

"Going with someone, steadily, is a commitment," she said. "It means accepting the good and the bad, because there will be bad. Boys like him, people like him, riding so high, are destined to have a great fall. Maybe he's Humpty Dumpty or he will be. We have a small school. He stands out, but if he gets into Michigan State or any big university, he might find himself a small fish in a big pond. It could destroy him."

"So you're going to help him survive? You're going to prepare him for all that? And that's why you like him, want to be with him? You really are Lady Jesus," I said.

She laughed and then looked thoughtful. Once again, she avoided my gaze.

"You're worried because you're the same, a big fish in a small pond who will go on to a bigger pond, too," I said. She didn't answer. "Right, Gloria?"

"Maybe."

"But you're not an egomaniac. In fact, you know your humility annoys me sometimes."

She turned to face me. "Maybe it's not humility. Maybe it's fear, Gish."

The way she said it and the way she looked when she did made me want to cry. I couldn't believe I was feeling sorry for her.

"Oh, why do you manage to get me into these deep conversations at the wrong time?" she said. "Let's just think great pizza."

She went to her closet.

"I'll find something close to what you're going to wear."

She chose her black and pink peonies shirt with her black jeans and put on a gold cap.

"What do you think?"

I was the sadder one again. She could put on a bloodstained butcher's apron and look beautiful. I might as well try to compete with Mother's Grace Kelly or Lana Turner. It was like the moon next to a star. I'd glow yellow, and she would twinkle.

Maybe she sensed my frustration. She put her arm around me when we were both dressed, and together we stood before her full-length mirror.

"Here we are," she said, "the famous John sisters."

She tightened her grip on my shoulders just like Coach McDermott might tighten his on Lee's to boost his confidence before the big game. Was that what she was doing for me? Even when I was alone sometime in the future, I'd feel Gloria's arm around my shoulders and the side of her head gently touching mine.

I did look good, I thought, maybe even better because I was beside her and, like always, her glow spilled onto me.

We laughed and headed downstairs. Mother had returned with a new catalog on 1950s movie memorabilia and was thumbing through it when we appeared in the living-room doorway. Daddy was in his office. We could hear him on the phone guaranteeing a client he wouldn't lose by investing in something. Mother looked up quickly when we stepped into the doorway.

"Where do you two think you are going?" she asked.

"Lee's picking us up to go have pizza at Mario's in Palm Desert."

"Picking us up? Why are you bringing her on another date with Lee? Who else will be there?" she demanded before Gloria could answer her first question. "Not that same clumsy boy from last night," she said.

That was when she focused those eyes of interrogation on me. "Well?"

"No, Mother," I said.

She smiled, coolly. "You have someone else you want to be with now, do you? Sneaking him in under the umbrella of Gloria's date?"

"Absolutely not," I said. As casually and matter-of-factly as I could, I added, "I don't have to sneak anyone into my life."

"We're just going for pizza with Lee. It's not a *date* date, Mother," Gloria said.

She looked from her to me, as skeptical as I had anticipated. "Did you ask to go along?"

"No."

"She didn't. It was my idea," Gloria said. I turned to her. I thought she had said it was Lee's. "We're sisters."

"Sisters can be very dangerous to each other. Watch *What Ever Happened to Baby Jane?* again, the movie with Bette Davis and Joan Crawford."

Neither of us spoke. How could she compare us to that? Did she think I was so sickly jealous of Gloria that I would deliberately harm her?

"Oh, Mother," Gloria said. "That's so not Gish and me."

"No one lies to anyone as much as they lie to themselves," she replied. I was sure it was a line from another movie.

The call phone from the gate rang. Gloria picked it up quickly and then pressed the button to open the gate.

"Lee's here," she said, hanging up the receiver. "See you later, Mother."

Gloria nodded at the door, looking like she was urging more of an escape than a simple departure.

"See you later, Mother," I mimicked in my best Gloria voice. She pressed those full lips of hers into her smirk and looked at her catalog.

We hurried out as Lee pulled up. Jack Gibson, another member of the basketball team, stepped out to open the rear door of Lee's obviously brand-new C-class Mercedes sedan. The sticker was still on the rear window. Shocked at the sight of Jack, I looked at Gloria.

"Didn't know," she quickly said. "Honest. I wouldn't have denied it earlier when we were dressing."

"Mother will surely think we were lying, I was lying." I looked back at the front entrance. Was she watching from a window?

Lee got out when he saw us hesitating.

"Jack just popped over, so I thought I'd bring him along," he said. "Hope that's okay?"

Jack Gibson was only a couple of inches taller than I was. He was broad-shouldered, with a muscularity that suggested he'd be better on a wrestling team. Daddy would surely say so, only we didn't have a wrestling team. Our school was too small for that and football along with basketball. Jack had chestnut-brown hair that always looked like it was cut at home, uneven strands more or less splattered over his forehead and down the back of his neck. His eyes were a flat brown and, to me, quite dull. I once heard Missy Sanders describe them as being on standby, waiting for him to wake up. They were deep-set, too, which made his cheekbones stand out at the crests. His smile looked like a facial accident because his mouth twisted a bit. He was nice enough but clearly one of Lee's idolizing pack who lived to be included in his shadow. I did see him watching me lately, but I was happy he was too shy to do much more. Of course, I wondered now what promises Lee had made him concerning me.

Gloria gave Lee one of her famous looks of disappointment. Her expression was as cold as an iceberg, and he did seem to freeze and hold his breath. Was she going to tell him to get back in his car and leave? I could almost see the words on the edges of her lips.

"C'mon," she said. She tugged me toward the car. "Thank you, Jack," she said, and got into the rear seat.

I was the one who stood frozen for a moment, not knowing whether to follow her or not. She wasn't moving over for me.

"Sit up front," she ordered.

At that moment, it was a question of who was more surprised, me or Lee. It was definitely a toss-up. I got in. Jack looked more puzzled than any of us but got in the rear. Lee stood there for a moment looking down, shook his head, and got into the car. It reeked of new leather and wood finish.

"Is this yours?" I asked him.

"One of our demonstrators. That's a perk for me. I have five dealerships to choose from," he said.

"Too much choice is not good," Gloria quipped.

"How can it not be good?" he asked.

"When you make a decision, you're more apt to wonder if you made the wrong one."

"Class valedictorian," he announced, as if it was suddenly a very bad thing to be.

We drove out of Cameo. I turned back to look at Gloria. She was sitting as far as she could away from Jack, who looked confused and a little frightened. I felt sorrier for him than I did for Lee or myself. With Lee in such deep thought and the confusion, and Jack too surprised to breathe, the new sedan felt more like a hearse. Who would break the funeral-like silence?

"Jack might start Friday," Lee said after we rode for a good minute. "Sonny Martin might have a flu or something."

"I bet you're excited, Jack," Gloria said.

"He'd better not go turnover-heavy on us in the game," Lee warned.

"I won't," Jack said. "You look real nice, Gish."

"Thank you," I said, surprised he hadn't included Gloria in the compliment. I looked at Lee, who was smiling. Then I glanced back at Gloria. She was staring out the window like a sulking child, looking more like me on endless family rides. "It's always nice to get an unexpected compliment from someone who was completely unexpected."

Gloria laughed. I smiled at her. Getting Gloria's approval of something I said or did would forever be important to me, no matter what I said or wanted to think.

"Be careful, Jack," Lee warned. "Her name is Gish, but it could as well have been Bee. She can sting."

"Or make honey," I said.

He smiled and nodded. "Sweet."

It seemed to break the ice. Gloria started a nice conversation with Jack, asking him about his plans after graduation. His father was a pharmacist, and he was thinking of following in his footsteps. Gloria could make someone feel comfortable in seconds, I thought. I understood why she was doing so with Jack. It wouldn't be fair to make him the target of any anger or disappointment. In the end, actually, he was the biggest victim of all. Lee had brought him along to feed his ego in front of us. Of course, I wondered whom he was aiming to impress more, Gloria or me.

Neither of us was apparently easy.

Years later, when I was alone and thinking about all this, I wondered what Gloria's purpose was after all when it came to Lee. And why it really angered her when he brought Jack Gibson along that night. Any explanation I would offer seemed insufficient.

The next crisis came when we arrived and entered the restaurant. Who would sit next to whom in the booth? Lee moved quickly, practically pushing Jack to the side when Gloria sat. She moved over for him, and then I sat and Jack sat.

"I worked up quite an appetite from today," Lee said. How much he had told Jack about his day with us at Cameo was anyone's guess. Like Gloria, I was sure he had exaggerated whatever he had said. "The John sisters can work your butt."

"When it gets right down to it, Jack, you men are really babies," Gloria said. "Lee whines a lot."

Jack's eyes widened. No girls were talking to Lee Aaron like that, especially these days with all the attention on the team and him.

"Ha, ha," Lee said. "She means W-I-N-E."

Jack eagerly smiled.

As soon as the waitress arrived, Lee ordered, pausing to be sure we all wanted olives on the pizza.

"Get us a salad, too, please," Gloria said.

The waitress heard but waited for Lee to say it.

"Cokes or what?" he asked us.

"Do you have something like Perrier?" Gloria asked her.

"I'm not sure what that is," she said.

"I guess you don't have it," Lee said. "It's like mineral water."

"You mean . . . oh, right," she said. "We have something."

"We'll have that, please," Gloria said.

"Jack?" Lee asked.

"Whatever you have, Lee."

Whatever you breathe, Lee, I wanted to say, but that would make more fun of Jack than Lee.

When the waitress left, Lee began to talk about his plans for the after-game celebration.

"My parents agreed to having it at our house," he said. "Catered and all. It will be better than a graduation party."

Gloria and I looked at each other. We'd love to offer Cameo, but without Mother knowing ahead of time, we'd never do it.

"After the game? That could be a very big party," Gloria said.

"Oh, we'd limit it, right, Jack?"

"Sure," Jack said, looking like this was the first time he had heard about it.

"Limit it to whom?" I asked.

"'Whom.'" Lee smiled. "You always speak correctly in front of your sister?"

I could feel my face flush.

"Why wouldn't she?" Gloria asked. "She has a better grade average than you do."

"Probably," Lee said. "Anyway, I was thinking the team, their girlfriends, cheerleaders, their boyfriends, some teachers, the principal, Coach, and their husbands and wives and *whomever* you would like."

"You're that confident? It could be a wake, you know," Gloria said.

It was Lee's turn to blush.

Jack smiled. "Wake who?" he said.

"Whom," Lee said, and looked at Gloria. There was fire in his eyes, but she kept her smile.

The salads and drinks arrived, and Gloria made the boys have some salad.

"Stay healthy for the game, especially if Sonny is sick. Something might be going around," she said.

Lee's demeanor lightened when Jack began to talk about Lee's athletic ability and how he was probably going to break a scoring record at the game. He suddenly became the team historian, relating one close game after another and describing how Lee managed to score the winning points in every one. Gloria glanced at me every once in a while, her eyes full of *I told you so*s.

"I did some research on the internet recently," Gloria said after our pizza had arrived and Jack was forced to take a break. "Seems never in the history of the league we're in, all the teams and all the players, did any of them make even the starting lineup of a major Big Ten school, much less the pros."

It was like she'd dropped a bomb at the center of the table.

"I'm sure someone came up with statistics like that for Magic Johnson when he was in high school," Lee said, relatively bitterly.

Gloria shrugged. "Just saying."

Jack went into a long list of unexpected basketball stars, none of whom had Lee's talent.

"So you're Lee's official PR rep?" Gloria joked.

"Huh?" Jack said.

"Never mind," she said. "You do a good job for him, Jack."

"What job?"

Lee changed the subject to the party again, listing the teachers he especially hoped would attend. We all got into a discussion about the school faculty, but the mood and the air still seemed testy to me.

Afterward, after Lee paid the bill and Gloria and Jack went off to the bathroom before we left, Lee reached for my hand, practically tugging me over the table.

"What the hell's gotten into her?" he asked. "I know she doesn't dislike Jack."

"Gloria's not used to being surprised. She's always been in control, even as a child," I said, of course not mentioning Mother.

"Yeah," he said. "Don't I know?"

Dare I ask what he meant? I wondered.

When they returned, Lee pulled her aside as we were leaving. Whatever he said to her was enough to get her to sit in the front for the ride home. After we had arrived and Gloria put in the code to open our gate, Lee got out to kiss her good night. They stood talking softly, and Lee kissed her again. Jack and I watched awkwardly. I told him it was an enjoyable evening and then waited at the front door. Lee waved to me and got into the car. We stood there watching them drive out.

"I'm not sure we had a nice time," I said.

She laughed and then looked coldly serious. "I'm going to say a terrible thing."

"What?"

"For his sake, I hope they lose Friday," she said.

I followed her in, not sure if I was feeling shock or surprise. Mother and Daddy were there in the living room, looking like they had been having a very serious conversation.

"How was the pizza?" Daddy asked. "I brought him his investor, you know."

"Is he Italian?" I asked.

Gloria looked at me, frozen between a look of surprise and a laugh.

"What? No. Why?"

"It's an Italian restaurant, Daddy," I said.

"Ridiculous," Mother said. "Come in and sit down. Both of you," she ordered.

I looked at Gloria. She had seen Jack, I thought. We sat on the settee and looked at them, anticipating one of their lectures, meant solely for me.

"Your father has an announcement to make," Mother said instead.

Daddy smiled. "The Financial Management Association has awarded its first-ever merit-based scholarship to Yale, and the recipient is Gloria John," he said.

Gloria simply stared.

I looked from her to Daddy. "Really?"

"It's a full four-year scholarship," he continued, looking at Gloria. "Remember when I told you that you were being considered, that your name had been submitted?"

"Yes," Gloria said.

"Aren't you happy about it? You're the first senior at our school to receive such an award, probably the first in the whole county," Mother said.

"Yes, of course," Gloria said. "It just was such a surprise to hear it now."

"We decided not to wait until tomorrow," Daddy said. "You deserve to know immediately. I was sitting here so anxious to tell you. I almost drove to Mario's."

Gloria glanced at me. "Thank you, Daddy. It's a lot to digest at once."

"We're very, very proud of you, Gloria," he said.

"Which brings us to your sister," Mother said.

"Why?" Gloria asked before I could. Mother turned to Daddy, practically ordering him to speak. "She's doing well in school. You should be proud of her, too."

"Oh, we are," Daddy said quickly, "which is why we're concerned about her future as well."

"What does that mean?" I asked. I could almost feel the exact question on Gloria's tongue and lips.

"Well, we've always been quite impressed with how close you two are. You do look after each other more than we see other siblings do in other families."

He paused, as if we had to wait for those words to sink in sufficiently.

"So?" I said.

"We worry how things will be for you, Gish, after Gloria leaves for college. It might be our fault. We haven't encouraged you to socialize properly with children your age."

"So when she leaves, I'll wither like a flower that's not been watered? Is that what you think?"

"Well, we don't expect it will be that bad, but why should it be bad at all? So," he said, smiling, "thanks to one of my more affluent clients, we have a solution, a real suggestion about your future, too."

"What solution?"

"We think you'd be better off in a proper all-girls school for your final high school year, the first year Gloria is away. It's an opportunity for you to carve out your own identity. We are quite aware of how wide and deep your sister's shadow goes at school now."

I stared at them both in disbelief for a moment. All this time, they knew I was standing in my sister's shadow but did nothing to bring new light.

"And you became aware of this when?" I asked.

Gloria was sitting with her head slightly bowed, her gaze on the floor.

"Well, we've been aware. We were always confident your sister would help you get through all that, but with her gone . . ."

"It's her senior year," Gloria said. "How can you expect her to leave?"

"Class identity never seemed that important to her," Mother said.

"Where is this school for girls?" Gloria asked, more like demanded. She had suddenly become my attorney.

"Phoenix," Daddy said. "Not that far away, and Gish wouldn't start there until you were on your way to Yale."

"So she'll be living there; it'll be like being at college," Gloria said.

"Yes, yes, exactly. Good chance to make new friends, as well as have a doorway to a number of good colleges."

"What will the ghosts say?" I asked.

"What?"

Gloria laughed. "C'mon, let's go to sleep," she said. "We can talk more about it once we understand everything, Daddy."

She rose and looked at me, so I stood quickly, too.

"Don't forget the big game Friday," Gloria told them.

"Right," Daddy said. "The Aarons mentioned having a celebration at their home."

"'Night," Gloria said. I followed her out without saying anything.

"I'm not going to any all-girls school," I said as we started up the stairs.

"Of course not," Gloria said. "Don't worry about it. I'll talk them out of that."

"Sure."

She turned at the top of the stairs. "I don't think I've ever failed to talk them into or out of anything, Gish," she said.

For a moment, she looked like she had absorbed all of Lee Aaron's arrogance.

And I was really unsure if that was something I wanted to see or not.

chapter ten

"Is that where you want to go to college the most?" I asked Gloria after we had gotten ready for bed and, like many nights, lay next to each other either in her room or mine until one of us confessed to being tired. When I was younger, I'd often lean against her when she put her arms around me. Sometimes we'd talk until one or two in the morning, whispering so low we could barely hear each other. Occasionally, Mother would stop by to tell us to go to sleep, but it had been years and years since she had done that. Right now, we were in my room and heard Mother and Daddy go to theirs, their mumbling like smoke trailing behind.

"It's on the short list of colleges Daddy had drawn up for me."

"Daddy? Why not our guidance counselor, Mr. VanVleet?"

"The suggestions from Mr. VanVleet were close. Daddy had spoken to him about me a few times."

"But are you happy with it, Gloria, this award and what it means?"

"I haven't set my mind on it yet. That's why I was so surprised and not sounding as grateful and happy as Daddy obviously expected. One thing about awards like this . . . they take away your choice."

"How? You would seem quite ungrateful to turn it down, and I know how Daddy would feel. You knew Daddy had submitted your name, didn't you? You knew this could happen."

"I was a little bit oblivious about it, I guess. The future always seems . . . in the future."

"But you're going to accept the award and go there, right? You'll tell him in the morning?"

"Do I have to decide everything tonight?" she asked, sounding annoyed.

"Everything but the epitaph on your tombstone," I said, recalling the discussion Mother and Daddy once had about that.

She laughed and then poked me lovingly in my shoulder with her elbow. "You're getting to be a real smart-ass, Gish. It took you a while, but I had faith you would."

"Whatever I am or become will be your fault," I said.

When I turned to her, she looked thoughtful and sad. "Yes, it will be, won't it?" After a moment of silence, she smiled and said she was tired.

We hugged. She got out of my bed and sort of glided out of my room, reminding me of one of Mother's spirits. I lay there for the longest time, thinking about everything: how we grew up together, the secrets we shared in the casita, and how she was still holding my hand figuratively and sometimes literally when it came to almost anything we did or anyplace we went.

How would I live here without her? What would the school become to me, and what would I be without her there? Perhaps Daddy and Mother were right. I should go somewhere else, too. For me, it wasn't going to be as traumatic to leave our school as Gloria had made it sound. I wasn't as attached to my class as my classmates were.

The friendships I had were so light and fragile. Whenever I went to anything without Gloria, I felt lost and beyond disinterested. Sometimes I was accused of being in a stupor. Everything I did and practically everything I said was measured against *What would Gloria think of that? What would Gloria have done?* We were like conjoined twins born attached at the hip and soon to be separated in a serious operation, only there was no operation that could separate us, and we were not born twins; we became like twins, or rather, I was slowly absorbed into my sister.

Suddenly now, confronted with the reality of her leaving for college and possibly her being quite far away at that, I felt myself slipping into a panic attack. How would I deal with everything? Even if I, too, left, would I be able to make new friends, think on my own? Despite time and distance, would I always hear Gloria whispering in my ear? *Don't do that. Don't say that.* All these thoughts rattled my mind. I felt like screaming, but if anyone came in to see why, I wouldn't be able to say.

Finally, my eyelids grew heavy, and I closed them, turned on my side, hugged my pillow, and drifted into what was an unexpectedly long and restful sleep. Maybe I was simply mentally exhausted. When I opened my eyes after a burst of sunlight on my face and turned, I was surprised to see Gloria sitting at the edge of my bed in her nightgown.

"What's happening?" I asked, pushing myself into a sitting position and grinding the sleep from my eyes into dream dust.

"You were sleeping so soundly. I wasn't here long, though."

"Why were you waiting for me to wake?"

"I wanted to tell you what I saw early this morning. I didn't sleep as well as you did, and I tossed and turned so much that I finally gave up and got out of bed. When I did, I looked out my window as the sun rose to see what the day looked like, and I saw Mr. O'Sullivan."

"That early? And on a Sunday?"

"That's what I was surprised about."

"What's the big deal anyway, Gloria? He forgot to do something, maybe."

"After he came out of the toolshed, someone else emerged."

"Who?"

"A young man with the most beautiful shoulder-length titian hair."

"What's that?"

"Titian is red hair, kind of brownish-orange. The name comes from the artist Titian, an Italian painter who used the color on the women he painted. I've used it on my paintings from time to time. It's not that common. Wait," she said, rising and going to my closet. "You have a Barbie doll with that color hair." She sifted through a trunk of my old toys and dolls and pulled out Midge. "Everyone forgets this color hair because Barbie dolls are mostly blondes," she said, holding it up.

I stared at her a moment, trying to figure out quickly why this was so important. Was she here just to tell me about some pretty hair and so excitedly talk about it? Was this because she loved to paint and was always looking for new subjects, new ideas, and new colors?

"What were they doing? Trimming hedges or something? You want to paint that?"

"No. That's not it," she said, putting the doll back. "They weren't actually working anyway. Mr. O'Sullivan looked like he was showing the young man around, describing the work done on the property and where things are located. That sort of thing. He's always been proud of our grounds. He fired one of his workers for cutting a bush awkwardly, remember?"

"Before Mother got to it. So?" I asked. I stretched and yawned. Was everything that had happened last night making her a little nuts this morning? "Are you annoyed with Mr. O'Sullivan? Proud of him? He's not exactly at the top of my list of favorite people, nor did I imagine he was at the top of yours. I don't get why you came rushing in here with that news, Gloria. Mr. O'Sullivan training some new worker on our property is a headline? Is that how desperate we've become for real excitement?"

"Don't you remember? He has a son who lives with his mother in Wisconsin. They had divorced years and years ago. I had the impression his son was disinterested in visiting him. We've never seen him, but from what he told us, I imagined him to be our age or just a little older. That's about the age of this young man. I really think it's his son."

"Mr. O'Sullivan has dark brown hair."

"There were other resemblances, and you don't always have the same hair as your father or your mother. We don't know the color of his mother's hair."

She stood there, obviously waiting for me to ask her something else, but I didn't see the point. Where was this conversation going?

"So, again, what's the big deal, Gloria?"

"Don't you see? What's he doing here? He's never been here."

I raised my arms. "You just said Mr. O'Sullivan is proud of our property. Showing him where he works might be a way of getting him to appreciate what he does. I don't know."

"Yes. That might be true."

"And that's important because . . . ?"

She smiled. "For one thing, he's good-looking." She nodded to emphasize it.

"So?"

"Very good-looking."

I squinted. This was my clear-thinking, feet-always-on-the-ground sister Gloria? She looked like a lovesick tween, more like I probably looked when it came to Lee.

"As good-looking as Lee?"

"Yes," she said, now looking thoughtful, looking more like herself. "But a different sort of good-looking. He had something else in his face and in the way he moved."

"What?" Now I really was bursting with curiosity.

"Manliness," she said.

I pulled my head back. "You could see that from your window?"

She shrugged. "I have the third eye when it comes to men." She thought a moment, and then her eyes widened with excitement. "Let's get dressed and see if he's still here when we go out. C'mon," she said when I didn't move instantly. "I don't want us to miss an opportunity to meet him."

"Okay. Jeez. Let me wake up," I said. I tossed off my blanket, but she was already out my door and back to her room. For a moment, I wondered if she was excited about this new boy for me or for herself. Maybe she was envisioning a real double date for me, or maybe she wanted to get my attention off Lee.

She was waiting for me in the hallway at the top of the stairs. I had just thrown on a school sweatshirt and jeans and slipped into my light blue canvas loafers, but she wore a pair of snow-white cutoffs with a light blue cotton shirt, the sleeves rolled up and the bottom tied, showing midriff.

Light bulb: she wasn't interested in this new boy for me.

"Let's just check it out first, and then we'll get breakfast going," she said.

Sunday breakfast was the big one of the week for us to prepare. Daddy usually had picked up bagels, which were waiting in the bread box. After we set the table, Gloria would make a platter of scrambled eggs with pieces of bacon while I toasted the bagels and put out jams, butter, and cheese. I also made the coffee. Daddy was always down first. Gloria would bring in his paper and have it by his place setting on the kitchenette table. Before sunrise, the paper was tossed over the gate and onto the driveway. Only on rare occasions, when Daddy was still on a business trip, were our Sunday mornings any different.

"We live lives according to a script written before we were born," Gloria once told me. "Most families do. Spontaneity is frightening. It takes you out of the safe zone."

She practically fell down the stairs ahead of me. She was acting more excited about this mysterious boy than she had been about Lee. Was it exactly that, the mystery? She loved something new and unknown. She didn't have to tell me. Lee was too easy to read? And when things were easy for Gloria, she could easily drift off. I thought I sensed that happening last night.

We practically shot out of the house, turned, and headed toward the toolshed. When we got there, the doors were closed, and there was obviously no one inside. We looked around. Except for some mockingbirds, it was very quiet. It was too early even to hear traffic on the other side of our wall.

"There's no one here, Gloria," I said.

She ignored me and walked to the right to look behind the pool house.

"Maybe it was a dream," I said, and laughed.

"Yeah, right."

"You told me sometimes people plant things in your head that you don't realize are there until they appear in a dream. Mr. O'Sullivan told you about his son."

"He didn't tell us that much," she said. "He was never really talkative about his life and family. It's mostly what we overheard him tell other people. And besides, he didn't describe him enough for me even to have him in a dream."

She stood a few moments longer, waiting to see if someone would appear from behind our house. There wasn't the sound of anyone talking.

"Maybe they had been here a while before you saw them, Gloria, and they already left."

"Probably," she said, the disappointment vivid. "It's still a puzzle as to why he is suddenly here. I definitely understood that they didn't get along and he'd rather be with his mother. I don't know if they even saw each other very much over the years."

"I'm sure you'll solve it."

"Right. Okay, let's do breakfast."

I followed her back inside and to the kitchen. I didn't want Gloria to think I didn't care about things that interested her, especially young men.

"He must have been some good-looking guy," I said as I began to set the table. "Probably not that surprising. I imagine when Mr. O'Sullivan was younger, much younger, he was handsome. Was he as tall and broad-shouldered?"

"He was about six feet, an inch or so shorter than Mr. O'Sullivan, and more lean and muscular. He wore a dark green short-sleeved shirt with nothing written on it, no images, and a pair of worn-looking jeans. He also had this wide-band dark brown wristwatch. You know, those leather cuff watches, and oh, yeah, sneakers with no socks. The sneakers didn't even have laces."

"What did you do, use binoculars?"

"He was practically under my window at one point. He didn't have Lee's pretty-boy look, but he could make the cover of a fashion magazine."

"Really? Looking like that?"

"Let's just say for more everyday clothes. A little scruffy can work."

"The spontaneous look?"

"Exactly," she said. I was really teasing her, but she was too into the description to realize it.

We heard Daddy coming.

"Let's get busy," she said. "You know how Daddy looks forward to this breakfast."

"You forgot the paper."

"Oh."

"I'll get it. You're in a daze," I said, smiling.

"Am I?" She thought a moment. "Good. I haven't enjoyed the feeling for quite a while."

I smiled. She was really happy that something, someone new, had stepped into our daily lives. As Daddy turned from the stairway, I hurried out for his paper. When I returned, I could tell from the look on Gloria's face and the way she widened her eyes that she had learned something about the titian-haired boy. Daddy was at the table, waiting. I handed him his paper.

"Thanks, Gish," he said, and began reading the front page.

I slipped close to Gloria. "Well? C'mon. You asked him. Right?"

"As I suspected, he is Mr. O'Sullivan's son. His ex-wife died, so he's come here to live with him. They didn't tell us anything about it yesterday, but Mr. O'Sullivan asked if it would be all right for him to employ him on his groundskeeper's team. I guess he's out of high school but not on to any college."

She made a face.

"What?"

"Mother apparently had a side talk with Mr. O'Sullivan."

"About what?"

"All Daddy said was, 'Your mother handled it.'"

"It?"

"Use your imagination," Gloria said. She waited for my response, but I really wasn't getting any answers ringing in my head.

"Him, probably having anything to do with us."

I smiled impishly. "I'm sure we won't be cooperative. What's his son's name?"

"Oh," she said, then paused. "You can be sure Mother picked up on that."

"On what?"

"Audie Murphy O'Sullivan."

I thought a moment. "Audie Murphy?"

"C'mon, Gish, you want to get sent to your room for the week?"

I thought, and a flow of Mother's celebrity photos a mile long streamed through my mind. "The war hero and actor?"

"Third book on the left, second shelf," she said, nodding toward the den.

"So Audie Murphy must have been a favorite of Mr. O'Sullivan's."

We heard Mother coming down the stairs.

"Surely." Gloria smiled. "The three of us have something in common. We were all named after movie stars."

"You know what I think of that," I said, just before Mother entered the kitchen.

I started to toast the bagels.

Mother eyed us for a moment the way she always did when we spoke low or whispered to each other, and then she went to the table to pour herself a glass of juice.

"Don't forget that I'm speaking at the senior citizens center tonight," I overheard her tell Daddy. "Those people, the ones with still something of a memory, know the movies and actors I discuss."

"That's great, Evelyn." He paused, lowering his paper. "You want me to be there, too?"

"It would be nice, Alan."

"Sure," he said, nodding. "Isn't Nick Temple's father their president?"

"Yes."

Daddy snapped his paper. "He just put a half million dollars into some mutual funds."

Gloria began to put the eggs on a serving dish. The bagels were ready. We brought everything to the table and joined them.

"Looks great as usual, Gloria," Daddy said.

"Thank you, Daddy," she said, and poured him a cup of coffee.

"I just made the eggs. Gish did everything else as usual." She held the pot of coffee over Mother's cup. Mother nodded, and she poured hers. "I saw someone new on our property this morning," she said. Gloria glanced at me with that small playful smile on her lips after she spoke.

Mother began to butter her bagel, pretending she hadn't heard her.

"With Mr. O'Sullivan," Gloria added.

Mother paused and looked at her. "What about it?"

"I just wondered why he was here on a Sunday and showing this young man around."

Daddy lowered his paper and wrinkled his forehead, wondering why Gloria was looking to have what he had told her reaffirmed.

"Mr. O'Sullivan has been here since we've had the property," Mother said. "Our grounds are probably the one thing that gives him pride and respect. I don't see the mystery. He's been here for something or another on a Sunday often."

Daddy put his paper down and began to eat his eggs.

Everything unsaid hung in the air. There was nothing about his son, not even an acknowledgment. How far was Gloria going to push it? I wondered.

"I just thought it was odd for him to be showing a new employee around," she said, and smiled.

Daddy looked at her, at Mother, and then back at his paper. Mother didn't respond.

Gloria glanced at me and then ate quietly, swallowing more than her food. Her frustration brought silence for a good minute or so. Daddy ate and read his paper, and then Mother began talking about what she would be telling the senior citizens.

Later, when we went out to the pool to read and do some

homework, Gloria said what I suspected was obvious, too. "I guess there's no doubt that Mother warned him to be sure his son has nothing to do with us."

"Audie Murphy O'Sullivan? Even with that name?" I joked.

She didn't laugh. "She really does think we're some royal family or something," she muttered. "Our money, her being a local celebrity, and my awards," she added, sounding like they were her sins, "make us so high and mighty according to Mother that we are lucky we don't wear oxygen masks."

"What?" I started to laugh. "Oxygen masks?"

"Sometimes I wonder if all I'm doing just feeds her ego. I should fail a few tests or something and bring her back to earth."

"Don't say that, Gloria. You're . . ."

"What?"

"Someone special," I said. "It has nothing to do with Mother's opinion of us. You don't get the grades you get because of who we are. I know I don't. You're Gloria John first and Evelyn and Alan John's daughter second."

"I know that, Gish, but it's how I'm wrapped when presented."

"What? How are you wrapped?"

"Forget it. It's all right. Let's enjoy the day."

She went back to her book, and I started to read my math assignment. Every once in a while, I glanced at her and then finally realized she hadn't turned the page for over ten minutes. But I didn't say any more. I was actually growing a little frightened. Gloria was showing me another part of herself, a part kept so well hidden that I didn't even suspect until this moment that it was there. And I wasn't sure it was good, because it reeked of sadness and anger, anger directed at herself. I felt like a surgeon who looked inside her patient and saw cancer.

Afterward, she fell asleep for a few hours. She had told me that she had gone through a bad night. I wondered if there was something more than Daddy getting her the award and basically choosing where she'd be going to college. I imagined it bothered her that anyone hearing about it would find any dissatisfaction inexplicable. All her life, she did exactly what everyone had expected and more.

Ironically, because I made so much fun of Mother's infatuation with her old films and movie stars, I thought that right now, Gloria resembled the actress that Daddy often compared Mother to, Audrey Hepburn, but the Audrey Hepburn in *Roman Holiday*, the princess who couldn't step out of who she had to be, even if it meant giving up love.

Could it really be that bad? I often wished Gloria would be unhappy about something, thinking it would make me feel better, but at this moment, I felt terrible for her. I hated myself for ever wishing she'd be upset, especially about herself, especially now. She was dating the most popular boy in the school. Her academic and artistic achievements already had her name on everyone's lips. Now this added glamour to it. Gloria was truly our local movie star.

How could she be sad or depressed when the prospect of having fun was supposed to be happening for us both, with the big game, the celebration, an evening of music, and who knew what during these high school moments that would be legendary? I knew it wasn't emotionally or mentally healthy for me to be living through my sister, but with one like Gloria, who could resist it?

She didn't tell me until dinner that Lee had wanted to come over but she had told him she had too much homework. I actually did more schoolwork than I had planned and began a term paper for my history class. Her gray mood didn't completely disappear either the next day or the day after. Some had learned about her college award thanks to Mother and Daddy's bragging to friends, but it wasn't big news yet. Lee was constantly trying hard to get her interested in the things he was saying. At times, when I was with them at lunch, I was the one who responded to what he had said.

"You all right?" he finally asked her on Wednesday.

"Yes, why?"

"You look worried."

"Well, I am."

"About what?"

"The big game," she said.

He nodded. "Oh. Sure. But don't worry," he said. "I'm feeling very up."

She smiled at me behind his back. She could manipulate and convince him of anything anytime.

Of course, I knew that wasn't the reason for her quiet withdrawal. She made references to Audie often, so I suspected that she was really disappointed every day because Mr. O'Sullivan and his team didn't arrive at our property until after we had left for school and were gone usually by the time we returned. She'd get out of the car quickly when we drove in and start looking around our property. On Thursday, however, it was different.

When we got out of the car, we heard a motor being started and stopped near the toolshed. Normally, neither of us would pay it the slightest attention. But she looked at me, smiled, and started across the lawn. I quickly caught up. Neither of us spoke until we saw him kneeling and adjusting something on one of the mowers.

He turned slowly and looked at us. She hadn't mentioned his stunning kelly green eyes. Right now, his hands were covered in grease, and there was even a streak of it over the bottom of his right cheek. On Lee, it would have looked quite out of place, even ugly, but it seemed like he was comfortable being in the thick of his work.

He had a light, Irish complexion, but there was a dark shade washed over his face, a shade that highlighted his eyes even more. He bit into the side of his cheek gently, looked at us again, and turned back to the engine he was obviously repairing.

"Can I help you?" he asked, without looking back at us.

"Who are you?" Gloria asked, smiling at me.

"Just hired on," he said, still without looking at us.

"Is that what we call you, 'hired on'?" Gloria asked him.

He paused and gazed back at us and then just turned a little more so he could sit on the grass. He wiped his hands with a rag and looked at us more seriously. "I have strict instructions not to be distracted by you two."

"Why?" Gloria pursued, stepping toward him.

He looked at me and then back at her. "I'm distractible," he said. "And my father's motto is 'Time is money.' Like I'm supposed to have this repaired by the time he returns with a part for somethin' else."

"So your father is . . ."

"You know who my father is," he said.

I actually blinked and stepped back. He sounded angry, aggressive, like someone who had no patience for childish games, even romantic ones. He turned back to the engine.

"Well, I'm Gloria, and this is my sister, Gish."

He looked toward the gate through which the employees entered Cameo and then at the house.

"What's your name?"

We knew it, but she was forcing him to say it.

He paused, looking like he was fighting the urge to spin around and throw a wrench at us or something.

"Someone else told me not to encourage any conversation with you two," he said, still not looking at us. "I'm just here to do some work, earn some money, until I decide where I'm going. Okay?"

"Yes, that's exactly what Gish and I are doing. Maybe when you're not working, we can talk about it. Doesn't have to be here, either," she said.

He looked at the gate again. "My father warned me more," he said. "I don't want to cause him any trouble."

"You don't look like the type who's afraid of too many warnings," Gloria insisted.

He turned and looked at her really for the first time, with just a slight hint of his attitude changing. "What do you want?"

"You look smart enough to figure it out. Fix the engine. We'll find you when we want to. We'll just look for someone with engine grease on his face," she added, which brought a smile.

She was right, I thought. He had something more substantial in his looks than Lee had. To me, however, it reeked of some danger because of the stream of rage lying just beneath the surface. Consider the conditions and events that had brought him here, I thought. I should get Gloria to realize that. It was just that it was impossible to think she hadn't or wasn't, and that seemed to make him more attractive to her.

"C'mon, Gish," she said. "We don't want to get him fired this quickly. We'd never see him again."

He turned back to the engine. I had never seen anyone resist Gloria like that.

She looked back as we started away and then stopped. "You're right. We know your name," she said. "What do you think of the man you're named after?"

He looked at us, unable to ignore her now.

"I'm named after Gloria Swanson, and Gish is named after Lillian Gish, both silent-movie stars."

"Never saw one of their movies," he said.

"When you learn how to sneak back, we'll watch an Audie Murphy movie in the casita one night. Be a first for all of us, actually."

We continued walking back to the house, Gloria with that tight little smile.

"You'll get him into trouble, Gloria," I warned.

She shrugged. "Maybe he'll think it's worth it."

Easy for her to say, I thought, until she added, "Maybe I will, too."

chapter eleven

We didn't see Audie again until after the big game. Mr. O'Sullivan and his employees were gone by the time we returned from school every day, which was usually what happened unless they were working on a new project or some longer repair. Neither Mother nor Daddy mentioned him, and of course, neither did Gloria or I. Our dinner conversations were built around two subjects only, the game and the soon-to-be-public announcement of Gloria's college award. Mother had all sorts of plans for the publicity. She even talked about how they would do some local television interviews together and how she would arrange for a reporter and photographer from *Palm Springs Life* magazine to interview us all.

"It's not out of the question to get the *Los Angeles Times* here," she said.

"Do we really need to do all that?" Gloria asked.

"Of course we do. Why shouldn't we be proud of what you've accomplished? Humility is overvalued," Mother said. She paused, tilted her head, and gazed at the ceiling. "I think Katharine Hepburn might have said that."

"No, what Katharine Hepburn is remembered for saying," Gloria said, "is 'If you obey all the rules, you miss all the fun.'"

Daddy smiled first. "That's right," he said. "I remember when you used that in a talk, Evelyn."

Mother grunted, her jaw tightening. There wasn't anything she hated more than being corrected about a movie star's quote or a quote from a film.

"Movie stars can say and do things like that, but not a young girl on her way to an exceptional college where she'll do exceptional things. This family doesn't need someone breaking all the rules."

She looked more at me, with the sparks still jumping in her eyes, put down her fork, and sat back. She could get so dramatic, I thought. My mother had been studying movies and movie stars so long that she believed she was living in a film. She probably heard theme music in the background wherever she went.

She calmed and looked at Gloria. "Good parents should always want their children to do better than they have done. We are proud of what we have been able to provide for you but far prouder of what you can and will provide for us. Alan?" she said, turning to Daddy for his memorized line.

"Oh, absolutely," Daddy said. "Your big achievements are yet to come, Gloria."

It really was almost automated, but I did see a deep look of joy in his face. He would never have that overwhelming expression of pride for me that he had for Gloria. I think I began to accept that before I was ten.

Gloria kept eating quietly. Perhaps no one but me could see when Gloria was churning and burning inside. It was another one of those many times when I felt as if I had stepped out of the present, out of the scene, and was watching just like anyone else in the audience Mother attracted. I might as well have not been sitting there. Gloria didn't say another word. Mother went on to talk about her publicity plans again, and Daddy mentioned how some of his political friends were quite impressed with Gloria's award. She continued to look very uncomfortable as both our parents heaped on their praise. As far as I knew, Gloria had yet to say she would accept the award.

"It will be all right," I told her, before we both went to sleep that night. "You always come up with a way to handle all this and make everyone happy, including yourself."

"What about you, Gish?"

"Me?"

"I want you to be happy. We're too much a part of each other for that not to happen."

"Whatever makes you happy will make me happy, Gloria."

She smiled, and we hugged.

On Friday, everything else we had done or said that week disappeared into the memories we usually kept under lock and key. The chatter was now all about the game anyway. Our small private school was going to soar above the tougher, grittier public schools that had always dominated. At school, everyone's eyes were on Lee and his teammates. They moved like gladiators in ancient Rome through our building, their shoulders high and their chests out, as if they were literally pumped up. I could see the anticipation even on the faces of our teachers.

As we were leaving the day of the game, Lee caught up with us in the parking lot. He had been held back by teachers wishing him well.

"Every basket I make I'll be making for you," he told Gloria.

"They should be for the school, not me," she said.

"I know. They will be, but they'll be more for you. And Mom and Dad are making some party for us. It'll be better than New Year's Eve."

"What did I tell you about the man on the tightrope looking down?" Gloria said, sounding quite angry, actually.

"I know, I know," he said, holding up his hands. "They can't help it, but I'll distract myself. Stay cool."

"You're the one who has to stay cool, Lee, not us. Let's go," she told me.

No hug or kiss for him and no wishing him luck. Maybe she thought that was best. He looked a little surprised and watched us leave.

"You were a little hard on him," I said as we drove out of the school parking lot.

"I hope so," she said. "It's his only hope."

Daddy came home early from work. He was very excited about the game, telling us it was the big topic of conversation at work. Mother talked about the after-party at the Aarons' and how she had helped Lee's mother plan it. She had her use the same caterer who did the film festival every year. We had a light dinner and then got dressed to go.

Before we went down to leave, Gloria came hurriedly into my room.

"Look," she said, standing by my window. I joined her and saw Audie shirtless at the pool, apparently patching some cracks in the tiles. He was lean and muscular in a harder, more carved way than Lee. "I guess he's an all-around handyman."

"Or he learns fast."

We saw Mr. O'Sullivan on the side watching him and shouting some orders at him, obviously criticizing how he was doing the chore and that he'd taken off his shirt, because he paused and quickly put it back on.

"Mr. O'Sullivan gets so anal about working on our grounds," I said.

Gloria nodded, but she wasn't thinking about Mr. O'Sullivan. "I wonder what he does with his free time. He doesn't know anyone yet, I imagine," she said. "It's difficult starting somewhere new, especially under his circumstances."

As she looked, I saw that soft, beautiful smile of hers brighten. I could almost hear her thoughts, hear her plan to spend more time with him despite Mother's warnings.

"Gloria. You'll just get his father angry or both of them fired."

She nodded, sighed. "I'm sure you're right. The game," she said, and we started out to join Mother and Daddy.

I had been to basketball games, even exciting ones, but none was anything like this. The gym bleachers were almost completely filled when we arrived, and we arrived a half hour early, even though my father wanted us there an hour early. All the way there, Mother had cried that she was going to hate sitting on those hard seats for so long, and now we had to crowd in beside Lee's parents and his brother.

"I brought you one of these," Lee's mother told her, and gave her a thin cushion.

"Oh, how thoughtful," Mother said. She was appeased for a while but complained incessantly about fans pounding their feet on the bleacher floors. It did sound like an earthquake, and the screaming of school cheers was so loud it made your ears ring.

There was never any question that it was going to be a close game. According to Gloria, the left guard on the Indio team was as good as he had been in the game she had witnessed with Lee. He had them out in front by four points before the end of the first half. Lee was doing well but not as well as I had seen him do. Any shot he missed reverberated in the moans of our fans and clearly impacted his confidence. I saw how Coach McDermott was lecturing him vigorously whenever they broke for a time-out.

"What's happening?" I asked Gloria. Even when it came to sports, she had more insight.

"I think he's messing up some plays because he's so intent," she said. "The coach looks like he might take him out to teach him a lesson for a while."

I looked at Lee's father, who did seem quite upset. Where was the college scout? I wondered as I gazed around.

Fortunately, Lee redeemed himself just before the end of the first half, when he drove in for a layup and was fouled. The layup counted, and he made the foul shot, tying the game.

At halftime, Mother looked so distraught I thought she was going to have a heart attack. My father and Lee's father rose to go get something to drink. I expected Mother would go, too, but when the stands opened up because so many people had left, she decided she'd be better off staying with Lee's mother.

"More air to breathe," she said.

Gloria and I joined some of the students who had gathered just outside the gym doors. I saw Lee's father talking to a man I didn't know. He must be the college scout, I thought. Daddy joined them with drinks. Lee's father and Daddy were both salesmen. Lee couldn't have had better spokesmen. Hopefully, he would do better in the second half and justify all the praise they were laying on him to the scout.

All the envious girls surrounded Gloria, who I knew disappointed them with her stoic attitude. "We'll see, we'll see" was practically her chanted reply to every over-the-top compliment of Lee. Everyone was quite excited, but I could feel why Gloria was being so cautious. The Indio player had been better than Lee. He had passed effectively to his teammates more and seemingly executed their plays perfectly. Gloria, who could keep track of and add numbers almost as well as some math genius, said he had eight points more than Lee.

"The scout will probably go after him," she muttered.

When a bell was rung, we flowed back into the bleachers. Everyone cheered at the sight of the teams, but that was followed by a tense relative silence until the players were back on the court. The Indio team scored six points in the first two minutes. Lee missed a shot, and Bobby Sacks fouled twice in a row. The coach called a time-out, but when they returned to the court, the panic made them wilder. Lee fouled twice, made a shot, and missed two in a row. We were behind six points with ten minutes left to play.

Every time I glanced at Lee's father, I could see that his face had darkened with more redness and rage, especially at the refs. Daddy tried to keep him calm with constant reassurances. Lee hit two shots in a row, and the score was closer. In the last minute, Lee forced a shot, missed, and tried too hard to follow up with the rebound. He picked up another foul and had fouled the wrong player, one of their best shooters. He hit both foul shots, and we were into the last minute four points behind. After another time-out, our team took the ball, and for whatever reason, Bobby's pass to Lee was weak and easily picked off by the opposition. With the ball in the Indio team's possession, Coach McDermott called the last time-out.

Our side of the bleachers was in a deep funk. The players returned to the court, the whistle blew, and a full-court press resulted immediately in Jack Gibson fouling.

When their player made his shots, the game was over. We rose and started out in a funereal silence.

"What kind of party is this going to be?" I asked Gloria.

"Hopefully short," she said.

We walked behind our parents, seemingly in a sea of gloom and disappointment, floating out to the parking lot in a pool of ink.

"There is a universal truth about life," Gloria once told me when we were talking about other girls from wealthy families in our classes one day in the casita. We were in high school by then. "The more you have when you start out, the more difficult it is to accept defeat and failure. Frustration cuts deeper and sharper. Let's try hard not to make that true for us, Gish."

"I doubt you'll see much defeat and failure, Gloria. But I don't doubt I will."

She had stared at me that day with so dark an expression that it made my heart pound.

"I won't let that happen to you," she'd said. It was a promise I laughed at. I was sure she had forgotten it moments after she had said it.

It didn't really surprise either Gloria or me that Mother was the most cheerful on the way to the Aarons' for the party that was supposed to be a celebration and now would be more of a wake. She was confident that the preparations she had made with Mary Aaron were so wonderful and extravagant that everyone quickly would lose their depression. "After all, it was just a basketball game."

"Yes, but it probably was an opportunity Lee lost," Daddy reminded her.

"He'll land something else just fine," she said. "My goodness. It's not like expecting the Academy Award and not getting it."

If Daddy had any comeback, he kept it smothered.

"I know what we can do to cheer up people," Mother said. "We'll talk about Gloria's achievement. That should add some joviality."

"No, Mother!" Gloria practically screamed. "It's the wrong time."

"She's right, Evelyn. We'll enjoy it as best we can and leave that for another day."

Mother spun around to look at Gloria. "Don't ever be ashamed of your accomplishments just because you're surrounded by mediocrity," she warned.

Gloria turned and looked out the window. Mother glanced at me and then sat quietly for the remainder of the trip to the Aarons'.

"You're going to have to cheer him up," I told her when we parked and got out.

"I think I'll leave it up to you," she said.

I looked at her sharply. Was she serious?

Everyone at the party put on the best face they could. Since it had been the basketball finals, the comfort of *You'll get 'em next time* wasn't available. Most told Lee he had played a good game and had nothing about which to be ashamed. Lies meant to comfort or compensate for failure and/or tragedy were gleefully accepted, but like leaking balloons, they crumbled and settled almost as soon as they were expressed.

Gloria's best sympathy for Lee came in the form of a warning. I stood beside her when she said, "Don't stand around feeling sorry for yourself, Lee. You'll just keep the cloud of gloom lingering over your and your parents' heads."

"Thanks," he said, and then leaned in to us to whisper, "I've got the right medicine."

His breath reeked of it. He winked and showed us his spiked glass of punch.

"Oh, that should solve it," Gloria said. "Brilliant." She stepped away to talk to some of the cheerleaders.

I stood by him.

His eyes narrowed and he took a bigger gulp of his drink. "She's so wise, so smart, so in control all the time," he muttered angrily.

"Not always," I said.

He looked at me skeptically and went to talk to Bobby and Jack, who were obviously into his special punch. When Mother decided to leave, Lee asked Gloria to stay, but she told him she was tired.

"Yeah, you worked hard sitting in the stands," he said.

His eyes looked like they were floating in his head by now, and Gloria wasn't hiding her disgust and disappointment. I was more forgiving, which was ironic, since that was her specialty, my Lady Jesus. Actually, I really was hoping he would ask me to stay to keep him company, but he looked right through me and joined some of the others.

"Well, what did you think?" Mother asked Daddy as we drove off.

"Fabulous food and quite the presentation."

"I thought so. That kept the mood from becoming too dark. The game will be forgotten long before the party, don't you think, Alan?"

"You're probably right, Evelyn," he said.

I didn't listen to any more of their conversation, and Gloria closed her eyes and looked like she really was exhausted. We entered the house in silence. I thought Gloria might want to talk, but she gave me a definitive "Good night" and went to her room. Even so, I anticipated her coming into mine after she had prepared for bed. But she didn't. I went to her bedroom doorway and looked in. She was in bed and looked like she was already asleep. I had started to turn away when she surprised me.

"I blame myself, Gish," she said.

"What?" I stepped into the bedroom. She turned onto her back and looked up at the ceiling. "Blame yourself for what?"

"Getting involved with him."

"Lee? You said you liked him well enough and might like him more," I reminded her. "Enough for *it*."

"Sometimes we see what we want. It's another kind of blindness."

"So you don't like him anymore?"

"Shoe doesn't fit," she said.

"I don't understand, Gloria. His unhappiness and trying to escape it isn't a surprise."

"In the end, it's how you react to unhappiness that determines who you are and will be."

She was sounding smug and superior, just the way Lee saw her, I thought.

"I'm confused, Gloria. What are you saying?"

"Let's talk about it tomorrow, okay? I'm exhausted. Between Mother and Lee and . . . everything."

"Okay," I said.

Everything covered so much. I wanted to stay and pursue it, but she turned over and embraced her pillow, just the way I always did, especially when I wanted to shut out the world.

I stood there looking at her a moment and then returned to my room.

This is not going to be pleasant, I thought. Lee and his friends would resent her for not being more sympathetic, and whether I liked it or not, that reaction would smear over me. The chances of my attending another school once Gloria left had just gone up threefold.

Lee called her late in the morning. I sat with her at the pool while she spoke with him on her cell. Her responses were mostly monosyllabic, except for phrases like "I can imagine."

When she hung up, she turned to me and said, "Breaking news. He's suffering a bad hangover."

"Don't you feel sorry for him, Gloria?"

"You'd think he'd want that, Gish, but Lee is really not the kind of person who welcomes sympathy. He'd rather spend the day finding other people, other things, to blame. But you're right. That only makes me feel sorrier for him. I'm just not ready to soothe his bruised ego yet."

"He wanted to come over, didn't he?"

"Yes."

"Is he coming?"

"No. I told him I had too much to do." She closed her eyes and lay back.

I couldn't imagine telling him that, I thought. We both sat up ten minutes later at the sound of the toolshed door being opened. Its hinges squealed. Audie entered and then emerged with the hedge clippers. At the rear wall, his father stood with his arms folded, looking at the bushes.

"He's making him do it again," Gloria said.

"What do you mean? You saw him doing it?"

"Yes."

"When?"

"Very early this morning, practically at daybreak."

Whenever she could, she had been looking out her window and watching him far more than I had imagined.

His father did look upset.

Audie began working on the hedges. His father looked back at us, said something to him, and walked off. I could see Gloria bracing herself to rise.

"Don't go there, Gloria."

"You want to offer someone sympathy, that's the one to offer it to," she said. She watched him and then, giving it more thought, lay back.

I watched him. His father was making him redo all the surrounding hedges. The late-morning sun brought the unusually warm weather down in what seemed like torrents of heat flowing through very dry air. What was this summer going to be like if it was like this now? I wondered. I saw Audie pause frequently to wipe his forehead. He started to take off his shirt, and his father popped out of the shadows on the side to yell at him. He worked on. Why wasn't Mr. O'Sullivan bringing Audie something to drink, at least? I wondered, but was afraid to mention it to Gloria.

She must have been watching out of the corners of her eyes, because she suddenly stood up more determinedly, reached into her insulated pool bag, and took out a bottle of water.

"Gloria!" I said.

She looked back at me. "The only thing to fear is fear itself."

"C'mon. You'll get him in trouble," I warned.

I looked at the house for signs of Mother and then at Gloria when she reached Audie. He paused, took the water, and they talked, looking a lot friendlier. Suddenly, Mr. O'Sullivan stepped out from behind the toolshed. He didn't speak. He just watched them. Gloria saw him and deliberately waved at him. He didn't wave back. After another few words between her and Audie, she returned to the pool.

As she walked toward me, I saw Mr. O'Sullivan move quickly to join his son. Audie continued to work as his father spoke to him, his arms flailing about.

"What was that all about?"

"Surprise. He's not happy here," she said, and sat. She smoothed on some sun protection.

"What are his choices?"

Mr. O'Sullivan walked back to the rear of the toolshed, and Audie snapped the hedge clippers with a vengeance.

"He has no uncles or aunts. The closest in his family live in Ireland. He said he was there once when he was a little boy and his parents were together."

"Will he go there?"

"I don't know. I don't think he has any money, don't think his mother left him anything, and I have the feeling his father isn't exactly sympathetic."

Her phone rang. She looked at it, looked away, and then, after it rang again, answered.

She listened, shook her head, and said, "Just a few minutes, Lee."

"What?"

"He's outside the gate," she said. "I'm so not in the mood for this."

"Why can't you at least pretend to be sympathetic?" I asked, getting up, too.

She turned quickly. "He lost a ball game, but his family is wealthy, and he'll have a good life, Gish." She looked toward Audie. "I'm tired of living on a movie screen."

I followed slowly behind her, my arms folded, my head down. I glanced back at Audie, who had moved down along the hedges until he was out of sight.

Lee stepped in quickly when Gloria opened the gate. He looked like he was being chased.

"So?" Gloria asked.

"I had to get out of the house. My father won't stop reminding me of what he had to go through to get me this opportunity."

"There are other good schools with basketball teams," Gloria said. She sighed, looked at me, softened a bit, and started back to the pool.

"Hey, Gish," he said. I smiled when Gloria was looking away. "What are you two up to?"

"We're solving the problems of the world," Gloria said.

When we reached the pool, she flopped onto a lounge chair. Audie had paused and was looking at us.

"My mother told me about your college award this morning," Lee said. "I guess I'll be one of the first at school to congratulate you."

"Thank you," Gloria said.

He sat on the lounge chair I had been using, so I sat on the next one over.

"I guess we should celebrate that, at least. How about we go to the Mission Inn in Riverside for dinner?"

She was quiet. I could see she was looking at Audie, who had started working again.

"I can pick you up at six."

"I think I'm coming down with something," Gloria said. "Maybe we'll do something tomorrow."

"What's wrong?"

"Gnawing headache and a little stomach upset."

"Ahhh," he said, looking at me. I knew he thought that was the whole explanation for Gloria's cool attitude. "How are you, Gish?"

"Okay," I said.

For a moment, I thought he was going to ask me out instead, but he slapped down on his knees and stood. "I guess I'll head over to Jack's house. Boys are getting together for a while. His parents went to Idyllwild with some friends for lunch."

Gloria turned and gave him a very sharp, hard look. "Don't get too deep in a well of self-pity, Lee. Move on."

His face seemed to explode with surprise. Even I wondered what she meant. Move on from the defeat or from her as well?

"I'll call," he said. "Feel better."

"Thank you."

He looked at me.

"Walk him to the gate," Gloria said, which was another surprise.

I stood and we started away.

"She really sick?" he asked.

"She's been different all day, so I imagine so."

I opened the gate for him. "It was a heartbreaker, but I know you tried hard, Lee," I said. "You shouldn't be blamed."

He smiled. "Maybe I'm with the wrong sister," he said. He hesitated and then walked out.

I stood there in the gateway watching him go to his car.

Did he mean it?

No one had ever chosen me over Gloria for anything, ever.

chapter twelve

For years afterward, I would think back to this time, and in my memory and even my dreams, I would see a dark shadow moving over our house the way shadows move when a large cloud floats over the sun. It really does seem to crawl, ooze over everything, when that happens. It intrigued, practically hypnotized me when I was a little girl. Gloria would think my infatuation with the shadow was funny. She'd jump up when we were at the pool or just sitting outside and scream, "Let's outrun it!"

I'd follow her all the way to the bushes at part of the wall surrounding our property, staying just ahead of the moving shade, and then crouch and screech with her when it reached us. It always annoyed Mother, especially if she was sitting on the patio and talking on the phone.

Eventually, I realized no one could outrun that sliding darkness, not even Gloria.

Mother and Daddy went out for dinner the night Gloria had claimed she wasn't feeling well. I was amazed at how surprised Mother was that Gloria wasn't going out with Lee. She just assumed it was Lee's fault.

"He's in that much of a depression over losing the game?" she asked.

I looked at Gloria, waiting to see what she would say.

"I'm tired," she said. "I might have a little head cold I want to nurse."

Daddy was immediately concerned and asked if she had a fever.

"No, but why push myself? There'll be plenty of date nights ahead," she replied.

"That's very mature of you, Gloria, but not at all surprising," he said.

"I hope you're paying attention to all the right examples your sister sets for you," Mother told me.

"I wouldn't miss one," I replied. I saw Gloria hide a smile.

She did go to sleep early that evening. I looked in on her. Once she awoke and told me she was fine and that I could stop worrying. I watched some television, read one of the novels Gloria had recommended I read months ago, grew tired, and prepared for bed. I was only dozing when I heard Mother and Daddy come home. Daddy looked in on Gloria. After, I heard him telling Mother that she was fine. He had even felt her forehead and decided she had no fever. I couldn't recall a time he had done that with me. Mother had done it very rarely. Both of them always relied on Gloria's examination and diagnosis, especially when we were older. Most of the time, even if I had a low fever, I'd hear Gloria tell them, "She's just bored silly. Nothing to worry about." Then she would give me something like Tylenol and a cup of hot tea and honey. I'd do the same for her. The only time either of us had to go to the doctor was to get necessary vaccinations.

Maybe fifteen minutes or so after I heard our parents go to bed, I thought I heard footsteps in the hallway. I turned onto my back and propped myself up on my pillow, anticipating Gloria coming to my door, but she didn't appear. It was silent again. Had I imagined it? Was it one of Mother's famous ghosts? I almost went back to sleep, but at the last moment, I decided to get up and go to her room. For a moment after I had opened the door, I thought she had gone back to sleep, but something made me step farther in and look closer. The blanket was up around the edge of the pillow, but that wasn't Gloria under it. When I looked, I saw it was another pillow. For a moment or so, I just stood there, a little shocked, and then I went to the window and looked out.

There, just at the edge of the ground lights, I saw two shadows move and realized one of them was Gloria. I didn't have to think too hard about the other. It was definitely not Lee Aaron. They merged with the darkness and then appeared at the door of the casita. I waited and watched until they entered and then returned to my room. I couldn't simply fall asleep again. I lay there with my eyes open, listening.

Despite my determination, my eyes eventually did close. Right before dawn, I woke because I heard what sounded like soft footsteps in the hallway. I got out of bed and went to her room. She was just getting back under the blanket. She had simply thrown a jacket over her pajamas.

"What are you doing?"

"Going to sleep," she said.

"Where were you?" I asked. She didn't respond. "What did you do in the casita?"

"Just talked," she said. "Why did you ask if you knew? You spy."

"How did you plan that? Did he text you?"

"No. His father won't give him the money for a phone." She paused and looked at me. "Remember how the highwayman and the rich girl met secretly in *Love on the Run*?"

"The scarf on the gate?" I said.

"When I see it . . ."

"You go to the casita."

"That's it, Gish. Now, go back to bed. We have to get up in an hour or so to make Sunday breakfast."

She got into bed and pulled the blanket up almost over her head.

I returned to bed, but I didn't go back to sleep. Even so, she was up and dressed ahead of me and quite chipper. No one would have guessed that she had been up practically the whole night, least of all Daddy, who was quite happy to see her quick recovery. I wanted to find out more about her secret nighttime rendezvous, but she spent most of the time talking to our parents about her coming to a decision. I cleared the table while they talked and then returned to listen.

"I think Daddy has gotten me a great opportunity," she told them. "I'd be a fool not to follow through."

Daddy's face was so quickly filled with joy that I thought it would explode from too sudden a rush of happy blood. His eyes had never been brighter. Mother looked very pleased. I could see her mind racing ahead with her publicity plans.

"We have our own little movie star," she said.

"Please don't do too much, Mother," Gloria said, but she might as well have told that to the wall of autographs.

Afterward, when I asked Gloria again about her meeting Audie, she only repeated, "We just talked."

The local newspaper sent a reporter over two days later. He and Mother were waiting for Gloria when we returned from school. I sat to the right side on the patio while she was interviewed. Her answers were long and detailed about her studies and interests. She said she was leaning toward a career in law with an emphasis on international business law. She even described some famous cases. I could see the reporter was overwhelmed.

She had never mentioned any of this to me or implied her enthusiasm for such a career. I had the feeling she was saying it more to please Daddy. Through some answers, she practically forced the reporter to talk to me as well. He immediately asked the questions I expected I'd hear for the rest of my life: "What's it like having a sister like Gloria? Does she inspire you to do better?"

Mother was very pleased and told Gloria they had a date and a time to do two local television interviews as well this week. "So don't dillydally after school."

"Okay, Mother," she said.

There was something about Gloria's suddenly embracing all this publicity that made me suspicious. When I asked her about it, she simply said, "I'm really doing it all for Daddy. He's more excited about it than I am. And I know how much he likes to brag to his friends."

She was right. At dinner, he told us about his old professors, some of whom were still working. He had written to them, and they were looking forward to meeting Gloria.

"It will be fun to visit you on campus. So many memories for me," Daddy said.

Mother announced that she was pursuing the *Los Angeles Times* through a wealthy friend who did a lot of advertising with the paper. She was sure they'd get that interview. She went on and on about how publicity helped build careers. Daddy was beaming. He intended to call his business associates in Los Angeles and alert them to the article whenever it was scheduled to appear.

"One of the radio stations might pick you up there, too," he suggested.

Mother vowed to work on it. The three of them were going on and on about it all as if they were planning a full-blown political campaign. Of course, no one paused to ask my opinion of anything.

"What kills a skunk is the publicity it gives itself," I blurted after a while. Gloria burst into a smile, but Mother glared at me. "Abraham Lincoln said that, right, Gloria?"

"Yes, she's right, Mother."

"How can you compare your sister to a skunk?" Mother asked, her eyes big and lit with that inner fire she could raise up inside herself. Daddy called her eyes "your mother's blowtorches."

"It was just a joke."

"We have no time for jokes," Mother said, and returned to her plans.

If Gloria had been something of a star at school before, she glowed and twinkled ten times as much after the television interviews and feature story in the *Desert Sun*. I don't know how many times I was asked if I was proud of my sister. It ranged from "Aren't you proud of your sister?" to "I bet you're proud of your sister."

I could see teachers and other students weren't satisfied with my "I have always been proud of Gloria." It was simply too matter-of-fact.

Nevertheless, I couldn't move out from under my cloud of suspicion about her behavior when it came to receiving so much adulation, despite what Gloria had told me. She was never embarrassed by the compliments that came her way, but she never seemed to embrace them as enthusiastically as she was doing now. Was she being sincere? Was she doing all this just for our parents? I continually questioned my reactions to the way she was sucking up praise. How unlike Gloria, I thought. Or was it? Was I simply evincing that jealousy that always crawled beneath my skin and in my thoughts?

What was lost at the beginning of all this was Lee Aaron's retreat from any relationship with her. He never called after she had rejected him that day at our pool. Once everyone began to realize and question it, the news of their breakup was practically on a marquee hanging above the entrance to the building, just the way Gloria had described his previous breakup. Because Gloria didn't talk about it, Lee was free to establish the reasons for ending the affair. The causes that he and his friends circulated ranged from Gloria no longer thinking it was prestigious to be his girlfriend after the lost basketball game to her being stuck-up because she had won this great college award, "and none of us are good enough for her now."

The jealousy and envy so many of the other girls had done their best to keep subdued burst out like a bad skin rash. The little clumps of gossipers whispered in every corner of the school. I worried for Gloria, but she didn't seem at all bothered. She didn't admit to these causes for her breakup with Lee or deny them, which at the start only reinforced them. It got so I was practically the only other student she talked to at school. Some of the brighter boys who respected her achievements tried to get her to pay more attention to them. She was polite, but she really did seem to have stepped out of this world into another. Of course, I thought I knew the real reason for that.

Over the next few weeks, Gloria continued her secret rendezvous with Audie, sneaking out late at night, practically every other night. Whenever he was on our property working with his father, both she and he did a good job of ignoring each other. I continually tried to get her to talk more about it, but she was resistant, always too busy or too tired. I finally grew quite annoyed and let her know it when we were finally alone in the casita, something she had been avoiding our doing.

"We've always shared our secrets," I said. "Why have you stopped trusting me with yours? You're shutting me out, avoiding me and my questions."

"I haven't stopped trusting you," she said. "The less you know, the less guilty you'll look if Mother especially grows suspicious and begins to interrogate you."

"I would never tell her anything."

"And if Daddy asks you?"

"The same."

"But can you lie to him?" she asked.

"Yes," I said, but not confidently. She knew it. She was quiet, thinking, and I didn't say a word.

"I'm just getting to know him, Gish. What he's been through was not pleasant."

"What does that mean?"

"His mother didn't just die."

"What's that mean? What happened?"

"She was an alcoholic and had moved into drugs. One night, she didn't come home, and the next morning, she was found dead in an alley. Someone had stabbed her. The police called his father. His father suspected he was doing drugs, too, so he had to prove to him he wasn't, but that's part of why he's so strict with him. He's going through some dark times, and his father doesn't exactly have sympathetic ears. He's one of these people who believe lots of suffering makes you a stronger, better person. Audie is suffering with all this locked up inside him."

"So what are you, like Audie's therapist now?"

She looked at me sharply. I did sound unduly unsympathetic, even mean, and instantly regretted it.

"Anyone who's in any relationship with anyone is something of a therapist, Gish," she said. "I would have thought you could see that in the way Daddy placates Mother so frequently."

"Yeah, I do. Sorry."

"Sometimes I think he's more of a therapist for me." She smiled. "Yes, Miss Perfect needs one, too."

"I thought I was your therapist."

She laughed. "You are, but it's different with a boy, a young man like Audie."

"Well, what's going to come of all this?" I asked, obviously a little frustrated with how casual she was being about a secret romance that to me couldn't have any sort of pleasing conclusion.

She shrugged. "He's saving his money. When he has enough, he'll leave," she said. "And I'll be off to college."

"That's it?"

"That's reality," she said. "In the meanwhile . . ."

"What?"

"We do the best, get the best out of it, until it's over."

Get the best out of it? She made it sound so inconsequential, but having a boyfriend could never be so simple for me. I didn't want to tell her, but when she wasn't with me at school, I often caught Lee flirting with me. Despite how much I wanted to, I didn't encourage it. He was doing this simply to get even with Gloria, I thought, and then fantasized that he wasn't, that he really meant what he had said about being with the wrong sister.

"I need you to do me a favor Saturday," Gloria said.

"What?"

"I want you to get Karla Bishop to invite you to a sleepover."

"What? She and I hardly talk anymore."

"Play up to her. She and some of her friends love gossip. Suggest you might reveal what really happened between Lee and me. I'll help you make up some stories."

"Why?"

"I'll take you there and explain to Mother and Daddy that I'm hanging out for a while with you and your friends."

I looked at her, smiling. "So you can have a real date with Audie?"

"Close to it. We'll go to Idyllwild or something."

"Where none of Mommy and Daddy's friends might see you."

"And Mr. O'Sullivan's friends, too. Mother really threatened him, and he threatened Audie."

"Oh. But a whole night with Karla and her friends?"

"You used to do it, Gish."

"They're so immature."

She laughed. "Now who's the snob in the family?"

"You'll owe me."

She laughed again. "I'll make it up to you, somehow."

I really didn't know if my distaste for Karla and her friends was what was bothering me or Gloria having a date with Audie, handsome, sexy Audie. Images of him shirtless and his dangerous stare, with those full, manly lips tight, rushed through my mind. Would I spend my whole life envious of my sister? Once I had been jealous of Lee and her, and now this. It saddened me, but I don't think Gloria suspected that. I was sure she thought my complaints were only my reaction to spending so much time with girls who gossip, chewing up innuendos and rumors like some of them click gum in their teeth.

"Whatever," I said.

She hugged and thanked me. How I wished I was as enthusiastic about someone the way she now was about Audie. It was really at that moment that I realized her little infatuation with Lee had been more like simply playing at a romance. Whatever she already had with Audie now was deeper set and, despite how she described their finale, not inconsequential. She was deliberately downplaying it. It made me grow even more suspicious.

"You'd better really be careful, Gloria." How rare it was for me to warn her about anything.

"I know," she said. "Don't worry."

She was right about how easy it was to get invited to Karla Bishop's house for a pajama party after I hinted at giving her the nitty-gritty about Gloria and Lee. Once that was secured, she started to create scenarios and details for her breakup with him, most of which were critical of him. They ranged from his being too demanding sexually, which most of the girls suspected anyway, to his being very immature when it came to any sort of rejection. She told me to say he sulked and made snide remarks under his breath. The real clincher was "When you get to know someone more intimately, you see and get turned off by some of his poor hygiene, his bad breath, and where he scratches himself in front of you."

It was fun creating the scenarios and acting them out. This was more like the way Gloria and I were in the casita, enjoying our free-flying imaginations. Later, at Karla's house, I held rapt attention when I, only when almost forced to do it, revealed some of this with the most dramatic flair I could create. What I was really doing was imitating Mother. She was the one who taught me how to be histrionic. By the end of the evening, most felt sorry for Gloria and were glad she had broken it off with Lee. I felt a little guilty about it but also a little proud of myself for how easily I could do it.

When Gloria picked me up the following morning, I described how they had reacted, the looks on their faces, and their own embellishments, some about him and some about other boys. Gloria and I laughed about it, but what we didn't anticipate enough was how quickly the stories I told would get back to Lee.

I wanted to know more about her and Audie, but I could see that she was reluctant to talk about it for now.

When we returned to school on Monday, Lee was looming in the hallways, fuming and eager to spit fire at Gloria. He accused her of being a tease terrified of losing her virginity. She walked away from him, but he followed right behind, spitting his venom. Mr. Madeo heard the commotion and came hurrying out of his classroom to defend Gloria. Lee was sent to the principal's office with a referral for his profanity.

It all put a new atmosphere in the building, and later, Mother received an earful from Mary Aaron. Daddy came to Gloria's defense immediately, not that Mother was going to blame her. However, it all threw a dark pall over us at dinner. I thought Gloria was going to regret what we had done, but she seemed quite indifferent to the aftermath.

"I'm just happy I saw what and who he really was before it was too late," she told our parents.

Daddy pointed out how maturely she was behaving about it. Mother reluctantly agreed. After all, she had touted Lee because he came from such a highly respected family. Of course, she turned the direction of the conversation to me.

"It often is too late if you're not as cautious as your sister," Mother followed.

I thought I'd regurgitate my dinner. I was inches away from throwing it back at her, but one look at Gloria told me to let it go.

As the next few weeks passed, Gloria continued her secret rendezvous with Audie in the casita. To me, she seemed to retreat into this and now lived for and looked forward only to it. She dropped no clues for our parents to see. Her work continued to be honors level at school, and she talked and planned continually with Mother about what she would buy and what she would take when she went off to college.

At school, Lee kept to his side of the school world and started to have a relationship with Mindy Leonard, a cute redhead with freckles splattering her cheeks. She was one of the shier girls in my class and more surprised than anyone by Lee's attention. To my mind, he was just trying to prove he couldn't be a loser, especially when it came to girls.

Gloria couldn't have cared less. I had the sense both of us were now drifting through the school day, still holding on to our cheerfulness together. As far as anyone else knew, nothing had really changed.

Of course, whenever I saw Audie working on our grounds, I watched Gloria's face and saw how she snuck looks at him and he at her. His father, surely sensing something, loomed in the shadows and gave him more to do. There was so much new planting and trimming at the start of spring. After a while, I avoided asking Gloria too much about her and Audie. I could see whenever I asked anything or mentioned anything, she became uncomfortable. Maybe because the end of their romantic trysts really was coming.

"Where do you think he'll go once he has enough money?" I asked her when we were sitting at the pool one Saturday. He wasn't on the grounds.

"He's a little more romantic than he seems," she said. "He thinks it might be exciting traveling across the country, hitchhiking, riding buses, getting odd jobs along the way to help pay for it. He likes poetry, you know."

"How would I know?"

"Oh, right. I introduced him to Dylan Thomas and Yeats. I read them to him, and then . . ." She smiled. "I had him read them to me. He has this resonant, deep voice, perfect for Dylan Thomas."

"That's amazing," I said. "Maybe he'll want to go to college."

"No," she said. "I don't think so. He likes working with his hands on engines, gardening, almost anything where it's just him and whatever. I don't think he ever had many friends. He never mentions anyone."

"You really are so much more fascinated with him than you were with Lee, aren't you?"

"Like I said at the start, there's something far more manly about him. Lee's a spoiled boy. I don't think he'll be as successful as so many believe. Honestly, I feel sorrier for him than anything else. I don't mean it to sound superior or anything."

"I know you don't," I said.

She closed her eyes and lay back. Whatever she was thinking brought that soft smile to her face, a smile I would try my best to duplicate. Watching her breathe softly, her breasts rising and falling ever so gently while she wandered in her thoughts, I realized how much I truly loved her. I memorized her that day, every strand of her hair, every crease in her skin, and every way her lips moved and settled.

Of every image of Gloria that was framed and mounted on the walls of my memory, that image, that day, would always come to me first.

During the following few days, I sensed something was happening or had happened between Audie and her, but she wasn't talking about it. In fact, she seemed to be cherishing every moment she could find to be alone. During those days, she left on errands without telling me why or what she was getting and never asked me to go along. I always suspected it had something to do with Audie, but once she left while he was repainting the toolshed, so it couldn't have been some secret rendezvous. Oddly, I was suddenly getting the feeling they were really ignoring each other and it wasn't part of an act for his father.

She was cheerful and talkative at dinner and eager to help me with some math homework, but she also went to bed early, explaining that she was reading. Daddy had gotten her two of the texts she'd be using in her freshman class, and she did seem very excited about that. If I asked her more about Audie, she would say there was nothing new except "The clock is ticking."

I didn't want to ask her what that meant. I imagined it meant he would be off, forever. Maybe it was painful for her to face it.

The end of the school year was looming, so I assumed she was really getting excited about attending college anyway. She had all the preliminary information and the pamphlets neatly organized on her desk. I began to think of myself as simply impossible, because I was actually annoyed at and even jealous of her excitement. She was going to have a whole new life, a life that didn't include me. It felt like a part of myself was slowly drifting away. I knew it made me more irritable. I had frequent snappy little arguments with Mother, and Daddy reprimanded me for being disrespectful.

A stillness descended, a stillness I hated because it was so heavy and so unusual. There was no music coming from Gloria's room, our conversations dwindled, and I found myself walking our grounds alone, even sitting in the casita by myself to listen to the old music. But nothing was the same. It felt like my feelings were twisting together under my chest like a ball of rubber bands.

Finally, I burst into her room one night and demanded she tell me what was wrong, why she was acting so different, and mainly why we weren't talking as much as we had. She was sitting at her computer, reading from one of the texts Daddy had gotten her, and writing something.

"Are you doing your first college assignment already?"

She smiled. "Something like that. I'm doing anything I can to take my mind off things these days."

"What things?"

She was silent.

"It has to do with Audie?"

"When you get too deeply involved with someone, you have to be willing to take on their burdens."

"What?"

She was quiet.

"Something else has happened. I sensed it, Gloria. Stop bottling it up inside you. You're making me feel like a piece of furniture and not your sister."

"Okay, okay, I'm sorry." She paused and then turned completely to me. "He says his father claims he's not really his son, that his mother had an affair and that's why he left her and had little to do with him. Audie and Mr. O'Sullivan had some big fights about it. Physical fights. A bad one two days ago."

"Can't they do blood tests for that?"

"He's afraid his father's right. His mother had many boyfriends after his father had left and was sleeping around before she was killed. The only solution is for him to get away. I gave him some things to pawn."

"Oh." She looked even more worried. "What else, Gloria?"

"His father suspects we're secretly seeing each other. That's not helping."

"So is this why you can't wait to go to college?"

"I suppose," she said.

"Maybe you should tell Daddy."

"Oh, I don't think that would help anyone, Gish."

"Well, what can I do?"

"Nothing. I'm sorry I've been so distant. We'll start doing things together again. Promise," she said.

"And no more secrets?"

"No more secrets."

I turned and started out.

"Wait," she said.

She rose and hugged me.

"Lillian Gish," she said, smiling.

"Gloria Swanson," I replied.

And we laughed.

Neither of us knew at the time that it would be the last time we laughed like this together.

chapter thirteen

I never felt terribly guilty about any secret that Gloria and I kept from Mother and Daddy, not that we ever did much that would be upsetting to them. But still, I couldn't help but worry about things we did without their specific approval or knowledge. Maybe my fretting was Mother's fault because of the way she described us in the community. According to her and often from what we did see, we were constantly under a spotlight. At least in my mind, our local celebrity status magnified anything we did.

When I was younger, I was actually afraid that our crossing Palm Canyon Drive other than at one of the designated places for pedestrians to cross would be witnessed and calls would be made to Daddy. Gloria was unafraid. She'd laugh as I screamed while she ran us across. However, as soon as Gloria was able to drive and I was as well, we were doubly aware of the traffic laws. What could be worse than Alan John's daughters being caught and ticketed for speeding or going through a stop sign? Gloria also would joke and say, "The fashion police will have the television stations video us wearing white after Labor Day." She had to explain to me why that had once been important to people like Mother who cared about fashion. What *didn't* Gloria know?

One night, a week after we promised no more secrets, Gloria stopped at my door and immediately brought her finger to her lips to keep me from speaking. I was half asleep. It was nearly eleven and a school night. She was wearing her dark blue sweater jacket, the one with the black-leather-tipped collar that Daddy himself had bought her for her last birthday. Even Mother had been shocked and skeptical of his claim to have chosen it himself.

I sat up, and she walked farther into the room.

"I want you to pretend you're asleep in case Daddy hears my car start and comes hurrying in to ask you where I am going."

"Where are you going this late?"

"I know I promised no more secrets, but let me do this without your knowing ahead of time. I want you to be believable when and if Daddy questions you, Gish. Please."

"I'm frightened for you. You've been sneaking around too much. And now? It's almost eleven."

"Don't worry. Again, if for some reason he sees I'm gone, even if he never heard the car, you really don't know anything about it."

"Will you be home soon?"

"Yes. Maybe I'll drop by when I return to let you know I'm back. Okay?"

"No. I'd rather you didn't go, but what good is my saying it?"

She smiled, kissed me on the cheek, and slipped out, gently closing the door behind her. I lay back, telling myself she was just on a quick errand, surely something for Audie. But what? And why did it have to be this late? *Forget about sleeping*, I thought, and listened keenly. I could hear her car engine being started and anticipated Daddy coming out to see what was going on at this hour. But obviously, he didn't hear it, and Mother was already into one of her movies. Despite my determination to wait up for Gloria, close to two in the morning, I closed my eyes and didn't open them until I felt Daddy shake me.

"What?" I said, rubbing my eyes. I searched my memory for a flash of Gloria coming to my bedside, but it wasn't even in a dream.

"Where's your sister? Where did she go so early?" he asked. He was dressed for work, as immaculately as ever, with his gray suit and silver tie. He was probably having an early breakfast meeting. He often had one of those. Miles was surely waiting in the limo. *Early*? He thought she had just left.

"I don't know," I said.

Then he did something he never did. He squeezed my chin between his large thumb and forefinger, twisting my head up and around, forcing me to look him straight in the eye.

"Where did she go? Why would she leave you and not take you to school?"

"I don't know, Daddy," I said.

His grip was telegraphing stinging pain through my jaw. It brought tears to my eyes. He held me a moment longer and then let go. After another scrutinizing look, he went out and woke Mother. I heard him questioning her.

"I have no idea!" she finally screamed. "Stop asking me the same question!"

I sat up, anticipating them both in the doorway.

"Where is she, Gish?" Mother demanded. Her hair looked like she had been running her fingers through it all night.

"I really don't know, Mother."

"When did she leave?" He thought a moment, the truth flashing in his eyes. "Did she leave last night?" Daddy asked.

"I think so," I said. "I heard her car start."

"What?" Mother asked. "She left last night?"

"Why didn't you say so when I questioned you just now? What time did she leave?" Daddy asked.

"I'm not sure . . . maybe eleven," I said. "I thought it was a dream."

I was hoping that saying I thought it was a dream helped me to not look like a liar, especially to Daddy.

"Did she go to see that boy, the O'Sullivan boy?" Mother demanded. Her eyes were wide with fury, those blowtorches.

"I don't know, Mother. She didn't tell me where she was going or say she was meeting someone."

"You'd better be telling the truth," Mother said. She looked at Daddy.

"If you're hiding something from us, it's not going to go well for you, Gish," Daddy threatened.

"I told you all I know. Really," I said.

He studied me a moment and then looked at Mother. Gloria was right. Not knowing for real made me believable.

"I'll make some calls," he said.

"Why am I not surprised at your lying?" Mother said.

"I'm not lying."

She turned and followed him down the stairs. I had been clutching my blanket, holding it close so they couldn't see how much I had been trembling.

Why wasn't Gloria back? I rose to look out my window to confirm she wasn't. She wouldn't simply go right to school and leave me. Where was she? After a few minutes, I heard Daddy come back up the stairs, his steps heavy, angry. I had put on my robe, thinking I would take a shower and start to dress, moving like someone in a total daze, my fingers numb.

"What did she say? I want to know everything she said," Daddy demanded, again in my doorway.

"When?"

"*Any when!*" he screamed. His face looked so twisted with rage. "Did she do something with O'Sullivan's boy?"

"Last night?"

He could see right through my equivocating. With his shoulders hoisted and his hands clenched, he stepped into my room. My father had never hit either of us. I should say *me*. He wouldn't even think of doing that to Gloria. If he was angry at me or annoyed at something both of us had done, he might yell, pound a table, or give us a very angry look. That was so rare it was practically nonexistent in my memory, but right now, he looked like he wanted to grab me and shake me so hard that everything would rattle inside me.

"Gloria would never do this. She'd never leave us worrying," he said, speaking through his clenched teeth.

Did he think I had made her do it? Why was he so angry at me?

"Well? Tell me what you know."

"She likes him," I said.

"And she's met him? Secretly?"

"Yes," I said, my tears of fear slipping out of the corners of my eyes and trickling down my cheeks. Every word I said was a betrayal of Gloria, but I could barely face down Daddy with a half-truth or an excuse even when he was calm, much less at this moment.

"How long has this been going on?"

"I don't know exactly, Daddy." That was almost true.

He stared at me, and then he pointed his thick right forefinger at me. "You're not going anywhere today."

"What about school?"

"You're not going anywhere until I get to the bottom of this. Get dressed and come down," he said, and hurried out again.

I gazed out the window. The gardeners were arriving. I watched for Mr. O'Sullivan and Audie. When I saw them both come through the gate, I breathed relief, but then, as I started for the shower, I stopped.

If she wasn't with Audie, where was she?

My growing fear had me moving like a sleepwalker. I skipped a shower, dabbed my face with cold water, and hurried to get dressed. I put on my jeans and chose a dark blue T-shirt. Mother was sitting alone at the breakfast table with only a glass of water. Daddy was on the phone in his office. I could hear him describing Gloria's car, probably to the police.

"Where is she?" my mother said when I entered the kitchen.

"I really don't know, Mother."

"If it turns out that I was right and you are lying to us, I'll have you sent to some school for tough love instead of a boarding school."

"What? What school for tough love?"

"This sneaking around," she muttered without answering. "This sneaking around you do."

"Me? I haven't been sneaking around, Mother."

"Your sister has never done anything like this."

"Well, why are you blaming me?"

Daddy stepped into the kitchen. "Charlie Siegler has an APB on the car."

"What's that?" Mother asked.

"It's been in enough movies," he said angrily.

He looked like he would lash out at anyone and anything. I rarely heard him take such a tone with Mother.

"An all-points bulletin so that the highway patrol as well as the local police and police in the other cities in the valley will be looking out for it. Maybe she broke down," he said, somewhat calmer.

"She has her cell phone with her, doesn't she?" Mother asked, turning to me. "Well?"

"I don't know for sure. I'll go up and look in her room," I said. I just wanted to get away from them for a few minutes.

I hurried past Daddy. When I stepped into Gloria's room, I saw that everything was neat and in its usual place except for those pillows used to fake her presence. Mother and Daddy were surely going to get angrier when they saw that, I thought, and quickly took them out and fixed the bed. Her phone was nowhere in sight and not in any drawers or on any shelves. I took my time searching, pausing to catch my breath. I felt like I had been running miles. I was about to go downstairs when I heard the shouting outside.

I went to the window.

Daddy was standing in front of Mr. O'Sullivan and Audie, who was looking down as Daddy shouted threats at them. When Audie looked up, I thought he was looking at me in the window, not exactly smiling but looking strangely calm. However, whatever Daddy said to them was enough for Mr. O'Sullivan to turn and slap Audie hard enough across his head to cause him to lose his balance and fall to the side. Looking more embarrassed than hurt, he leaped to his feet, glanced at me in the window, and hurriedly walked away. Daddy spoke more softly to Mr. O'Sullivan and then returned to the house.

I hurried down.

"Her phone's not there," I said as soon as Daddy burst back into the house.

"What did they tell you?" Mother asked him.

"The boy admitted they had been seeing each other but swears he didn't see her last night."

"I don't want them here anymore, Alan."

"Oh, he knows that."

He went to his office. He had fired Mr. O'Sullivan? No wonder he had slapped Audie. I took a deep breath. I could feel how thick the tension had become. Everything was exploding around us.

Stay calm, I told myself. *Do what Gloria would do.*

"Do you want me to make you something to eat, some coffee, Mother?"

She shook her head. "If she's been kidnapped, your father wouldn't be like Glenn Ford in *Ransom!*, would he? I'd be worse than Donna Reed. You remember Donna Reed. She won the Academy Award for Best Supporting Actress in *From Here to Eternity*."

I didn't remember, and without Gloria beside me to remind me, I stood with what I was sure was a blank look. Mother didn't notice. She was at least a mile into her own world.

"I read that every mother was angry at Glenn Ford through most of that movie. When I watched it, I hated him, but I cried for him at the end, just the way most mothers did in those days. I'll cry for your father, but go tell him not to be like Glenn Ford in *Ransom!* if she's been kidnapped. Go on. We always worried about something like that. We have a lot of money. Evil people look for people with a lot of money. And everyone for miles and miles around knows who she is. She's been on television and in the papers. Don't look at me like that. It's not my fault. Any mother would have done those things for her daughter, proud things. Well? Go on," she said, waving at me. "Tell your father what I said."

I turned and went to his office. He sat slumped in his chair, staring at his desk. I could see he wasn't aware that I was standing there, at least for almost a minute. I was afraid to interrupt his thoughts.

"Daddy."

He turned as he sat up. "Your sister wouldn't do this," he said. "She wouldn't stay out all night without telling us. She doesn't lie to us. Your sister wouldn't do this." He looked up at me, his eyes already quite bloodshot from a mixture of fear and rage. "Who can you call? What kids?"

"Everyone's on his or her way to school by now, Daddy," I said.

"I'll call Mr. VanVleet. I'll have him start questioning students. Who should he question? Make a list," he said, and pushed a pad and a pen toward me.

I knew in my heart that whatever Gloria had done, wherever she had gone, she would never confide in someone other than me, but Daddy wouldn't believe that. In his mind, Gloria was too popular not to have good friends, friends with whom she would trust with secrets. I started listing the names of anyone who did cherish talking with her, including some of the boys who fantasized about her as their girlfriend.

"Good," he said when I stopped writing names. "I'll just scan this and email it to him."

I stood there for a moment wondering if I should mention what Mother wanted me to mention. She might get angry that I hadn't.

"Mother wanted me to tell you about Glenn Ford and Donna Reed in *Ransom!*" I began.

He looked up at me with his eyes even more furiously bright than Mother's could get. Again, I thought he was going to lunge at me. I didn't wait for his comment. I returned to the kitchen. She wasn't there. I found her in the den, sitting and looking at one of her movie books.

She looked up so calmly that it was frightening.

"I forgot that Leslie Nielsen was in *Ransom!* and it was his first acting role."

She returned to reading. I stood there a moment, my heart so heavy that I felt like I had swallowed a chunk of old, stale bread. I left her and went to the kitchen to make some coffee. *Daddy's going to want it soon*, I thought. *We'll all sit at the table, and Gloria will walk in, apologizing for not calling.* Whatever she told them would work. They'd be so happy to see her that they'd instantly forgive her. Later, she would tell me the truth. We'd go to the casita. I'd have to tell her what Daddy had said to Mr. O'Sullivan and what he had done to Audie. She'd be so upset, but at least she would be back.

I laughed, thinking how she would do more to comfort me. *I'm sorry I put you through all that*, she would say. I knew exactly what Gloria would say, almost all the time. We were truly in each other's head.

Fear vibrated in our very walls. Even Mother's ghosts were probably shuddering. It seemed like we were all moving in slow motion as the day ticked forward, every phone call causing me to hold my breath. Just before noon, Mr. VanVleet called to tell Daddy he had interviewed everyone on my list, and as I had expected, no one knew anything. The local police had searched the city and practically every street under their jurisdiction with no sight of Gloria's car. Other police departments in the valley were reporting in with the same non-result. Neither Mother nor Daddy would eat any lunch. I nibbled on a cracker and sat in the living room, gazing toward the gate, willing it to open and reveal Gloria driving in.

Finally, at close to four o'clock, the gate did open, and Police Chief Siegler and one of his patrolmen drove in. I sat frozen as they parked and stepped out of their car. Daddy had rushed out to greet them, and Miles, who had been on standby with the limo, joined them. Mother was lying on the sofa with a cool washcloth over her forehead, almost in a dull stupor. She had heard no one. She wouldn't answer her phone all day. I had to do it and tell every single one of her friends that she was resting and we hadn't heard anything. The questioning of the students at school had sent the news of Gloria's disappearance sizzling through the community. When I related the calls to Mother, I could see that their names floated in and out of her ears.

I rose and stepped out. Daddy turned away from the policemen and looked at me, his eyes so startlingly accusatory.

"Why would Gloria go to Idyllwild?" he asked.

The four of them stared at me, waiting for my reply. I swallowed down the lump that instantly had lodged in my throat.

"She went there with Audie. I don't know how many times."

The two policemen and Daddy talked softly, out of my hearing.

"Stay with your mother," Daddy said, and got into the rear of the patrol car. Miles got in on the other side.

I watched them leave. When the gate closed behind them, I turned and went into the house without realizing I was tiptoeing to the living room. Mother still was unaware of anything new happening. I wondered if I should leave it that way. She sat up slowly. When she turned to me, she looked like she was waiting for the fog to clear.

"What time is it?"

"It's just four, Mother."

She tilted her head.

"It's Wednesday, right?"

"Yes, Mother."

"I forgot what we are doing tonight. Would you go to the kitchen and get my daybook? There are so many events, dinners, I get confused."

I stood there staring at her. Did she completely forget what was happening?

"Well? Get it," she snapped.

"You're not going anywhere tonight, Mother. I'm sure."

"Just get my book," she insisted.

I hurried out, found the daybook, and returned to hand it to her.

"Thank you," she said. She started to thumb through it.

"Mother," I said. "We're all worrying about Gloria, remember?"

"Gloria?" She blinked rapidly and then shook her head. I practically could see her memory rushing back at her. Her lips trembled, and she put the daybook down. "Where's your father? What is happening?"

"I don't know yet," I said.

"Where's your father?"

I bit down hard on my lower lip.

"Gish!"

"The police came, and he and Miles went off with them about ten minutes ago."

"Why didn't he tell me first? Where did they go?"

"I don't know exactly, Mother. Somewhere in Idyllwild, I think."

My face felt like it was shattering.

"Why are you always lying to me?" she said, rising.

"I'm not lying."

The phone rang. She looked at it and then at me. "Answer that. I don't wish to speak to anyone right now."

There was no chance it was Gloria. She would have called me first on my cell.

"Hello."

"This is Bruce Lafner of the *Desert Gazette*. Is this Mrs. John?"

"No. She's indisposed at the moment," I said. Not another of Mother's publicity people, not now, I thought.

"Oh, sure. Who is this, please?"

"This is Gish John, her younger daughter. But we . . ."

"Well, do you have any comment about your sister's car and what was found? Have you heard anything?"

"What about my sister's car?"

There was silence.

"I'll call back," he said, and hung up before I could say another word.

Mother paused in the doorway. "Who was that?"

"Bruce Lafner."

"Now he calls? I made a complaint about him. He didn't return my calls about Gloria's award. They'll have to assign someone else to the story."

She turned and walked out, leaving me standing there with

the receiver in my hand. I hung up and hurried out to find my cell. There were no calls on it, but I hit speed dial and called Daddy. He picked up instantly.

"Is she there? Is she home?"

"No, Daddy. What's happening? A reporter just called and said something about her car."

"They listen to police scanners for news scoops," he said, really talking more to himself.

"What about Gloria's car, Daddy?"

"It was found on a side road out of Idyllwild, Coyote Court, with the driver's door open, the engine run down to empty."

"Why? I don't understand."

"I'm not there yet. Her dark blue sweater jacket with the leather tips I bought her was on the passenger's seat."

"Oh."

"Streaked with blood," he added, and either lost the phone signal or he had switched off.

The phone bonded with my hand as if it had been covered in superglue when I had clutched it. I didn't move for a good minute. I was trying to get my heart to stop pounding on my chest like someone locked behind a door. It was hard to breathe. Any attempt to take a deep breath was met with resistance. I felt dizzy. When I turned just a little to the left, I saw Mother standing there staring at me.

"Who was that?" she asked.

"Daddy," I whispered.

"What?"

"It was Daddy. I called him."

"And? Well? Don't stand there like a fool."

"They found Gloria's car," I said, and described the rest, fearful of how angry she would be if I didn't.

She put her hand on the doorjamb to keep herself standing steadily.

"They're on their way to the car," I added. "It's on a side street in Idyllwild."

"She must be lying there, hurt," she said. "I'm getting dressed. You'll drive my car."

"But Daddy said . . ."

"The same thing happened in *Ransom!* They found the little boy's T-shirt stained with blood. Don't you see? He won't pay the ransom now. Get ready," she ordered, and left to get dressed. I debated calling Daddy to warn him but decided instead to do what she wanted. I wanted to see the car myself. Maybe Gloria was hurt nearby. Maybe I could help find her.

During most of the trip to Idyllwild, Mother described the movie, almost scene for scene. I didn't stop her. I could see it was her way of coping, and for a few moments, I was jealous of her, envious of her ability not to go completely mad and scream and cry, which was what I felt like doing.

When we were almost there, my cell phone rang.

"Where are you?" Daddy demanded. "Why didn't you answer the house phone?"

"Mother wanted to go to Idyllwild."

"Oh, great. I have to deal with her right now."

"What's happening, Daddy?"

"She's nowhere near the car. We're gathering a search party to comb the area, bringing in tracking dogs. Forensics from the state police are here going over the car and the scene. It's taped off, so your mother can't get close. Just park where you see other vehicles, and I'll come to you," he said.

"Okay."

I related it all to Mother. She didn't speak. I practically could see her physically sinking deeper and deeper into herself.

"Gloria Swanson," she finally whispered. "My Gloria Swanson."

I smiled, which anyone would think was odd at this moment, but I was remembering us making fun of each other's name. It was so easy to visualize her beside me. I realized that when you loved someone the way I loved Gloria, you memorize her the way you would memorize lines in a play to be repeated in dreams and visions for the rest of your life. As a child, I often mimicked her gestures, deliberately chewed on the side of my lip gently as she did whenever she had to think about some decision to be made. Sometimes I would sit in front of my vanity mirror and try to move my eyebrows the way she did when she became excited about something. I think she realized it very early on. I'd see her smile when I cupped my hands the way she would when she was adamant about something we had to do.

After Daddy had organized her art studio, I sat with her and tried to draw and paint as well as she did. She never belittled what I had done, even though a blind man could see the talent and skill in her work and the ordinariness of mine. If Daddy saw our two pictures side by side, he became partially blind and saw only hers. He might say "Nice" to me, that hateful word. The real praise always flowed to Gloria.

Was I bitterly jealous? Was that why I tried to emulate her as much as I could? At a certain point, I did stop and search for my own identity, and to Gloria's credit, she saw me struggling for it and whenever possible stacked compliments on my work or how I looked.

"You're so lucky, Gish," she would say. "You can be who you want."

It took a long time for me to understand that. She had told it to me in many different ways.

But my response was and probably always would be: "I want to be you, Gloria."

I want to be you.

Even now.

Especially now.

chapter fourteen

The sight of so many police cars and police officers was stunning and shocking for both Mother and me. After I had parked and informed Daddy that we were here, we both sat watching and waiting for him. Everyone was rushing about frantically. Dogs had arrived and almost immediately started barking. Night was falling quickly, the sunlight already being blocked by trees. Daddy came walking toward us. I had never seen him look this flustered. He was always calm, sometimes too laid-back for Mother. Gloria said it was that part of his personality that enabled him to think more clearly and make the right choices. She was already very much like him, and I knew she wanted me to strive for the same personality, especially now.

He opened the door on Mother's side but held his hand up to indicate she shouldn't get out.

"There's nothing new yet," he said. "You have to stay out of their way."

"Where's her sweater jacket?" Mother asked, as if that was the entire reason for us to come here.

"It's with the police, Evelyn. It's evidence now," he said, expressing uncharacteristic impatience with her. "They have it at a lab to see about the bloodstain. I've already given them DNA samples."

"Don't they need it for the dogs?" I asked. I had seen enough movie and television scenes like this.

Mother nodded. "Yes, yes."

"They took what they needed of it," Daddy said. He leaned on the opened door as if he had to or he'd fall.

"Are you all right, Daddy?" I asked.

"No," he said. He stood straighter quickly. "I'm going back to help in the search. There's no point in your just sitting here."

"There's no point in us just sitting anywhere," Mother said, which surprised me with its truth.

"I'm not coming home until we know something," he warned. "Even if it takes all night."

"We'll wait a while, Daddy, and then go home."

"Yes, good," he said.

The sight of us, especially Mother, did not give him the comfort I was hoping it might. On the contrary, he looked more frantic now and spun around to hurry back toward Gloria's car. I could see they had left the door open just the way he said they had found it. Forensics people were inside and outside of it. Dogs shot into the woods barking, the policemen holding the leashes running to keep up. Had they already smelled something? The image of Gloria lying dead on the forest floor was enough to drain my world of its energy. A cold numbness flowed through me. I noticed there were no birds and no other cars, but on this road, there was probably little traffic anyway.

"There are no birds," I said.

Mother looked at me and then at the woods. "They're in the shadows, holding their breath," she said.

We waited, watched, and listened, struggling to hear what some of the policemen were saying. More patrol cars arrived and some unmarked vans and cars behind them. More men and some women got out to join the search. One man who was surely a local resident, based on the way he was explaining and gesturing toward the woods, brought his own dog along. The flashlights in the darkened forest looked more like fireflies. I had the window open and leaned out of it so I could hear anything that might indicate Gloria had been found. They were calling her name, seemingly on every side of us now.

Mother slapped her hands over her ears.

"Let's do what Daddy said and go home, Mother."

She didn't answer. She kept her hands over her ears. I started the engine and made a U-turn. She kept her hands over her ears all the way home and finally took them off when our gate opened and I could drive into the sanctuary of Cameo. I shut the engine, and she turned to me with excitement.

"Maybe she's home. She doesn't know what's happening. She's calling everywhere for us."

"Mother . . ."

I was going to tell her that Gloria hadn't called me, that I'd be the first call she'd make, but Mother practically leaped out and hurried to the house. I followed her in slowly. When I stepped into the entryway, I could hear her calling for Gloria and rushing through the house, opening doors to every room. I went into the kitchen and began to make a salad. I wasn't sure what to prepare for dinner, but when I opened the refrigerator again, I saw Gloria had done her meat loaf, probably just for me and her. There didn't seem to be enough for the four of us. Mother was probably right. They had a dinner or some event tonight, something Gloria was more aware of than I was. She kept track of Mother and Daddy's events and sometimes even put them in Mother's daybook for her.

I took out the meat loaf. Maybe I could get Mother to eat something, I thought.

"Gloria!" I heard, and turned to the doorway. Mother was standing there, her face recapturing some of its color and brightness for a moment.

"What?" I said.

She stared at me and then let the truth seep in.

"Oh, I thought you were . . . Gloria does that," she said.

"I'm making us a salad, and then I'll warm up what Gloria left in the refrigerator. We both have to eat something, Mother."

"Yes," she said. "We're canceling whatever we had tonight."

She went to the living room, and I continued, trying not to think about anything but the dinner preparations. Would Daddy eat when he returned? He hadn't eaten anything all day. Maybe the police would take care of him, I thought. Carefully, as if it was a bowl of precious diamonds, I put the last meal Gloria had made into the oven. She was whispering over my shoulder, telling me the degrees and the amount of time to bake it. I suddenly understood why it was so easy for Mother to convince herself that the spirits of famous actors who had been here still haunted this house. What was an easier way than that when it came to bestowing immortality on those you respected, cherished, and loved?

The deep shadows made me aware that darkness had completely fallen. Our outside lights on timers had clicked on hours ago. I fought back the vision of Daddy blindly charging through the brush and the woods, calling desperately for Gloria. Now the glow of flashlights was surely more like the gleaming eyes of wolves around him. I imagined that panic was running through his veins; he had probably lost his voice and was merely mouthing her name. I stood there, leaning over the sink, embracing myself, and sobbing.

"Why are you crying?" I heard Mother ask. I turned as she entered the kitchen, smiling. "There's no reason to cry. Don't cry. What are you making for dinner?" she asked, forgetting everything I had said minutes ago.

"Gloria made it. I'm just warming it."

"Of course. My darling Gloria Swanson," she said. "Always thinking of us." And then she did something I had longed for her to do so often. She hugged me and kissed my forehead, brushing my hair away from my eyes. "So long. Your hair is so long." She sighed. "I think I'll lie down for a while."

"You should eat something. You haven't eaten all day. It'll be warm very soon. I have a salad prepared."

"I need to rest, just a little. Besides, I want to wait for your father."

She turned, nearly walking into the doorframe.

"Did you take something, Mother? What did you take? How many?"

"Better lie down," she said, nodding. She walked out.

I followed to watch her go up the stairs. Once, when she

paused, I shot forward to get behind her, but she put out her hand to tell me she was fine and continued. I listened to her walk to the bedroom, and then I returned to the kitchen and set the table as if all four of us would be eating dinner. How could I think otherwise?

But then I sat and stared at the dishes and silverware as if I could will us all together. I debated calling Daddy. His phone might not work, and if I called, he might think Gloria had come home. The false alarm would be too painful. I'd better try to eat. I had to be strong for them, I thought, and went to the kitchen. I brought in the salad and some bread, filled a pitcher of water, and sat to start pecking on the food. I paused, thinking Mother was returning, but there was just a deep echo of silence coming from every hallway and every room.

When I looked at my watch, I leaped to my feet. The meat loaf would be overcooked. I couldn't ruin what might be Gloria's last meal. I brought the hot dish to the table and served myself a few forkfuls of it. I couldn't eat much more. My stomach was shutting itself. I drank some water and sat there, doing my best to conjure up Gloria in her dining-room chair. When I looked at my watch again, I realized I had been sitting at the table for nearly an hour. Gloria would tell me to wrap everything and put it in the refrigerator so I could reheat the meat loaf when Mother came down or Daddy returned.

After I did that, I left everything the way it was on the table and went to the living room and sat on the sofa so I could have a direct view of our driveway. It didn't surprise me that no one had called. Everyone who would was probably afraid of what they would hear, including Mother's friends.

The phone finally did ring nearly two hours later. It was Stanley Hemsley, Daddy's business partner.

"Gish," he said after I answered. Somehow he never mistook me for Gloria on the phone, even though our voices were quite similar and most everyone else did. "I tried calling your father's cell practically every hour."

"He's not home yet, Mr. Hemsley. He might very well still be in the woods, and either his phone isn't working or he's not answering."

I left a silence for the words that might explain why he wouldn't answer.

"How's your mother?" he asked.

"She took something, one of her sedatives, and is sleeping. I'll be checking on her in a few minutes."

"There are no clues, nothing yet?"

I knew I sounded cold, even angry, at the question. "The only clue is blood on her sweater jacket."

He was silent.

"There are a lot of people searching the area," I said in a friendlier tone.

"Yeah, I figured. All right. I'm here if you need me."

"Thank you," I said. Mr. Hemsley was a heavy man in his sixties. I didn't think he'd be of any use out in the forest with the others, or I would have suggested it. "'Bye," I said, and hung up.

I rose and went up to look in on Mother. She was lying on her back with her face turned away, but she must have sensed me and looked toward the doorway.

"Gloria?"

"No, Mother. It's Gish. Daddy's not back yet. You want something to eat now? I can bring it up to you."

"Always smart, always thinking," she said, and turned away again.

I'll just wait for Daddy, I thought, and went back to the living room. I fell asleep on the sofa but woke instantly when I heard the front door open. I had never seen my father look this disheveled. There was a rip in his left pants leg. Through the opening, I could see his leg had bled. His face was flushed with fatigue, and his shoes were muddied. He seemed unaware of it, of everything.

"Daddy?" I said, because he was just standing there and staring at me.

He shook his head. "We didn't find her. The police think she was in the woods because of the way the dogs tracked, and then . . ."

"Then what?" I asked, my heart hitting my chest with every thump.

"We found one of her shoes. Tony Miles, a California Highway Patrol officer, thought someone might have been carrying her and it dropped off . . ." He paused, almost saying, *dropped off her body*. "Dropped off her foot. What footsteps they found were too large for Gloria's. It was at least a size ten, man's size. They kept her shoe for more evidence. We followed in that direction, but the footsteps disappeared as if whoever it was had taken off his shoes. We walked in a large circle, about a hundred or so by now, but we didn't find her or any more clues. They're bringing in helicopters at the break of day, and a bigger search party will begin again. In the meantime . . ."

"What?"

"They picked up Audie O'Sullivan and his father for questioning. They took both their fingerprints and shoe sizes and seized all their shoes, boots."

"Audie's been in her car," I said. "His prints will be there."

He nodded. "I don't know anything about that yet. He's being interrogated."

"Audie wouldn't hurt her."

But his father might, I thought, but didn't say.

"You don't know anything when it comes to what someone like that would do or wouldn't do," he said, his angry tone rushing over the words. "Where's your mother?"

"She took something, went to bed, and wouldn't eat anything. Did you? I have everything ready, a salad, the meat loaf Gloria . . . the meat loaf."

He looked at me for a moment and then rushed to the stairway. I got up and went to the food just in case he decided he would eat. He didn't come down for so long that I went up to check. When I looked into their bedroom, I saw he had sprawled out beside Mother and both of them were asleep. I just stood there with the tears streaming down my cheeks. I returned to the kitchen and put everything away before I went to the living room and sat on the sofa, close to the phone.

I fell asleep and woke to the sound of someone in the kitchen. It was Daddy. He was making some coffee. He had changed into a pair of jeans and a sweatshirt. Most of the night had passed, but the sun had not risen yet. He glanced at me and continued getting himself some coffee.

"Did you hear anything new?"

"No. I'm returning to the site," he said with his back to me. "When your mother wakes, give her some coffee and something to eat. I'm leaving Dr. Littlefield's number out here on the counter. You explain what's going on. He'll come by and see if there's something better to give her to keep her calm. Those damn pills she has always turn her brain to mush, and I think she took too many."

He turned to me.

"I want you to stay here all day, and don't let anyone come into

Cameo except the doctor if he decides he should. I'll call you if we . . . if there is something. Got it?"

"Yes, Daddy."

"You're sure there isn't anything else you didn't tell me that would help us, tell us about when she left?"

"She didn't want to give me any details. I asked her."

"Why not? I thought you two were like conjoined twins."

"She knew I could never lie to you successfully, so when I said I didn't know where she went, I would be telling you the truth."

He nodded. "That kid," he said. "Always thinking ahead. Incredible."

He started out.

"Daddy," I called when he had opened the front door. He paused and looked back. "I'm scared."

"So am I, Gish, down to the very bones of my body," he said, and left.

I got Mother to drink a little coffee and nibble on a biscuit, but she was still quite dazed. When she made references to Gloria, I had to remind her what was happening. I could see she just wouldn't let those thoughts enter her head. Friends did start to call, but I couldn't let her talk to anyone, not the way she was. Hours later, when Daddy called to see how she was and I told him, he asked me to call the doctor immediately. He said nothing had changed in the search and nothing yet had come out of the interrogation of Audie and his father. They had even dug up some places in the forest because the dogs were interested in this spot or that, but there was no sign. Then he added something that did frighten me even more.

"You call me immediately if someone calls and claims they have her. Maybe there are a few people involved in this. The FBI is on standby."

I thought, *What if Mother was right?* I almost decided to sit and watch that damn movie. I called the doctor, who, like probably everyone else in Palm Springs, knew what was happening. He said he'd be over in about twenty minutes. Mother really liked him, so I was hoping he would get her up and about enough to eat. After he came and spoke to her, I made her some scrambled eggs. She said they were prepared exactly how Gloria prepared them for her whenever she made them. Consequently, she ate most of it. Dr. Littlefield gave her a different medication.

"Let her rest now," he told me on his way out. "This is going to be pretty hard on your mother and your father. Just support them as best you can," he added.

I told myself it was just my imagination, but I thought he put more emphasis on my father. Everyone knew how much he doted on Gloria and how proud of her he was, but there was something more, something else, in the doctor's voice.

Every time the phone rang, I felt the blood drain from my face. I know I wasn't pleasant when I spoke to Mother's friends. I was curt and almost accused them of pricking us with darts with every ring. After she nibbled on some food, Mother continued to doze on and off.

Daddy called twice to ask if anyone had called claiming to have Gloria, so I didn't have to ask if anyone had found any trace of her. I told him about Dr. Littlefield's visit and the new medication. When I asked him how he was, he said, "Don't think about me. Think about your mother."

"What about Audie O'Sullivan?" I asked when he called the second time.

"You were right about him having been in the car. Forensics has checked their shoes and boots, but there were no traces of the area on them. One pair of boots had been cleaned recently."

"Whose?"

"Nick's, but the police followed up on his and Audie's alibi for some of last night. They had dinner with a neighbor, and according to the neighbor's wife, O'Sullivan drank too much and fell asleep. Audie and the neighbor put him to bed. The police are following up with a warrant to search their home and O'Sullivan's truck. No matter what, I can't have them back at Cameo," he quickly added.

"What are you going to do now, Daddy?"

"I'll be home in a few hours. We're just covering a few other places up here."

"I can warm up that meat loaf for you and make some pasta for Mother."

"Whatever you want, Gish. I had something up here, so . . . whatever you want."

During the day, Mother ate some buttered and jellied biscuits with tea, nibbled enough of them, at least. She didn't want to come out of her room. Just before the sun started to fall behind the mountains, Daddy returned, looking as tired and drained as he had the previous night.

"No calls for ransom?" he asked me instantly.

"No, Daddy."

"I don't know if that's good or bad," he said. He went up to shower and change and visit with Mother. I worked on preparing some dinner. He ate some and brought some to Mother, using the fact that Gloria had made it to get her to eat some of it. After I had cleaned up the kitchen, I showered and went to my room. It was impossible to watch television or read. Daddy came to my door.

"Miles is taking me back up there," he said.

"Now? It's so dark, and you haven't rested enough."

"We have lights, and some of the search party is still at it. I couldn't sleep anyway."

"You're exhausting yourself," I said.

For a moment, he looked like he was going to cry—my father, cry. He stiffened to get hold of himself. "Keep an eye on her, and call me should anyone . . . just call me."

"Okay, Daddy."

He hurried down the stairs.

I did look in on Mother a little while later, but she was fast asleep.

Because of what Daddy now suspected, actually I suppose hoped for, I shuddered so hard every time the phone rang that I actually had trouble grasping it. Once it fell to the floor. Some of the callers were Daddy's clients, and Mr. Hemsley called again. He said he would be coming over tomorrow, and I should tell my father even though he would call first.

There wasn't any other call on our landline. The one call I received on my cell was surprising, but afterward, I realized it shouldn't have been. It was Lee.

"Everyone's talking about Gloria," he said. His voice did sound shaky. "No matter what, I'd never wish something like this on her."

"I know."

"I drilled everyone I know, searching for a clue. No one knows anything, but I'll keep at it."

"Thank you."

"Call me if I can help in any way. I can organize ten, twenty people to help the search."

"Thank you. I'll mention it to Daddy when he returns."

"I'm here for you, too, Gish."

I could feel my throat closing. "I gotta go," I said. "I need to keep an eye on my mother."

"Sure. I'm sorry," he said.

I held the phone at my ear for a few moments, and then, almost as if the call had triggered something in my mind, I walked out of the house and to the casita.

chapter fifteen

She wasn't there. She would never be there again in real life, but she would always be there in my imagination. Funnily enough, when I thought about all our times here, I envisioned both of us as little girls again and not teenagers with more exciting things on our minds. It seemed more comfortable and safer to think of us that way. There were all those afternoons when Gloria read to me from books and studied with me, helping me with my homework, especially when I was in the fifth and sixth grades.

And of course, there was the list of wishes, the experimenting with dancing, and watching Gloria sketch out a new drawing she might or might not turn into a painting in her studio while I kept track of the cookies or cake we had made. Recalling how we'd smuggle in some of Mother's vintage clothes, put them on, and imitate actresses in some of the old pictures she forced us to watch, I opened the closet in the bedroom, and sure enough, there were two dresses we had forgotten to return to Mother's closet. I couldn't help putting on the one I had worn. When I looked at myself in the mirror, I easily imagined Gloria beside me, dramatically reciting film lines.

What fun those innocent days were. Little did we know how dangerous it could be to dive in and out of your imagination, fleeing from your own reality. But we could pretend more when we were little girls. You had license to explore your imagination. There seemed to be no boundaries, and if you thought you were skirting something forbidden, you would giggle with fear or embarrassment and then quickly move on to something else. Most people, especially parents, laughed and were amused at us fantasizing about being princesses or pirates. Gloria was always the more imaginative one, creating the scenarios and the sometimes terrifying crises we had to manage and navigate to get to safety.

Our world in the casita wasn't always born from what we imagined or pretended. The casita was the safe place for the revelation of our real dreams, our confessions about defiant or mean thoughts we had, and always, our most frightening fears. Gloria's haunting concern was not living up to expectations our parents had anticipated for her. I feared being forgotten or ignored. I didn't have to explain it; Gloria understood. Something about our casita, about it being ours in our minds, permitted us to be honest with each other and ourselves.

Growing up at Cameo, we resented, hated, any of our parents' guests occupying the casita, even though that was its original purpose. Gloria would get angrier about it than I would, but she would never reveal that to our parents. Once or twice, I did and was reprimanded for being either too selfish or too arrogant.

Soon after the guests had left the casita, we would attack it with cleaning rags and soaps, even though the maids had done so. They could never restore it to what it had been the way Gloria and I could. It wasn't personal enough for them. They didn't know where we wanted little things to be placed or how we wanted our furniture arranged. Of course, while the search continued for Gloria, I wondered if it could ever be restored for me. Could there be a happy ending to this if every phone call, every car, and every voice brought heart-stopping anticipation and then disappointment?

I took off the costume dress, hung it up in the closet next to the one Gloria had worn years ago, and, feeling as if I was stepping off a stage, the curtain being drawn closed behind me, I returned to the house to check on Mother.

In very short order during the days that followed her disappearance, we learned that the blood on Gloria's sweater was definitely hers and that the police had acquired a search warrant but had found nothing incriminating at the O'Sullivan home or in Mr. O'Sullivan's truck. Daddy told me Mr. O'Sullivan had been hired to care for the grounds of a home in La Quinta, despite him not giving Mr. O'Sullivan a reference. He said he believed Audie was working for him there. As far as he was concerned, they remained suspect.

The detectives on the case came to our house to question me in Daddy's office. They had me go over that night Gloria left, repeating her words, describing her mood and her urgency despite the hour and how it would upset our parents.

"Was it like her to do something like that?" the older detective asked. His last name was actually Hamlet. I couldn't stop thinking how Gloria would have had fun with it.

"No."

"And she refused to tell you what it was?"

I repeated what I had told Daddy about why she wouldn't tell me.

The second detective, a younger man, thinner, with eyes washed in skepticism and accusation, leaned in toward me and asked, "What do you think would draw her away like that, that time of night?"

I knew Gloria would hate me for casting more suspicion on Audie, but helping him was the only thing that came to mind. The detective nodded. It was the answer he wanted. The investigation of Audie and his father would get more intense. Weeks went by, though, and nothing new came of it.

"Perhaps they didn't have anything directly to do with it, but they did something," Daddy mused when he received another empty report.

I didn't want to believe Gloria would endanger herself to that extent, even for Audie. Maybe it wasn't a belief; maybe it was simply a hope and a prayer.

But every time I envisioned Nick O'Sullivan, I envisioned him with that look of distaste or resentment. Perhaps he had used Audie, manipulated him into something that even today he was unaware of. I couldn't let myself believe anything worse.

The search in the woods in Idyllwild ended. Literally hundreds had scoured the area. Daddy didn't tell me until much later, but Detective Hamlet, based on his prior experience, was convinced it was probably a kidnapping, but something had gone wrong.

"People who are asked to pay kidnappers usually are persuaded to pay by pictures or by hearing the victim's voice," Detective Hamlet had told Daddy.

The reason that might not happen this time was left unsaid, but it was still clearly heard, especially by Daddy and me. Mother seemed incapable of hearing anything that wasn't positive or hopeful. She withdrew into a shell as if she literally had stepped into one of her movies and could see or hear nothing else. She wanted that happy ending that most of her films had.

For weeks after Gloria had disappeared, I would spend most of my free time in the casita, especially on weekends. Nothing at Cameo was the same. The housekeepers worked at almost a frenzy to get in and get out, as if the tragic events were infectious. I could see the relief on their faces when they left.

Daddy didn't return to work for nearly two weeks and even then for only short periods, always thinking that while he was away, someone might have called or, as in all our dreams, Gloria miraculously had reappeared with some very logical explanation. Sometimes he pretended he had gone to work, but one look at him when he returned at the end of the day told me where he really had been. He hadn't cleaned his shoes well, or there was a part of a leaf or a bush clinging to his pants. He lived with the hope that despite how many people had searched, they had missed something, something only a father might know or sense.

Although nothing tying Audie or his father to Gloria's disappearance had been discovered, Daddy often asked me questions about Gloria's relationship with Audie. I explained how, at least to my mind, she had felt sorry for him and was merely trying to ease the pain of his losing his mother in a dreadful way. Daddy always looked skeptical, as if I was simply too young or inexperienced with love relationships to know what really had gone on between Audie and Gloria.

And of course, he believed, although he didn't say it in so many words, that anyone who had gone through what Audie had with his mother could be somewhat unbalanced, vulnerable to acts of rage himself. He had seen how physical Mr. O'Sullivan had been with him and, most likely, still was.

He chipped away at my prayers and had me wondering if I, in some way, helped all this to happen. If I had betrayed her earlier, she might be up in her room right now, angry at me but alive.

I never saw Audie again on our grounds, of course, but I did see him once in downtown Palm Springs. I thought he saw me, but when I slowed down, he turned down a side street. I was going to park and go after him, but I didn't. Daddy's insinuations frightened me. At a minimum, I knew he would be upset to find out I had anything to do with Audie now. I continued driving to the store to pick up some groceries and never saw him again.

The police had returned Gloria's car after they were satisfied forensics had scoured it of any possible clues. Daddy told me there were some unidentifiable fingerprints and some hairs that didn't match Gloria's or anyone in our family, but Audie's prints were there and strands of that titian hair. He never denied having been in the car, so that wasn't enough to make any conclusion about that very night. The leads the police had were thin and ghostlike, drifting into the rear of some file.

Still, both my parents hung their hopes on every possible police activity, especially the search for any witnesses. Gloria's picture had been in the newspaper enough for anyone to report having seen her anywhere, but no one did. Of course, Daddy put out a reward for any information leading to her return or whereabouts. There were the usual false reports. It was ugly to see that there were people who wanted to extort us even with something as sad as this.

By the end of the first month, Dr. Littlefield tried to get Mother to ease up on the drugs. Whenever she did skip a dose, she spent most of her time sitting either on the patio or in the living room, rereading some of her movie books, moving and talking as if she was still on the medicine. She resisted talking to any of her friends on the phone and literally shook if my father suggested permitting this one or that to visit.

Daddy wasn't all that different. He didn't encourage his friends to visit him or join any of them for golf or lunches. Instead, he spent his free time on the computer searching sites that helped find missing persons, most often replying angrily to cruel, sick people who thought it was funny lighting up his hopes. He ranted about it to both of us, Mother looking at him with a blank stare, as if she had no idea what was upsetting him. The frustration deepened the lines in his face. His eyes looked like candles burning down and throwing off less and less illumination.

As for me during this aftermath, I hated school so much that I faked one illness after another to avoid attending, and when I did, I desperately tried to elude talking to most anyone, except Lee now and then, because he looked almost as much in pain sometimes. My teachers were terribly understanding, not realizing that the more they were, the more difficult it was for me to be in their classes and see the pity in their faces and hear it in their voices. I felt like I could stand up and scream in the middle of a lesson in any class or tear up the textbook and throw it in the air, and no one would get angry about it. That made me angrier.

The looming end of the school year was practically the only thing I looked forward to with any enthusiasm. Daddy saw all this in me more clearly than Mother did. She continued to move about with that haze over her eyes. If anything, it seemed to thicken. Sometimes she looked totally blind and shocked to realize where she was in the house. Time had lost meaning for her, too. She couldn't keep track of the days, nor did she care to. Her daybook began to look like an ancient volume you'd dust off and open gingerly for fear the pages would crumble in your fingers.

Dr. Littlefield had suggested a therapist, a bereavement counselor, Laura Garson. Daddy refused to see her, and I wouldn't, either. In my mind, I always had Gloria to talk to and still could conjure her now. Laura Garson visited Mother weekly and, with Dr. Littlefield consulting, suggested alternatives to her medication. But nothing seemed to change her very much. She was comfortable being snugly in her shell.

The next time I feigned some illness, headache, or stomachache to avoid school, Daddy first insisted I should talk to Laura Garson, too. When I refused, he thought that it might very well be the best thing for me to attend another private school some distance away, as they had been planning once Gloria had gone off to college to enjoy her award and pursue what was surely intended to be an outstanding education, filled with her new accomplishments. He still had the pamphlets and gave them to me to consider. I didn't say yes or no. Actually, I began to think that our, or at least my, pretending Gloria was off to college was a comforting illusion.

Because Daddy was home so much of the time, Mr. Hemsley was at the house more often. I could read the concern in his face, and it wasn't stemming from his fear of their losing money. A great deal of the business that they had was practically cemented into the firm, and from some of the things I heard him say, I gathered that a few of their very wealthy clients even had increased their investments, maybe out of some effort to console Daddy. That irony was surely lost on him. I could see the meetings between him and Mr. Hemsley were not as successful as Mr. Hemsley had been hoping. Something had happened and continued to happen to Daddy's ability to concentrate and do that wonderful analysis of potentially profitable acquisitions the way he had been so capable of doing.

It wasn't only his mind, his thinking, that was indicating the damage to him that he was suffering. My once strong, handsome, and formidable father was moving more slowly, stooping more, falling asleep at his desk often, and eating poorly. His mental and emotional agony was taking a toll. When Dr. Littlefield stopped by to examine Mother, I could see more and more concern for Daddy than for her. He had lost too much weight and, something I hadn't been aware of, wasn't taking his medicine properly. I didn't know he was taking anything. Dr. Littlefield wanted him in for a full examination, but Daddy kept putting it off.

Dr. Littlefield wanted me to keep after him, but I was caught in the middle of another enigma. A little more than a week after Gloria's disappearance, I had begun to assume all the duties and chores she often had fulfilled. I had watched her prepare food enough times, especially on weekends, to do it almost as well. Because they weren't going out for dinner or to any events, I thought it would please my parents, but I caught Daddy, especially, looking at me with mixed feelings. He was happy the work was done, but there was something about the way he watched me that made me feel he almost resented my imitating Gloria. To him, it surely was a verification of Gloria's permanent disappearance.

But the reality was, she was gone.

And I was slowly stepping into her shoes.

I knew he struggled with the contradictory feelings. Mother was becoming strangely indifferent at first. Her depression was taking her to different places where she could find rationalizations: she was putting up with me until Gloria had returned, everyone had gotten everything all wrong, and this was only a big mistake.

These thoughts, as strange as they were sometimes, kept her somewhat sane and enabled her to take breaths like an underwater swimmer rising to the top of the deep pool of depression. Neither I nor Daddy shattered these hopes, but ironically, I thought they only intensified Daddy's anxiety. There was no question that he was trying to do what Mother was doing, denying reality. Once, when he wondered, probably more to distract himself than anything else, what we were going to eat on Saturday night, he began with "Ask Glor—" and stopped. I quickly told him what I had suggested the day before, and he nodded. It could have been a plate of tar. His interest diminished that quickly as the truth set in again.

And yet, despite all this, there were moments when I thought we were all going to get through it. There was another side to reach after we had completed our mourning and accepted what was true. Life would be different, but we would have some semblance of what we'd once had. Mother would revive her celebrity teas, Daddy would regain his enthusiasm for his work, and I would seriously consider and then go to a new school, where I would make new, real friends who liked me for myself and not because I was Gloria John's sister.

Almost as soon as these thoughts occurred, a waterfall of guilt cascaded over me. Wherever I was in the house, whatever time it was, I would hurry to the casita, where I would lie on the bed and quickly conjure Gloria beside me, apologizing for even thinking of forgetting her. Of course, in my world, she was always forgiving and understanding. Lady Jesus.

Because I found relief in the casita at times like those, I was able to return to the world of darkness that had found what looked like a permanent home in our house. I could contend with it after I had one of my imaginary Gloria talks. I did my Gloria chores and actually tried to improve on the homework I had. I didn't even mind or feel guilty about talking to Lee at school and occasionally on the phone. I knew he was grateful for my not holding any grudges or blaming him in any way.

But as the final month of school began, I could see the anxiety and the sadness return with a renewed vigor in my parents. Mother had developed a nervous twitch and some palsy. Dr. Littlefield started treating it, and there were always side effects to whatever medication he prescribed, chief among them being a loss of appetite. I knew the panic she experienced every time she looked at herself in a mirror. Like Daddy, she had lost too much weight, and she either messed up her makeup or didn't use any.

I had anticipated their deeper depression during these final weeks. This was supposed to have been Gloria's graduation. She was going to deliver a valedictorian's address, and they were going to be the proudest parents in the valley, maybe in the state. That was all gone. The Magician of Sorrow and Pain had whisked it away with a turn of his wrist. In my nightmares, hundreds of parents in the graduation ceremony audience voiced an awesome groan and looked upon me with eyes so flooded with pity that they resembled pools without bottoms, only deepening darkness and emptiness.

And then, one morning, I awoke and, just as I did every morning, dressed quickly so I could prepare breakfast for all of us. I had slept late. I was at the coffee pot, refilling it with fresh water, when I heard Mother's scream. Her voice seemed to deepen and distort the longer she screamed. I hurried to the stairs and rushed to their bedroom.

She was standing at Daddy's side of the bed and struggling to get him to sit up. I started to run in and stopped. My breathing stopped, too.

"He won't get up," she said. "Get him up."

I moved in between her and the bed and felt Daddy's face. It was so cold that it chilled my hand, the chill rushing up my arms and then curling around my heart.

"Daddy," I said.

I looked at Mother. She looked more angry than frightened.

"Why can't you get him up?" she asked.

I shook my head.

"Call Gloria," she whispered. "She'll know what to do."

My body felt as if it was literally melting. I gasped and backed away.

"I'll call Dr. Littlefield," I said.

She turned back to Daddy and shook him.

When I reached Dr. Littlefield on his cell phone, he said he was calling an ambulance and he would be right behind it. A voice inside me was saying, *It's too late*, but, like Mother, I refused to believe what I saw and knew. I went to the module for the gate and opened it so the ambulance wouldn't have to wait a second more, and then I opened the front door and stood there waiting. I didn't want to go back upstairs.

Because we were located only minutes away, the ambulance was there seemingly just after I stood outside. The paramedics rushed to me, and I blurted about my father being upstairs in his bedroom. Dr. Littlefield came a minute or so after they had entered. He took one look at me and then hurried up behind the paramedics.

I closed the door and sat on the leather wood-framed entryway bench. I heard Dr. Littlefield comforting Mother, trying to get her to sit. I knew I should be up there helping him, but I felt too frightened to move, almost too frightened to breathe. I had no idea how much time had passed. The paramedics came down first and stopped in front of me. They were two very fit-looking young men, more like soldiers standing at attention.

"We're sorry, miss," the taller one said. "We did what we could."

Still stunned, I stood, but nearly toppled to my right. They both reached out to steady me.

"Maybe you should just sit for a few more minutes. I'll get you some water," the shorter one said.

I sat. The taller paramedic kept his hand on my shoulder until the other one brought me a glass of water. I drank some and felt my body slowly returning. The blood that had drained from my face rose up my neck.

"Take some deep breaths," the shorter one said. I did.

I heard Dr. Littlefield call me from the stairway. I rose. They kept their hands on my elbows.

"Easy. Go slowly," the taller one said. I knew they remained behind me as I walked to the stairway.

"I'm taking her to your bed," Dr. Littlefield told me. "Between this and everything else, she's very confused. She keeps asking for Gloria. I'll make the calls we have to make, Gish. I'm so sorry."

I started up the stairs and paused as he walked Mother to my room. Instead of following them, I returned to Daddy and stared at him, wondering, even though he'd had a sharp, fatal heart attack maybe sometime during the night, could he still be fighting to stay with us? Maybe he hadn't just been switched off, but he had held on enough to life to make his leaving gradual.

"I'm sorry, Daddy," I said, as if everything had been my fault somehow. "I wish I could have filled you with almost as much pride and happiness as Gloria did. You would have felt more hopeful, cared more about living, and found your way back to us. I'll still try," I said. "In some way."

I touched his hand, stroked it, and, ignoring the cold cheek that wanted me to believe he was as unmoved and as uncaring as anything without a pulse, I kissed him and went to help Dr. Littlefield with Mother. It was then that the doctor told me he and Daddy had been planning for him to have a stent. It was being set up right before Gloria had disappeared.

"We had him on blood thinners and warned him about stress, but there wasn't much we could do about that. I was hoping he would get through it all and we'd get the procedure done. Don't blame yourself or anything else, Gish. Even a man without his issues could have ended this way."

I couldn't help wondering if Gloria had known anything. I doubted Mother had. She remained under heavy medication afterward, lightened for a short time to make it possible for her to attend Daddy's funeral, but she remained very confused, the palsy returning. She collapsed almost as soon as the service had begun. An ambulance was called, and Dr. Littlefield accompanied it to the hospital. I, with Mr. Hemsley, our attorney, Mr. Tiegler, and a number of Daddy's friends remained at the church and then went to the cemetery. Mr. Hemsley remained at my side, embracing me. He was more than my father's partner; he was more like the brother he never had. For now, Daddy's grave had only a marker, but I almost laughed aloud recalling his discussion with Mother about tombstone inscriptions. How I wished Gloria was there to help me find the right one.

After they stabilized Mother somewhat at the hospital,

Dr. Littlefield recommended home care for her. She was quite fragile and often delirious for days afterward. We had two nurses splitting the day and night shifts and using the guest bedroom, even though the night-shift nurse often fell asleep in the chair in Mother's bedroom. I was there to help as well, making meals and dealing with the housekeeping help and, from time to time, answering the new head gardener's questions about some landscape trimming.

I didn't return to school for the final week. No one gave me any trouble about it. I was even offered the choice to take my finals at home. At first, I wasn't going to do it, I didn't care, but I kept thinking, what would Gloria do? I even went to the casita to ask the imaginary her. In the end, I spent time studying and took the finals two at a time at home. One of the substitute teachers was hired to bring and administer them to me. She waited while I completed them in Daddy's office, which was where I imagined Gloria would have taken them.

I passed everything and received final grades in each subject that kept my B-plus final average intact. I didn't think of anyone but Gloria being proud of me. Mr. VanVleet called to tell me he would mail me my schedule for next year, my senior year, but I told him my mother was seriously thinking of sending me to a different private school. I'd had no conversation with her about it, of course, but I was still seriously considering the idea, although I couldn't see how I could leave Mother. He was surprised but assured me he would have everything prepared to send on when and if I needed it done.

The following week, Mr. Tiegler stopped in to speak to Mother about our legal matters, but he quickly realized she wouldn't be able to mentally digest any of it right now. He asked to meet with me in Daddy's office while Mother slept. He had been with us for over fifteen years, and Daddy had given him power of attorney when need be. He explained how all our bills and expenses would continue to go through his office. He and Mr. Hemsley were in close contact.

It seemed empowering for me to sit behind Daddy's desk. I imagined how Gloria would be, sitting firmly, intense, and taking notes. She had taken business management in her junior year, and I had been taking it this year. She had been helping me get through it.

"Your family still holds a fifty-percent ownership in the business," Mr. Tiegler began. "Mr. Hemsley could offer to buy you out. I do anticipate that sometime down the road. Or he might hold it back until his retirement and sell the company for your family and himself. We'll see. In the meantime . . ."

He showed me the account from which I could draw "hard cash" when needed. I worried about Miles, but he assured me he would find him new employment quickly. Most all of Cameo's financial obligations were automatically paid, and he promised to take a personal interest in its upkeep.

"Until your mother is well enough, of course."

"From the way you talk and all that you have shown me, Mr. Tiegler, I wonder how aware my father was that this would all need to be done this soon."

"He was just being a careful man, a good father and husband," he said. "Most don't have the foresight to prepare like this." He paused and looked at the doorway for a moment. "Your father never thought your mother would be capable of handling all these business concerns in a real crisis."

"As opposed to one in the movies?"

He smiled. "Both you and your sister were always quite mature and capable for your age."

"More so Gloria," I said. "But I'm learning."

"Well, they say necessity is the mother of invention, but it might be more accurate to say it's the mother of maturity. It was for me, too," he said. "When she's up to it," he said, handing me a copy of Daddy's will, "read it and go over it with your mother, and then call me with any questions."

With great timidity, he added that wherever I saw Gloria's name mentioned, I could assume it would only be me now.

"Although we have to follow the state's rules for recognizing when one is considered . . ."

"Dead?"

"Yes," he said. "We'll file a petition with the court in five years to declare her so if nothing changes. I'm sorry," he quickly added. "Lawyers and undertakers have to say things they'd rather not have to say."

"Doctors, too," I added.

"Yes, of course. Is there anything you need now, anything I can help you with?"

"Turn back time," I said.

He smiled again. "That's a watch with no dial, I'm afraid." He hesitated a moment and then gave me a hug, his eyes tearing. "Hang in there," he said, and left.

He was right about what necessity did to you. I did feel older. It was as if I was truly becoming wiser, becoming more like Gloria overnight.

I left Daddy's will on his desk, avoiding reading it. Weeks went by, and although Mother became more active, eating more and reading, I hesitated to confront her with all the legal and business realities. She seemed so comfortable living in a cloud. Now that summer had begun, I suggested that we close things up the way Daddy always did and go to our beach house in Laguna. Dr. Littlefield was having one of the nurses make only weekly visits by now.

However, one afternoon, two of her friends from the celebrity teas stopped by unexpectedly, Mrs. Adamson and Mrs. Masters, who had been a widow but remarried recently. Mother behaved as if she had never met them before, just smiling or nodding at their desperate attempts to get a conversation under way. The tragedies occurring one after the other had damaged her to the point where she continued to have long periods of confusion.

They finally gave up and wished me luck before leaving, their faces so soaked in pity I couldn't wait to close the door. I knew they'd be on the phone as soon as they drove away and would advise any and all of Mother's friends not to bother visiting just yet. Maybe never.

Mother was still sitting where she had been in the living room, in the chair from which she used to narrate her wonderful celebrity stories. She looked incapable of recalling a single one. I wasn't even sure she realized she had just had visitors. I told her I was getting our dinner together. She smiled and opened one of her film history books. After a moment, I left her.

I decided going away was simply not possible. Actually, Mother had not yet returned. Not Dr. Littlefield, not our therapist, not the nurses or our lawyer and Mr. Hemsley, not confronting her with Daddy's will, and certainly not just me would bring her back even halfway from the dismal place she had gone to deny all that had happened.

No, there was only one person who could bring her back to something of herself.

Gloria.

First Gloria had to return.

That night, I went to Gloria's room and took out everything, trying it all on and deciding what I would keep and what I would bundle with my things to give to the housekeepers. In the morning, I called our beauty salon for an appointment, scheduling it for when the nurse would be at Cameo. Our stylist didn't question what I wanted done with my hair. Everyone in the shop had words of sympathy but also looked a little terrified of continuing much of a conversation with me. No one dared mention my sister having the exact hair color and style.

When I entered the house afterward, Mother was sitting in the living room, and the nurse was having a cup of coffee in the kitchen. I looked in on Mother, who didn't look up from her book, and then I went to the kitchen to tell the nurse that I was back.

"You look very pretty with that hairdo," she said.

I thanked her. She told me all was well with Mother, which meant nothing much had changed. Then she left, and I went up and changed into one of Gloria's khaki button-front miniskirts and a white vest top. I looked at myself in her full-length mirror and decided to bring all my remaining things, shoes, socks, underthings, and my jewelry, into Gloria's room. This was where I would sleep now.

When I started down, I trembled a little. Mother could get angry, and then everything I had done would have to be changed back. I held my breath and entered the living room. She looked up and stared at me a moment, and then, as I feared, her face hardened, those eyes turning into what Daddy called her "blowtorches." In moments, I thought, I would run out of the house to the casita to apologize to my imagined sister.

But that wasn't what happened.

"Where have you been?" Mother asked. "We were all so worried."

epilogue

I had my seventeenth birthday July 15 and celebrated in the casita by baking a birthday cake, lighting candles, and talking to my imagined sister. Anyone hearing me singing would have thought I had gone as nutty as my mother. Before the end of July that year, I decided I didn't want to attend any school.

However, in California, someone not yet eighteen couldn't quit school himself or herself. He or she needed parental permission. I met with Mr. Tiegler, who had my parents' power of attorney, and explained how I felt about it, considering Mother and all.

"You're at a disadvantage without a diploma," he warned.

"Have you looked recently at our net worth?"

"Well, it's not only money."

"I need time to find myself," I said.

He had no idea what that really meant. "What will you do with your time?"

"Between caring for Mother and studying the business with Mr. Hemsley, reading, and my artwork, I'll be fine."

"Don't you have friends you want to get back to?"

"There's no one as important to me as my sister was," I said. "There were plans being set for me to go to another private school, out of the area. I don't want to return to this school, and I don't want to start with new friends right now. I need the time, and there's no better place to step back a while than Cameo."

"Yes, but if you really want to step into your father's shoes, you're going to have to have a good business education."

"I don't intend to be more than another adviser," I said, and he laughed.

"Why don't you let me arrange for you to get your GED, at least? I think I can arrange that test, even though you usually have to be eighteen to get it. We can get Hemsley to agree to your prospective employment, which is one way to get you qualified."

I saw that he was throwing that down as a stipulation, so I agreed.

The only person I spoke to from our school that summer was Lee. He called just before he left for college. He had been accepted at the University of Arizona, among others, and he chose it because he had a good shot of making the basketball team. I wished him luck. He had no idea what I was going or not going to do, and I didn't mention anything. He just ended by saying he was sorry.

It was the first time I had cried in nearly two months.

Despite my not having an organized, formal school day, my life fell into regular patterns. The nurses I kept on to help with

Mother all complimented me on how maturely I was running the house and caring for Mother when they weren't there. They admired how I would spend so much time reading, exercising, and working in what had been Gloria's art studio. I began by trying to reproduce some of her paintings and drawings. I never did as well, but I did improve enough for the nurses who saw one or two to praise them.

They spoke with admiration but also with pity between the lines. I was too pretty to be locked up this way all the time. I should be with young people my age.

I didn't bother to tell them that none of my school acquaintances took the time to find out about me, invite me to anything, or offer to visit. They were too wrapped up in and protected by their own lives. Who wanted to even touch someone so wounded? What was the promised result? Depression? It took a big effort to cheer up someone like me and get me to forget my family tragedies.

No, both Mother and I drifted away, slipped off the screen, were rarely mentioned in conversations. Mother was not seen in public. People probably asked about her at the charity events or film festival galas, but no one knew much, and why bring up such a dark topic anyway amid all the fun?

I didn't resent the silence; I welcomed it. And of course, I always had my sister times in the casita. There were the new books I had read and my efforts at art to be the subjects of my imaginary conversations. Sometimes I returned to the house in tears, and sometimes I felt energized. I was becoming like Mother in the sense that I, too, would bounce between reality and wishful thinking. I could refuse to accept the past. I could wait for Daddy to come home from work and hear him telling one of his stories about foolish clients.

It was like I could sit, reach over, and switch on the old film projector Mother had restored. But instead of one of her famous films, I would see our lives, the way they were, the two of us, Gloria and me, running over the lawns, splashing each other in the pool, playing badminton, or just walking and talking, Gloria's cupped hands going this way and that as she explained something so gray and mysterious to me.

Occasionally, when I was out and about, someone would nod or wave or even dare to say, "Hello, how are you? How's your mother?" But for the most part, they avoided eye contact, turned away, and started a conversation quickly with someone else. Tragedy had turned us into lepers. Victims, I thought, we'd never stop being victims.

Once, when I went to the dry cleaner's to pick up some of Mother's and my clothing, the owner, Mr. Kuan, paused while he was preparing my bill and took a real look at me. Most people didn't look at each other. We live in a world of passing glances, brief hellos and goodbyes.

"I thought," he began, and paused, realizing what he was going to say.

"Yes?"

"I'm sorry. I thought you had . . ."

"Disappeared?"

"Yes. I'm sorry."

"Don't be," I said, smiling. "People you really love don't disappear."

He nodded and rushed the bill, happy to have me pay and leave. I looked back from my car. He was staring at me. I waved, and he smiled.

What Mother had believed and I had dreamed of being was

happening. My sister was returning, seeping into me slowly over time. I wasn't upset. I had always felt insubstantial, like just another of Mother's spirits. Whenever she had a conscious moment and asked about me, I reminded her I was to be sent to a different private school. It didn't matter that I was there seemingly forever. It was an explanation that permitted her to have Gloria back.

I cried about it, for sure, but I always had cried about it. I had learned to live with it and certainly could live with it now.

Just after my twenty-first birthday, I told Mr. Tiegler that I wanted to sell Cameo.

"I want to start a new life living in our beach house. Mother's not improving any being here, either. I think the Golden Ages home slash mental clinic would serve her better. I have discussed it with Dr. Littlefield, and he agrees. You can call him, if you wish. I gave him permission to discuss it with you."

"I see. Yes, maybe that would be best," he said.

"And I've talked business with Mr. Hemsley. We've agreed on a settlement. Ironically, he'll be investing my money through the company he and my father owned."

"What are you going to do in your new home, your new life? Are you thinking of school?"

"No. I'm going to keep working on my art. At least for now," I said.

"Okay, let me get started on all this for you," he said.

We stared at each other for a long moment, neither of us willing to be the first to say it. I did. I had to do it.

"It's been two months past five years."

"Yes. Be good to have that done before we put together all the financial arrangements."

"Thank you," I said. "Oh, I want to donate all of Mother's books and films to the library."

"Good idea. Nice write-off."

"That's not why. I didn't want to stay with the business because I can't think like my father. I think more like . . . like my sister."

"Understood," he said.

I was grateful for him. He was a good friend. My father had been wise to choose him to be our family attorney. With his efficient help, everything went smoothly. Two months later, I began my move to the beach house, and in something of a record sale, Cameo was sold, ironically, to a new movie star.

One week after Gloria was legally declared deceased, I woke up with an idea that wouldn't let go. Days later, I petitioned on my own to change my name. I filed for a new driver's license as well and then gradually changed everything I could. I hadn't met anyone new yet, so there was no confusion to clear up. The only ones who were surprised, but not critical, were Mr. Hemsley and Mr. Tiegler.

When Mr. Tiegler called to let me know he had made whatever legal changes had to be made on accounts and documents, he asked a little more about it.

"I always hated my name," I said. "You know Mother insisted on us being named for silent-movie stars."

"Yes." He laughed. Then he grew serious and said, "Just be careful. Not knowing who you really are is quite painful. You see that in your mother, I'm sure."

"It's not hard for me," I replied. "It's like changing shoes."

He laughed, but skeptically.

Perhaps he was right.

Perhaps I had lived among Mother's spirits too long. Maybe the damage was already done.

One night, my boyfriend Brad was over preparing one of his restaurant's most popular dishes, chicken piccata. I was sitting on the patio and looking down at the beach when something caught my eye and made my heart pound.

"I'll be right back!" I shouted.

"Whaaa," he said, but I was already marching quickly down the hill. It would take me only a minute or so in a fast walk. I crossed the busy highway, challenging some cars, the drivers leaning on their horns to voice their anger, and rushed onto the sand.

She was standing looking out at the water, her back to me. I slowed but walked toward her. She didn't turn until I was almost there.

"I thought it was you," I said.

The moonlight revealed that soft smile.

"And I thought you would be out there on the patio this time of night, just like we often were, waiting for stars, hypnotized by the yellow-silver light gliding over the water."

"You said it looked like the moon was painting the earth."

"The artist in me."

"What did you do?"

"I stepped off the screen. We often talked about that, remember?"

"But you had an Academy Award life ahead of you."

"Too many other people were writing the script. Remember? I envied you."

"I never believed you."

She nodded.

"You know what happened?" I said.

"Yes, but once I had jumped, it was too late to stop it."

"Was it?"

"Yes." She looked up toward the beach house.

"It's all gone, you know," I said.

"No," she said. "It's just beginning. Go home. Continue my Academy Award life."

She started away.

"Where are you going? Where have you been? You can't leave me now!" I shouted after her.

She paused. "I never left you, Gish. You know that," she said, and walked on until the darkness swallowed her.

I ran after her, but she wasn't there.

"Hey," I heard, and turned to see Brad. "What's going on? Everything's ready."

"Nothing," I said, walking to him. I looked down the beach. "Just one of the spirits of Cameo."

"Following you here?" he asked, putting his arm around me.

"Following me forever," I said.

We walked back slowly.

Behind me, the moon continued to paint the ocean.

A week later, I returned to the Golden Ages home to visit Mother for what I didn't know at the time would be the final visit. When I entered her room, she looked farther away then ever, her eyes glassy, focused on some deeply buried thought. I pulled a chair up to the bed and took her hand in mine.

"Gloria visited me, Mama. Maybe I dreamed it, but you always believed in dreams. She said she would always be with me."

I waited. Her eyes blinked, and then, I would swear forever and ever, she smiled before she closed her eyes again.

When I left, I saw the old man I had spoken to in the lobby just weeks ago. He had just arrived.

"Your mother?" he asked.

"She's comfortable."

He smiled and looked around. "Going to be a beautiful day, isn't it?"

"I think so."

"Hope always seems to come in the morning," he said. "It's the gift that never stops giving."

"Yes," I said, and smiled before I walked on.

For all I knew, he was a spirit of Cameo, too.